WILLIAM DEMBY

KING COMUS

William Demby was born in Pittsburgh, Pennsylvania, on December 25, 1922, and attended college in Clarksburg, West Virginia, before enlisting in World War II and serving in Italy. He graduated from Fisk University in 1947, then moved abroad to Rome, where he spent the next two decades working as a novelist, journalist, and script translator and screenwriter for the Italian cinema. In the late 1960s, Demby joined the faculty at the College of Staten Island, dividing his time between the United States and Italy. His works include *Beetlecreek*, *The Catacombs*, *Love Story Black*, and *King Comus*. In 2006, he was the recipient of the Anisfield-Wolf Book Award for Lifetime Achievement. He died in Sag Harbor, New York, in 2013.

Books by William Demby

Beetlecreek

The Catacombs

Love Story Black

King Comus

King Comus

King Comus

A novel

William Demby

Introduction by Melanie Masterton

Vintage Books
A Division of Penguin Random House LLC
New York

FIRST VINTAGE BOOKS EDITION 2026

Published by Vintage Books, a division of Penguin Random House LLC, 1745 Broadway, New York, NY 10019. Originally published by the Ishmael Reed Publishing Company in 2017.

Library of Congress Cataloging-in-Publication Data
Names: Demby, William, author | Masterton, Melanie, writer of introduction
Title: King Comus : a novel / William Demby ;
introduction by Melanie Masterton.
Description: First Vintage Books edition. | New York : Vintage Books, 2026. |
Includes bibliographical references.
Identifiers: LCCN 2025052973 (print) | LCCN 2025052974 (ebook)
Subjects: LCGFT: Novels
Classification: LCC PS3507.E5346 K56 2026 (print) |
LCC PS3507.E5346 (ebook) | DDC 813/.54—dc23
LC record available at https://lccn.loc.gov/2025052973
LC ebook record available at https://lccn.loc.gov/2025052974

Vintage Books Trade Paperback ISBN: 979-8-217-00737-0
eBook ISBN: 979-8-217-00738-7

Book design by Steve Walker

penguinrandomhouse.com | vintagebooks.com

Printed in the United States of America
1st Printing

The authorized representative in the EU for product safety and compliance is Penguin Random House Ireland, Morrison Chambers, 32 Nassau Street, Dublin DO2 YH68, Ireland, https://eu-contact.penguin.ie.

Acknowledgments

From James Demby: Special thanks to Ed, Claire, and Jacob Margolies for their steadfast friendship and strong support of William Demby and his family through the years; to Bob Baker, for his artistic collaborations with the Dembys during many summers at the Villa Podernovo; to Quincy and Margaret Troupe, for their decades of friendship and support of Demby's writing; to Jeff Biggers, Silvia Lucchesi, and Giovanna Micconi, for each interviewing Demby from a unique and complex angle in his later years and promoting his work; to Richard Courage, for paying homage to Demby's career at the CUNY memorial; to James C. Hall, for his rich scholarship and for shepherding a reprint of *Beetlecreek* (University of Mississippi, 1998), and organizing Demby's only public reading of *King Comus.*

From Melanie Masterton: Special thanks to Richard Yarborough, for his depth of insight and for facilitating the reprint of *The Catacombs* (Northeastern Library of Black Literature, 1991).

Both James Demby and Melanie Masterton extend their deepest gratitude to Ishmael Reed and Carla Blank for the care and devotion they put into realizing William Demby's wishes for his final novel's publication and with whom it has been a privilege to collaborate.

Introduction to the Vintage Books Edition (2026)

In a 1971 interview at the Brockport Writers Forum, William Demby reflects on his writing practice and his recent return to the United States after working for two decades in Rome as a novelist and journalist, as well as an actor, screenwriter, and translator in the Italian cinema. Demby's comments about his participation in a landmark 1962 meeting in Florence of the European Congress of Writers introduce a key metaphor: the *tapestry*, an artistic preoccupation that runs through his novelistic practice for decades to come and culminates with his vision for *King Comus*. Demby describes at length his fascination with a Renaissance-era tapestry hanging in the hall of the Palazzo Vecchio:

> And while we were standing there in the intervals of the speeches discussing the novel, I suddenly looked at this tapestry and saw that it was a sixteenth-century tapestry in which there were huge armies moving. Events were taking place, maidens and castles

> and great movements of people, all on an enormous tapestry that was, it seemed to me, very much like the large screens that our film epics are using. So it seemed to me that this movement on this tapestry was not horizontal and in a horizontal sequence of events, moving from the beginning horizontally to an end. No, the movement was *here*. The eye would have to choose from all that was happening on the screen to focus on that episode. I tried to do the same [in *The Catacombs*].

In *The Catacombs*, his most well-known novel, narrator "Bill Demby" takes up the period of 1962 to 1964, collaging this tumultuous era from Rome for the reader with tidbits and headlines cited directly from the daily news: the nuclear brinksmanship of the Cuban missile crisis; the Birmingham bombing that killed four Black girls at Sunday school; the March on Washington for Jobs and Freedom; the advent of the birth control pill; and Marilyn Monroe's death, to name just a handful of events. Demby shared in an interview, "The sixties were like that. It was a gothic age, an age of migration, of horrible mass diseases, of mendicants and beggars, of religious fanaticism, of miracles, and I recorded all of it" (Micconi, 136).

King Comus, first published posthumously in 2017, continues and expands Demby's sustained work of recording historical cycles by bringing together three interrelated settings that span centuries and continents. In the first half of the nineteenth century, an enslaved musician undertakes a perilous journey to elude his enslaver. During World War II, King Comus's descendant, Tillman, imparts his legendary ancestor's story to his fellow Black serviceman, D., while crossing the Atlantic. And at the turn of the twenty-first century, Tillman reunites with D. for a whirlwind plan to stage a global Gospel Summit in Rome, with the aid of their white commanding officer from the war.

The Tapestry of Time offers *King Comus*'s semiautobiographical narrator, here named D., a narrative device to conceive the novel's lofty aims. Demby initiates his opus with this central image: "I am an ant traveling over one of those enormous Tapestries of Time, and I shall make mistakes of fact and observation, and may not see in time what was there to see before attempting to climb up yet another mountain of colored thread." *King Comus*'s tapestry demonstrates a striking use of repetition: in phrases and events that recur, patterned in a postmodern vein, recalling Italo Calvino at times and presenting the reader with a proliferation of narrative possibilities. Tillman half-jokingly acknowledges to D. that "this is one of those stories that feeds upon itself and therefore seems never to end—." We might hear Demby, too, in that utterance, working as he did for some twenty years to bring his sprawling tale toward completion.

Throughout each of his novels, Demby braids aspects of his biography readily into his fiction, and his final novel is no exception. Like *The Catacombs*'s narrator, *King Comus*'s D. is a Black American author living in Italy. D. serves in World War II in Italy, as Demby did, and makes a life there after the war, marrying an Italian writer with whom he has a son. D. imparts that he has been living in a "somber villa [his wife] had inherited from an aunt (herself the widowed wife of the last male descendent of the aristocratic family that had built the villa in 1842 as a hunting lodge to entertain the new Napoleonic elite)." The author himself worked on drafting his novel-in-progress while spending summers in Italy with his wife, Lucia Drudi, and their son, James, at the Villa Podernovo, their historical residence in the Tuscan woods near the village of Consuma. When Tillman, Stabat, and Little Antioch materialize near D.'s home in the novel's turn-of-the-twenty-first-century setting, D. is mourning the death of his "beloved wife Lucia." D.'s wife's passing is an irreparable crisis and the occasion for the muse to appear in the unlikely trio of Tillman, Stabat, and Little Antioch in a stretch limousine. Demby the author, meanwhile, continued to return to Italy in the summers following Drudi's passing in 1995, and would continue working on *King Comus* until 2007.

When Demby set to work on *King Comus* in the mid-1980s, he was writing in the aftermath of the cultural phenomenon of the television miniseries *Roots* (1977), whose premiere ushered in a national conversation about slavery. Demby features its broadcast in a key satirical section in the novel. In multiple registers, Demby's final novel thinks through the lens of the neo-slave narrative, the latter a term coined by Ishmael Reed in relation to his novel *Flight to Canada* (1976). The genre had gained considerable traction by the time Demby commenced writing *King Comus*, with virtuoso authors like Reed, Octavia Butler, and Toni Morrison conducting their own distinctive experiments in content and form. In *King Comus*, Demby weaves himself, like his fictive creations, King Comus, Tillman, Stabat, and Little Antioch, into an epic tapestry of clashing armies and world-making epochs; at the same time, in characteristic postmodern fashion, he holds the reader at arm's length, playfully blurring fact and fiction and dispensing with modernist interiority and depth. A prime example of the latter is a refusal to furnish commentary from Tillman or from D. regarding Tillman's decision to sign a contract to become "Stabat's perfectly legal slave" in the novel's contemporary setting.

Always attuned to the literary zeitgeist, Demby interlaces Afrofuturist elements into his neo-slave narrative's temporal fabric. Tillman promises D. that the Gospel Summit in Rome will make "Campo di Constantino . . . look like some kinda futuristic Garden of Eden, all silver and gold and lavender and white, glistening in the night like a beacon of hope and salvation for a world gone sour and just about ready to vomit its fear and violence all over the fucking universe." As with many Afrofuturist artists who turn to deep time to conjure an image of the future, Demby conjoins African antiquity in the figure of Prester John, "that wise Ethiopic king of antiquity," with the avant-garde in his Tapestry of Time. In an excised passage from the novel's ending, Demby delivers King Comus to the banks of the Tiber in a glowing cocoon ("The William Demby Papers at the Villa Podernovo"), registering his interest in Afrofuturistic possibilities.

Infusing his own writing career into his novel, in its final section, Demby draws on his early work in journalism to report playfully on the buzz surrounding the Gospel Summit. These missives, for instance, take up the controversy of the event being financed in part by conflict diamonds sent to Rome by "The Lord Demby Evangelical Choral Society" from Sierra Leone. The Gospel Summit is held on the banks of the Tiber, where Constantine is said to have had his vision of the cross. Through the lucrative promise of the Gospel Summit and Stabat's suspect role in the enterprise—which echoes Stabat's smuggling of Etruscan art objects during World War II—*King Comus* positions Rome as the ultimate site of the sacred and the profane. Ugo Rubeo aptly observes of the city's role in Demby's text, "Open to international operators in all kinds of business—whether related to religious practices, or to the prosperous underworld—Demby's Eternal City is closely reminiscent of Fellini's fantastic visions in which it becomes impossible to draw the line between the city's spiritual and secular attitudes." This blurring of attitudes is similarly at work in Demby's appeal to multiple tones and styles, ranging from the comical and satirical to the allegorical and spiritual.

King Comus's Tapestry of Time also affords crucial insights into Black servicemen's diverse experiences in what D. terms "the segregated Army of those racially benighted days." Unlike the famed Tuskegee Airmen and the 92nd Division, in which Demby's brother, Frank, served and saw active combat in Italy, Demby's troop had their mission shifted from cavalrymen to that of truck drivers. As D. puts it: ". . . our sudden transformation from romantic Indian-fighting cavalryman to your everyday average truck driver was a letdown almost too great to endure—." To ease this crushing shift in their wartime mission and its impact on their collective identity, Tillman (D. presumes), circulates a "rumor" as a means for the troop to recover the narrative of war they had been groomed during training to embrace:

> . . . as soon as our ship landed on Italian soil, and on special orders from the White House and Franklin D. Roosevelt himself, our legendary and historic Negro horse cavalry battalion was going to be issued brand new 19th-century horse cavalry uniforms, theatrical costumes but authentic in every detail from

> the wardrobe stocks of Italy's famous Cinecittà film studios in Rome along with thoroughbred horses from the Royal Stables just outside Rome so that, the moment the Fifth Army broke out of Anzio and was ready to march north to liberate Rome, we Negro troopers of a glorious Indian fighting tradition were to be invited to ride at the head of the Fifth Army's armored column as it made its triumphant entry into Rome—

The reality for Demby, and for D. and Tillman alike, was a nighttime entrance to deliver supplies to a warehouse near Rome's Termini station at the anonymous tail of General Clark's heralded march.

Like this whimsical reference to Cinecittà studios and Demby's imagining here of his troop riding victorious into the ancient city on horseback, having vanquished fascism and its racial laws, Demby's professional experiences in the Italian cinema inform several aspects of his final novel. Demby served as Roberto Rossellini's assistant director of dialogue on *Europe '51* (1952) and acted in *Anna's Sin* (1952), a retelling of *Othello* set in postwar Rome. With his wife Drudi, his close creative interlocutor, Demby wrote multiple screenplays in the 1960s, including *Eruption* (1962). *King Comus* channels these experiences into his final novel, particularly through its sustained use of dialogue. This is most obvious in Tillman's soliloquys, delivered in the Black oral tradition. Demby's attention to voice and character is also on full display in Stabat's striking opening monologue to the troop that traces his impoverished Italian lineage to an unknowable Etruscan past and loops it into the wartime present of the novel's tapestry.

Demby develops in Tillman a singular critical voice that lends a political context to the men's sudden demotion from cavalrymen to truck drivers. Tillman chides the troop, "Jim Crow is Jim Crow in the Army or out of the Army and I KNOW all you bona fide country Negroes ain't forgotten my man Jim Crow, so what I'm hearing on the grapevine is that since Jim Crow's always been the boss man in Rome, Georgia, now that you're in Italy—what did all y'all chumps expect?" Tillman's commentary succinctly tracks Jim Crow's portability abroad, as do the Army's segregated forces and white command structure. D. and Tillman's troop enters Italy through Naples, in a region with its own history of disenfranchisement and poverty, adding further complexity to Tillman's commentary. Compellingly, Demby generated a great deal of material in his decades-long drafting process, much of it focused on Tillman's experiences in the decades after the war. Demby edited his own manuscript into a slim volume that distills his central narrative vision.

This Vintage Books edition of *King Comus*, alongside editions of Demby's earlier novels, spotlights Demby's vital place in American letters. As a recipient of an Anisfield-Wolf Lifetime Achievement Award in 2006, Demby garnered acclaim for his experimental daring in form and style and the eclecticism of his work. Not long after receiving this honor, he would complete *King Comus*, signing the novel, "The End, Sag Harbor, N.Y., May 29. 07." Nevertheless, when Demby passed in 2013, his opus had not found a publisher.

With the knowledge that Ishmael Reed published Demby's *Love Story Black* in 1978, when I first learned of *King Comus*'s existence in Demby's *New York Times* obituary, I queried Reed about the novel's status, citing his own tour de force *Mumbo Jumbo*: "For Jes Grew is seeking its words. Its Text. For what good is a liturgy without its Text?" Reed replied in short order that he would publish *King Comus*, and its journey from Italy into print began. With this new edition, the novel continues to seek its Text, its readers.

While Demby's themes remain grand, and the novel's content the stuff of history and legend alike, Demby compresses time and space, so that we travel from the nineteenth century to the twenty-first and across continents in a matter of paragraphs. Such narrative moves identify the enduring role of the racialized past in our present, even as Demby suggests that traces from the past are the very means by which we might chart new futures. The novel leaves unsettled the direction the masses gathered at the Gospel Summit waiting for a Messiah figure will take. But Demby's keen eye for gothic happenings in and across the sweep of Time return us to his invocation in *The Catacombs* that "life is existence and existence is sacred."

MELANIE MASTERTON
2025

Melanie Masterton is a lecturer at the California Institute of Technology. Her scholarly work appears in journals including *Modern Language Notes*, *Modernism/modernity*, *Pacific Coast Philology*, *California Italian Studies*, and *Italian Quarterly*. William Demby is a key protagonist in her current manuscript devoted to a cohort of African American writers, artists, and performers in postwar Rome and their Italian creative circles. With Ugo Rubeo and James C.

Hall, she guest-edited *New Perspectives on William Demby*, a special issue of *African American Review*.

Works Cited

Biggers, Jeff. "William Demby Has Not Left the Building: Postcard from Tuscany." *Bloomsbury Review* 24, no. 1(2004): 12–13.

Demby, William. Interview with Peter Marchant and Pat M. Ryan. Brockport Writers Forum, October 6, 1971. https://dspace.sunyconnect.suny.edu/server/api/core/bitstreams/ad4be7db-3f82-435d-964f-d0fece10cf09/content.

Masterton Sherazi, Melanie, Ugo Rubeo, and James C. Hall, eds. "Introduction." *New Perspectives on William Demby, African American Review* 55, no. 2–3 (2022): 111–19, https://doi.org/10.1353/afa.2022.0016.

Micconi, Giovanna. "Ghosts of History: An Interview with William Demby." *Amerikastudien / American Studies* 56, no. 1 (2011): 123–39.

Rubeo, Ugo. "Roman Landscapes in William Demby's *The Catacombs* and *King Comus*." *Konch* (2022), https://static1.squarespace.com/static/5a258a1e0abd04962c1cae34/t/634fd85642fcb6158b79d73e/1666177110343/Roman+Landscapes+.pdf

Yardley, William. "William Demby, Author of Experimental Novels, Dies at 90." *New York Times*, May 31, 2013. https://www.nytimes.com/2013/06/01/arts/william-demby-novelist-and-reporter-dies-at-90.html.

Part I

1

(If, God willing, the prescient and guileless spirit of the angel does indeed continue to bless our understanding—not only of those things already come to pass but also of certain other events and coincidences now being revealed to me even as I hasten to write this all down—then, perhaps, you, too (who for whatever reason will have undertaken to follow us through the tortuous byways of this tale) will also become convinced as I have long since been convinced that the enigmatic and prophetic lyrics of a gospel song written by a black teenage gospel singer from a Bedford-Stuyvesant housing project in Brooklyn, New York, known to her millions of fans around the world as "Little Antioch," provide us with the only plausible interpretation of what took place in clear view of everyone present at that improbable "Gospel Summit" in Rome billed by its enthusiastic though perhaps overly venal promoters as "A Day of Glory Reenacting the Roman Emperor Constantine's 'Vision of the Cross,'" a unique once in a lifetime media event featuring thirty-three gospel/rock choirs from all over the world which in spite of the perhaps overly enthusiastic hyperbole of its promoters is now believed by sociologists, advertisers, religious conservatives and gospel/rock fans all over the world to have actually saved our planet from its hysterical rush to nuclear disaster—

For then and only then, that is if you, witness or reader, can in your heart accept as flesh and blood truth that a Negro slave with the fanciful name King Comus, born in the year 1817c. in the New Orleans slave market while his mother was being sold on the block was, both in legend and fact, the reincarnation of Prester John, that wise Ethiopic king of antiquity, in our day all but forgotten, but whose amazing and otherwise inexplicable reappearance a few short weeks ago at the above mentioned Gospel Summit, had in fact been predicted in the lyrics of the title song of the Angel, Little Antioch's most recent and most sensationally successful album, "Lord, Lordy Lord, I Need an Explanation!" which album, in the few short weeks since the astonishing sequence of events which I will now attempt to relate has sold more copies worldwide than any previous album in the history of pop music; only the Holy Bible has beat it on the bestseller lists.)

2

But forgive me for I am rambling and the truth is I don't know quite how to proceed, for I am an ant traveling over one of those enormous Tapestries of Time, and I shall make mistakes of fact and observation, and may not see in time what was there to see before attempting to climb up yet another mountain of colored thread—so first things first, and so as to doubly reassure ourselves that what follows is the workings of Our Lord and not the workings of the Demon it may be wise for us, at least for the time being, to abandon certain vain and useless literary conventions as to the nature or not of narrative realism (which in any case in light of newly discovered laws of physics make such guarantees at best illusory and academically vain) and so, therefore, and without further ado and unseemly apologies before the fact, let us now hasten swiftly back in time to a certain night in Vienna, the night of June 8, 1815, where in this very instant, just moments before the church bells will begin to toll at midnight, a talented young musician with blue eyes and a straggly blonde beard, a virtuoso instrumentalist who has mastered almost every instrument in the orchestra of his day, including the rarely used musette and his first loves, the pianoforte and violin, an orphan steeped in the Hassidic lore of doting grandparents, they too emigrants from the claustrophobic oppression of the Warsaw ghetto, with whom our soon to become hero shares a dank, windowless and rat-infested basement but from whom, alas (perhaps because of certain wild and golden dreams that have recently begun to torment his nights), he has begun to feel estranged—summoned that very morning to the royal court orchestra's rehearsal hall to substitute for the second violinist, a Freemason whose sudden death the night before had had (so it was whispered) something to do with the man's surly and ill-advised opposition to the concertmaster's choice of the very Catholic Bolinski's crowd-pleasing "Te Deum" as the final number on the program of the Royal Gala Concert to be attended by all the crowned heads of Europe and which, in the words of Viscount Castlereagh (whose elegant but alas evasive proposal for ending the slave trade had been met with pious indifference by the now bored and distracted delegates impatient to adjourn), "will hopefully and with the Grace of Our Lord bring this oft cantankerous Congress of Vienna to a most joyous, harmonious, and optimistic conclusion—"

This talented young Polish musician, who for the time being shall remain without name, instead of heading straight home with the money paid him for three rehearsals and the gala concert (and where his aged and loving grandparents were eagerly awaiting his return so as to surprise him with a rare pot of rabbit stew and a cup or two of real Peking tea) and alas with characteristic perversity, joined two of his fellow musicians on their way to a nearby brothel and tavern where, in the course of two hours of feckless drinking, he managed to spend every farthing in his pocket buying drinks for one and all while running up an astronomical tab he had no hopes of ever being able to pay while getting so drunk himself he no longer knew who or where he was—

So now we find him, still drunk but sober enough to be tormented by gnawing all-too-familiar feelings of inadequacy and guilt, staggering aimlessly in the middle of the main highway that from the northern suburbs leads north to the sea and south to the Italian Alps, conversing wildly with himself—

"Abolish the slave trade indeed—!" he ranted, shaking his head back and forth with theatrical disgust, "—these so-called aristocrats, hypocritical assholes every single one of them, it's easy for them to talk! Me, I'd gladly sell myself into slavery if I thought it'd get me out from under this mountain of debt and I could live out the rest of my days on some cozy plantation in the American Southland with nary a worry about who's going to pay for the rent and food—!"

No sooner were these words out of his mouth than a wayward cloud suddenly darkened the dazzling full moon and the silence of the night was shattered by the urgent wild clatter of rapidly approaching hoof-beats.

Immediately sober and alert, the young musician staggered to the middle of the road to see from which direction the unholy commotion was coming—just in time to leap out of the way of a runaway team of horses pulling an elegant but wildly careening carriage, its lighted lamps banging furiously against the crested doors, its driver struggling to keep his balance as with one hand he waved the drunk musician out of the way and with the other strained backwards on the reins in a vain effort to bring the horses to a halt—

But almost frozen stiff by fear, though still capable of admiring the elegant lines of what obviously was a royal carriage, the bulging eyes of the high-born horses were almost upon him before, and at the very last moment, he managed to leap out of the way and in doing so (and in response to some entirely unexpected playful instinct) seized hold of the dangling reins as they came slapping against his chest and thighs, leaned back, dug in his heels, all the while pulling back as hard as he could, until suddenly the carriage toppled over on its side and the wild-eyed frothing horses came to an abrupt halt—

His hands bruised and painfully seared by the whip-like slapping of the reins, the by now sober but frightened young musician came running up to the overturned carriage, its wheels still spinning wildly, only to discover the phantom driver was nowhere in sight—

Thinking the man had been bounced off the driver's seat and was lying in a ditch nearby, perhaps unconscious, he got down on his knees—finally flattening himself face down on the rocky slope—and had snaked his way halfway to the opposite side of the toppled carriage when suddenly two strong hands began yanking on his ankles—

Twisting his head around he caught a glimpse of a pug-nosed giant with enraged bloodshot eyes—

"You shitty bugger of a sheepherder!" the man shrieked in high-pitched but surprisingly cultivated German, "—how dare you block the Imperial Highway! How!!! Dare!!! You?!!!"

Then as enraged spittle sprayed the young musician's face and as the full moon soared from behind a cloud, he suddenly recognized his assailant as a certain Baron von Gugelstein, a notorious young man-about-town whose signature caricature (usually the head and face of a foppishly-dressed dandy on the body of a pig with a tiny weenie) appeared almost daily in the satirical broadsheets of the day, usually in connection with some largely fictitious amatory exploit, which nevertheless had earned him the satirical accolade, "The Boudoir Prince"—

"You were trying to rob me, weren't you, you shitty bugger?! Who are you? You look to me like a Jew!"

And as the stinging blows of the whip continued to rain over his face the humiliation and rage the young musician was beginning to feel slowly became directed, not at the handsome pampered face shouting obscenities at him (so close he could smell the baron's expensive cologne and garlicky breath) but at himself for being so desperately poor, so irrevocably uncouth and unpresentable, while this monster of a baron no doubt had just finished dining on oysters and snails in one of the plush private parlours of the Café Royale while frolicking obscenely on a velvet divan between the cunning perfumed thighs of a royal whore—

"Well let this be a lesson to you, you flea bag of a dog! How dare you! HOW DARE YOU!!" "The Boudoir Prince" continued to shriek, while at the same time lashing his victim with his whip—

It was then, suddenly, and to the great surprise of the victim himself, that the young violinist abruptly stopped ducking and cringing and instead rose to his full height, paused dramatically to catch his breath, and then threw his arms around the baron (almost as if greeting a long lost brother) and began fiercely to squeeze him tight—

"Ho what's this?" the baron exclaimed, wrenching his face out of the way as if afraid his victim was about to give him a kiss—

Instead the musician kicked the baron violently in the groin. And when the young nobleman doubled over and coughed with pain, the musician struck him yet another even more violent blow, this one on the back of the neck and with his doubled fist—

Now suddenly buoyed with a great wave of unexpected joy and furious energy, and as both tumbled to the ground atop each other like frantic lovers, both emitting breathless sub-human grunts and growls, the young violinist found a soft depression on the baron's neck, twisted the baron's head around until they were almost touching face to face, straddled him and like a cowboy about to brand a heifer, slowly began to grind his boney kneecap deeper and deeper into the baron's slackening flesh, pausing only to turn his head away politely when the baron let out a garlicky dying grunt—

When the young musician awoke the sun was high in the sky. And though he had long since lost all awareness of the passing of time, he realized he had been sleeping several hours and now found himself stretched out on the footpath that lined the highway on both sides with his thumb in his mouth, wondering what he was doing there lying asleep on the side of the road and not in his bed.

And when he remembered where he was and what he had done he got up and relieved himself behind a bush, shook himself dry, buttoned his fly and only then, and most reluctantly, acknowledged the presence of the corpse already discovered by a swarm of quietly buzzing flies, gnats and fluttering moths and which now, reluctantly and with fastidious distaste, he dragged to the edge of an embankment and clumsily rolled down a steep slope to the briar-choked copse below, and finally slid clumsily down the slope himself for one last look—

Yes, no doubt about it—he mused silently to himself while shooing away the voracious preening flies buzzing contentedly around the brownish liquids dripping from the dead man's nostrils and mouth—no doubt about it: that puffy powdered arrogance could belong to no one else but the Baron von Gugelstein, "The Boudoir Prince" himself—

But then, suddenly remembering talk the night before at the tavern about the shocking murder of an African slave child dressed up as the Whore of Babylon and then raped and murdered in the course of some obscene orgiastic ritual which several journalists present described as a crude plot engineered by a cabal of reactionaries to discredit the growing ranks of certain humanitarian and outspoken delegates in favor of totally abolishing the slave trade, the young musician realized he may unwittingly have involved himself in some momentous international plot that could well result in his ending up hanged on the gallows, or at the very least locked up for life in some windowless prison for the criminally insane—

But then, just as he was about to flee the scene of his crime (for if the young violinist lacked one essential characteristic of his revolutionary age it was courage) the soaring strains of the finale of Bolinski's "Te Deum" began to resonate through the chambers of his mind as if being played somewhere out of sight by some heavenly orchestra, absolving him of all further doubt and guilt while at the same time pointing his way to an optimistic future—

And so it was—tears of joy streaming down his cheeks—he got down on his knees next to the baron's corpse and, surrendering himself completely to God's inscrutable will, began painstakingly, piece by piece, one luxurious garment at a time, pausing only to admire the exquisite workmanship and fine materials of this garment or the other, to take off the dead man's clothes—

First the wool gabardine and silk outer garments which he carefully brushed off, folded with care, and arranged in a neat pile, and then the splendid linen shirt with its embroidered royal crown and monogram, and finally the baron's highly polished boots which he saved for last (which, however, because of the swelling of the dead baron's veins and muscles as rigor mortis began to set in, at first seemed glued forever to the corpse's cold white feet)—

In fact, and as many would say, miraculously, when after much yanking and twisting and coaxing the young musician finally succeeded in wrenching the first boot off, and then, after taking off his own scarred worn shoes, began to ease his claw-like toes bumpy with calluses and bunions into the heavenly glove-like softness of the handcrafted boot's lining (discovering as he did so, and to his amazement and delight, that the boots were a perfect fit, he happily put on the other boot and danced a royal jig)—

Indeed and in no time at all he had donned all the dead baron's finery including the exquisite linen underwear the corpse had been wearing which, to be perfectly honest, was somewhat less than immaculately clean—

Nevertheless, and now barely recognizable in his new "to the manor born" attire (which, of course, was more a matter of how he felt than what he could see of himself, there having been not a single mirror among the dead baron's effects), the young violinist scrambled back up the escarpment to the side of the road where the thoroughbred black stallions were politely waiting to be fed—

It was then, as the sun of a glorious optimistic sunrise rose over the horizon and after, having just finished feeding the stallions their morning ration of oats and hay he was replacing the folded canvas feedbags inside the box under the seat where he had found them, and at the very moment the sun's rays burst gloriously over the horizon, he suddenly discovered the baron's personal trunk which apparently the night before he hadn't noticed because, evidently during the crash it had become wedged out of sight between the driver's seat and the springs—

Mostly the trunk contained nothing more exciting than more hastily packed clothing—

But then just as he was about to slam the lid shut and return the trunk to its place underneath the seat he discovered a small coffer of ancient Moorish design secreted beneath a jumble of sundry toilet articles and stacks of letters tied with ribbons—

Unfortunately the coffer was locked but when finally he managed to open it with a mysterious and oddly-shaped key, the last of some twenty keys he had found on a key ring in one of the baron's outer coat pockets, to his tearful astonishment and joy he discovered that the coffer contained an incredible fortune in gold and silver coins and jewelry including, all mixed up together, a king's ransom in loose diamonds, rubies, amethysts and pearl necklaces, some of which were over two meters long—

But then, as he began to weep uncontrollably with joy while dancing yet another jig, the young musician found something of far more interest to his as yet unformulated plans—the baron's travel documents which he found neatly folded inside an envelope of heavy parchment that had been secreted away underneath the silk lining at the bottom of the trunk, each document stamped with the seal of the highest authority in the land—

But of most immediate use to the young violinist's as yet unformulated plans, was the original patent for the baron's title and family name, inscribed in the flowery medieval Latin of an earlier age and with the imprimatur of the Holy Roman Emperor stamped in a blob of hardened red wax, a priceless document without which the newly optimistic but perhaps a bit overly self-confident young violinist would have had no proof of his new identity.

Be that as it may, six days later and now elegantly dressed in the baron's luxurious garments and wig—and after a pleasant and mostly uneventful journey with many leisurely stops at hospitable inns and public houses where he found ample opportunity to perfect a highborn German accent complete with languid hand movements, slightly arched brow and petulant disdaining lips, he finally arrived at the bustling North Sea seaport town where a retired custom house inspector seated at his table in the inn the night before had told him he would be most likely to find a buyer for his carriage and team as well as passage aboard a ship willing to run the blockade—

"It's a whole new world out there and a rotten one at that and I say it's this blasted war that's to blame!" the old gentleman had observed while they were saying their goodbyes in the foyer of the quaint country inn where they had just finished dining on pheasant and grouse and now, finally, after a dangerous moment of suspicious astonishment the innkeeper agreed to accept one of the gold coins as payment for the sumptuous meal the young musician had insisted on paying for, he was finally able to breathe and force a smile—

"I agree—," he'd replied, swallowing his moment of fear, "—but it is also true that the confusion of war has stimulated the economy and created many new opportunities, though I agree things have become so topsy-turvy these days it's become practically impossible to know who one can trust—"

"Permit me—," the retired custom house inspector said effusively (now that the matter of who would be paying for the extravagant meal had been settled), "—what you say is very true, but from my point of observation, I'd say you're a young man with his head screwed on tight, and it's bold and courageous young men like yourself who are going to be the salvation of the Fatherland—"

"So kind of you to say so—in fact my late father, the Baron's favorite motto was 'Prudence Above All!' "

"Well said! Bravo! With excellent advice like that I venture you're guaranteed to stay out of harm's way!"

Instead in less than an hour after he'd arrived at his destination the apprentice baron had fallen victim to the seductive charms of Madam Maloka—

"Do you like the Germans?" she asked, dismissing with a wave of her gaudily bejeweled hand the impish Moroccan boy who had stabled and fed his team and then guided him to Madam

Maloka's lair on the second floor of a ramshackle commercial building that overlooked the waterfront.

"I'm afraid it's the topic of the day," she said while brazenly sizing him up.

"I'm afraid I haven't given it much thought," he replied, avoiding her penetrating gaze.

"Well, it's always seemed to me the Germans are unhappy with their lot and secretly long for the carefree life of Negroes. As you see I am black and an African, but I am not a Negro. I am an Ethiopian—my father was the half brother of the Emperor and my mother was his concubine from a Moslem kingdom far to the south—"

"Me, I'm an Austrian—," the violinist said recklessly, "I've just arrived from Vienna and I am headed for America to begin a new life—"

"America! How wonderful! I'm so happy for you! And you'll be starting a new life! You must be very rich—"

And lifting aside the light blanket covering the lower part of her body, she swung her legs around the heap of silk cushions upon which she had been reclining, then slowly and with a complicated twisting of her hips and thighs she slowly rose to her full height while at the same time she continued to hold the young violinist in her mesmerizing gaze—

She was wearing a green and purple dressing gown of some exotic glistening fiber that rustled like tin-foil as gracefully, like a circus acrobat, she slowly paced around him like a wrestler at the beginning of a match.

"How I envy you—," she said, letting out a theatrical sigh while at the same time settling down heavily in one of the two chairs on either side of a cafe table that faced a large double window that offered a sweeping view of the port, "—as for me, I suffer from the vapors and from loneliness and I am afraid I shall never travel again—"

She had closed her eyes dramatically but now suddenly she opened them, in this way catching the young violinist stealing a glance at the opium pipe she had been sucking on when he first came in—

"I understand you have a carriage and a team of horses you wish to sell—," Madam Maloka said, her voice suddenly sharp and cold like the cracking of a whip. "Mustafa says the horses are thoroughbreds from Morocco, and that the carriage bears a royal seal—"

"My late father, the Baron, was a connoisseur—," the violinist said, trembling and alert at her mention of a royal seal while at the same time avoiding her eyes.

"Mustafa, too, is a 'connoisseur—,'" she said slyly, "—but unlike your late father, Mustafa is a Moor and a thief, tell him how much you want and I will pay you—"

He assumed then that she was dismissing him and couldn't hide his relief but then he realized that her constantly meandering gaze had fallen on his boots—

Then on his shirt, his jacket, his vest—

"Mustafa is growing so fast," she said, settling back on her cushions to take one last puff from her opium pipe before putting it out of sight if not out of reach behind some curtains.

"He's become such a little man. He wants to take care of me, the darling boy, but he's very mischievous and says you're a Jew—are you a Jew?"

She looked deep inside his eyes and cocked her head like a bird—

Then she motioned him to come closer.

When he did so and was standing over her she tilted her head back, opened her mouth wide and gestured for him to look inside—

Her teeth were solid gold!

"When I was a child and just becoming a woman," she began, settling back on her cushions like a mother about to tell a story to a child, "I became sick of the rickets and when my teeth began to rot my father, the Emperor, sent his privy secretary to Khartoum to persuade a surgeon with Napoleon's army to come all the way from Khartoum to Axum to cure me—"

She motioned him to pull up a chair and waited for him to do so before she would continue with her tale—

"Can you imagine such a journey?" she exclaimed. "In those days it took almost a month. Anyway, this famous surgeon, when he finally arrived at the palace he put poison in my mouth where the base of the teeth had rotted down to the gums and then built new teeth of balsam wood and solid gold and planted them in my gums! He was a German but he also was a Jew. And when I became pregnant with his child he asked my father if he could bring me back to Germany as his wife. I was twelve years old, and I lost the child in a terrible storm at sea that lasted over a week.

"Then on that same voyage my husband died from the croup—this was twenty-three years ago, has it really been that long? You see, I've lost all track of time thanks to my pipe—

"His mother, my dead husband's mother, a pious Lutheran

woman gave me this house to make up for the suffering her son had caused me, but she gave me no money, which is why I had to renounce the privileges of royal birth and become a tradeswoman and a whore—

"But enough talk about me, what about you? Am I wrong to surmise we have much in common?"

A bit startled by her question the young violinist was about to stutter a reply when Madam Maloka smiled and placed a finger to his lips and motioned for him to bend down so she could caress his cheek and give him a feathery kiss—

"If we are to become friends and perhaps even business partners, then there must be no secrets between us—"

Her tone of cold and total possessiveness sent a wave of tiny shivers down his back and involuntarily he pushed his chair back as if to increase the distance between them.

Which sudden move caused her eyes to darken and her expression to become fierce and grave.

"You will never pass as a baron," she said in a sharp contemptuous tone of voice which chilled him to the bone. "The police here are well schooled in such matters and you are wearing the waistcoat inside out—the red silk goes on the inside and the gray gabardine must be worn outside. And look at your nails, they are like the claws of a seagull and just as filthy—"

She thought a moment, her gaze riveted on his eyes and then said, but now not unkindly: "You're such a dear helpless child! Take off your clothes and I will give you a bath—"

From the moment they met the young violinist had been suspicious of this brazen self-confident Ethiopian woman just as sooner or later he had grown suspicious of every woman (his adoring but aged grandmother the only exception) in his cramped and stunted life.

But realizing now that for better or worse he had become totally dependent on this exotic and improbable black woman and that without her help he might not only never escape to America, but might well end up for the rest of his days in some grotesque horror of a German prison, he abruptly decided he must change both attitude and tactics and, smiling sheepishly, he began to undress, docilely handing each elegant garment in turn to an old crone dressed entirely in black who had materialized from behind a curtained alcove in a far corner of the cavernous all-purpose room.

Now, naked and trusting and feeling grateful and privileged as a boy visiting a whorehouse closed for the holidays of which he was now the only guest, he followed the old woman into a tiny dark room where a huge ornate bathtub made of copper but with a gleaming white ceramic lining took up almost all the space, and stood there patiently swathed in a sheet while the old woman slowly filled the tub with steaming hot water from pots and a kettle lined up on the top of a stove—

When the tub was filled and the temperature just right he lowered himself into the hot sudsy water almost up to his neck while, in the meantime, the old woman placed his clothing on a table next to an ironing board and then came back to the tub and began to scrub his back vigorously with a stiff brush—

A few minutes later Madam Maloka came into the darkened room and waved the old woman away—

When the two of them were alone she reached into the bosom of her blouse and pulled out a tiny blue apothecary bottle which she wore on a chain like a necklace and poured a few drops of the liquid into a cup of tea which she held to his lips, explaining as she did so that it would calm his nerves and expel the demons from his brain—

Then as he began to sip the bitter-tasting brew and almost immediately became drowsy she continued to stand there beside the tub, watching closely as his eyelids became heavier and heavier and finally closed—

Smiling knowingly to herself she leaned over the tub to make sure he really was asleep and not just pretending—

But the moment she straightened up and turned away he reached out suddenly and lewdly began to caress her buttocks—

"It is not me you want," she said, smiling coquettishly while brushing his hand away, "—but your long-dead mother who has come back from the dead and is here in this room with you to see you on your way!"

Then, continuing to watch him closely, she added:

"A little while ago I told you I was your friend so now that your mother is here with us and you have no reason to distrust me, I want you to tell me who you are and where you come from and what is the secret you so unjustly are trying to hide from me—"

The last thing he remembered was Madam Maloka's deep theatrical voice telling him not to be afraid—

But by then he had fallen into a deep dreamless sleep.

When, many hours later, he regained consciousness and found himself naked in a strange bed he began shouting hysterically at the top of his voice for the Ethiopian woman to bring him his clothes—that she was a witch and had tricked him and robbed him and that as soon as he could find a policeman he was going to have her arrested for having taken advantage of the good graces of an innocent traveler—

At the sound of shouting the old crone came scurrying into the darkened chamber where apparently she and Madam Maloka had carried him when he passed out in the tub—

"You are in no position to threaten anyone, me nor anyone else, you ungrateful wretch—!" the old crone shrieked, hitting him on the head with a dust pan and then scurrying off to the window to violently bang open the shutters, "—least of all Madam Maloka who is a saint and has given you far more than you deserve!"

A few moments later as sunlight and a strong sea breeze suddenly began to brighten the room, Madam Maloka appeared in the doorway carrying the young violinist's ironed and brushed off outer garments and freshly laundered linen which apparently had been hanging in front of the fireplace to dry, for they were very warm and snugly to his touch.

"Shame on you—," Madam Maloka said, feigning great disappointment, "—you had not a soul in the world to trust but me and the ghost of your long-dead mother, what must she be thinking—?"

Then she began to lay out his freshly laundered underwear and brushed and neatly folded outer garments on the top of a table, all the while reasoning with him quietly as if to calm him down—

"While you slept and dreamed you told me where you had hidden your treasure and pleaded with me to go fetch it and bring it to you here before the Kaiser's police found it and arrested you for murder—"

She paused with her hands on her hips and a smug smile on

her lips and stood there waiting for his doubt and confusion to subside—

And then before he could speak, all of a sudden and with an impatient toss of her head, she began to scatter the precious contents of the Baron von Gugelstein's coffer all over the floor—

"Don't worry, you can see for yourself it's all there, you ungrateful dog of a peasant!"

But then, taking a few steps backward as if to avoid stumbling on the glittering jewelry scattered all over the torn and tattered rug she suddenly broke out in a smile of hilarious complicity, lifted her skirts and began dancing a jig, all the while singing at the top of her voice like a drunken sailor's ditty, "Don't worry, don't worry, it's all there! See for yourself! I may be a whore but I'm not a thief!"

Until finally, her eyes twinkling, she moved back against the wall and she too began to feast her eyes on the glittering heaps of pearl necklaces, gold coins, and huge sparkling diamonds scattered all over the tattered rug—

Now suddenly the stunned young violinist, naked and skinny as the day he was born, dropped to his knees and frantically began to scoop up handfuls of his treasure which finally and with trembling hands he began to arrange on top of the ironing table into a number of manageable heaps—

"Have no fear it's all there," Madam Maloka repeated inanely, chuckling with delight, "I may be a sorceress and a harlot out of hell, but one thing I'm not is a thief who'd rob a poor innocent traveler!"

This time she laughed so loud and hysterically the young violinist began looking at her as if she had lost her mind—

And when he continued staring at her with suspicious defiance she walked up to him and kissed him maternally on the cheek—

"Tell me the truth! You are a virgin—?"

Yes, the violinist thought to himself without answering, I am a virgin because I would not join my drinking companions on their weekly tour of the brothels, because I never had money for whores and in any case I was afraid of catching the pox that drove my father mad and caused him to kill my mother with an ax—

For three months "The Baron"—as the Ethiopian woman insisted he be addressed by everyone they had reason to speak to in that small seaport town—and Madam Maloka lived as husband and wife and in a state of domestic bliss.

Every evening his exotic benefactor cooked elaborate meals for him and after the meal the two of them would take long strolls along the waterfront, watching the sun go down and holding hands like a newly married couple on their honeymoon.

Indeed, on one of these walks when the young violinist told Madam Maloka about the poverty he was born into and about how he had undertaken a music career hoping to earn enough money to buy his grandparents a house but how, no matter how hard he worked as a court musician, there was never enough money left to even pay for the next week's food and rent, she stopped to hold him close and wiped tears from her eyes, and he quietly explained that because of his father's pox which he had inherited he could never have children of his own—

But that did not mean he could not experience in the New World the same domestic bliss he was experiencing now—

"What God denies men of, men of wealth can buy for themselves," she said, kissing him lightly on the cheek while giving his hand a reassuring squeeze.

"And though to pay me for my silence you have been so kind as to give me half of your ill-gained riches, you are still a man of considerable wealth and when you arrive in the New World you will see that domestic bliss can indeed be bought!"

And then finally and irrevocably the day came for the young violinist and his Ethiopian benefactress to say their farewells—

On September 14th of that year the young baron—for such was his title on the ship's manifest—set sail for the United States aboard the brand new Yankee clipper, the *Philadelphia Triumph*, which was on its maiden voyage—

Madam Maloka, Mustafa and the old crone stood on the dock waving handkerchiefs and as tears welled up in their eyes and the sleek gray vessel began to rise with the tide and a shifting breeze began to puff out the sails and cause the proud new red white and blue flag to flap bravely against the gray-edged autumn clouds the baron wept for, at least for the moment, he was safe and secure in his new status and identity, and he continued waving to the tiny receding figures on the fog-shrouded German shore until they were so tiny they could no longer be seen, and for the first time since childhood he muttered an almost forgotten Hassidic prayer—

A month and twelve days later the *Philadelphia Triumph* dropped anchor in a war-weary but nonetheless boisterous and boastful New Orleans where, as soon as the French and American port authorities allowed him to disembark, but before he retrieved his trunks and could make inquiries as to a suitable place to live, he hired a luxurious cab, complete with two Negro footmen who had unkindly mocked his German accent, and had himself driven posthaste to the slave market which on that date was still located in the old quarter of the rapidly growing city and where with the hope of experiencing again the domestic bliss the Ethiopian woman had taught him could be bought, he paid a handsome price for a comely slave woman in her midthirties and her eleven-year-old son whose name he promptly changed from Cato to Comus in loving memory of the smiling eyeball-rolling blackamoor who had presided as King of the Revels atop a dazzling float in the first and only carnival procession of fools he was to see in Europe and which, as with measured gaiety the carnival parade passed by a crack in the wall that enclosed and circumscribed his stunted Polish childhood, he was never ever to forget.

3

One hundred and eighty-three years (give or take a year) after the neophyte Baron von Gugelstein arrived in New Orleans determined to begin a new life in a new country and to find once again the domestic bliss he had briefly experienced with Madam Maloka and Mustafa but this time with a new family of newly purchased slaves, and only a few days after my beloved wife Lucia had been entombed in the tiny walled cemetery at the top of the mountain pass that overlooked the somber villa she had inherited from an aunt (herself the widowed wife of the last male descendent of the aristocratic family that had built the villa in 1842 as a hunting lodge to entertain the new Napoleonic elite) and where for the last eight or nine years she and I and our son James had sought our own eccentric version of domestic bliss, I was slouched heartbroken and despondent on a park bench in the municipal park of Pontassieve, gazing blankly and with morbid rapture at the foaming muddy flood-swollen waters of the Sieve River surging by over the rocky junk-littered bottom like the noisy flushing of some cosmic toilet, wondering glumly if I would ever be able to put my life together again when suddenly out of nowhere a chubby little girl wearing a tattered T-shirt with the faded slogan "Glory Now!" on the front came peddling furiously down the sidewalk on a bicycle much too large for her to handle, holding up something for me to see which, as she sped by without slowing down, she tossed on the walkway at my feet while yelling something in Italian at the top of her voice—

"A man black like you told me to give this to you, they're back there in that long white limousine, Americani, two of them are black like you, *AMERICANI-RICCHI, ANZI-RICCHISSIMI*—!!!"

What she had tossed on the sidewalk at my feet was a note scribbled on a sheet of tightly folded parchment-like note paper in a barely legible scrawl:

"You used to at least look like a man, now you look like some poor-ass piece of welfare shit the cat dragged in! Straighten up, SOLDIER, and look behind you! We can see YOU but you can't see US, so get off your sorry overeducated ass and come over here where we're parked so you can tell us before I lose my bet how many years it's been since WE THREE OLD ARMY BUDDIES seen each other last!"

Now more convinced than ever that the improbable language of the note was somebody's sorry idea of a joke meant to jolt me out of my grief, I reluctantly twisted my head around in the direction the girl had pointed and, suddenly, improbably, there it was—looking more like a glistening white yacht than the custom-made super-stretch Rolls-Royce limousine which it was in reality, it had been parked recklessly, cater-cornered and illegally, in front of a busy neighborhood municipal health clinic and in a no-parking zone reserved for police and fire emergency vehicles only—

Fortunately at that time of day the neighborhood is deserted for the siesta hour and when I rushed over to where the outlandish glistening white Rolls-Royce was parked and peered through the dark-tinted glass of the rear window and saw no sign of life inside except a lighted TV set with the sound off, I sullenly became convinced that someone was playing a stupid joke on me to jolt me out of my doldrums—

Then suddenly someone had grabbed me from behind and was holding a long sharp knife blade against my throat—

"Where you think you're going, you sorry excuse of a Buffalo trooper? And when you talk to me, stand at attention, nigger, so I won't have to shoot you a second hole where before you had only one—!"

Twisting myself loose and turning, I saw a tall lanky black man wearing a black silk high-fashion baseball cap and a black silk Eisenhower jacket and black, obviously tailored jeans studying me with shrewd mirthful eyes that seemed to be mocking me from some shared but distant vantage point in time—

He had a dainty pearl-handled revolver in his free hand which he put back in his back pocket just as the door on the opposite side of the stretch limousine swung open and a tall young and very handsome black woman, she too dressed in a high-fashion black silk Eisenhower jacket and jeans, got out of the Rolls-Royce stretch limousine and came around the hood to stand next to him.

"Turn him loose—," she said, "—you're hurting him!"

At the same time a short plumpish swarthy middle-aged European-looking man chomping on a cigar, he too wearing a black silk jacket and black designer jeans materialized from around the opposite side of the limousine and stood next to the handsome young woman after clamping a powerful possessive hand around her sinuous bare waist—

"You see? What'd I tell you? He hasn't a clue who we are? I don't blame him, man's been living over here in the lap of luxury, probably forgot all about his old Army buddies!"

"He knows who we are, all right, he's just fucking with us!" the tall lanky black man who still had his arm clamped around my neck said, an expression of disgust and disappointment on his face as he put the tiny pearl-handled revolver back in his pocket and comically pushed me away with disgust—

When he turned I was able to read the logo on the back of his black silk Eisenhower jacket: STABAT/INC, and in a flash it came to me who the two men were—

"Tillman, my god, you're TILLMAN!" I shouted wildly while jumping up and down as though I'd just got religion, "—and, I can't believe this, this gotta be a joke! CAPTAIN JOE STABAT, Chief Commanding Officer 3284 Truck Battalion, 9th Horse Cavalry Division, Fort Sill, Lawton, Oklahoma, Fort Riley, Texas, shit! Where you guys come from, scaring me like this?"

In the meantime, as we three men began hugging and kissing and slapping each other on the back, the tall sexy black girl opened the front door of the stretch limousine on the passenger side and fumbled inside the glove compartment until she found a tiny movie camera with which she immediately began to film our grotesque reunion.

But even as the camera began to roll and I was jumping around mugging and grinning along with everybody else a warning bell began to sound urgently in my mind—

What in God's name were the company commander and company cook of my old World War II battalion doing here in Pontassieve in the company of a beautiful and sophisticated high-fashion young black woman who looked like a vaguely familiar movie star I must have seen in one of the old copies of *EBONY* my oldest sister had begun sending me once a year "so I wouldn't forget my roots—"

"Come on, guys, that's enough. We've really got to get going if we're going to stay on schedule!" she said in a disappointingly nasal 5th grade teacher tone of voice that collided with her otherwise flashy show business flair—

She had already put the camera back in her purse and was studying a clipboard and had just stuck her head back into the limousine's front seat to retrieve something and was now running her finger down the edge of what must have been several pages of typed instructions—

"It says here, and it's underlined in red, there's no margin for being late because RAI, that's the Italian government TV, will be handling the feed and apparently here the government unions are still Communist and don't take any shit from amateurs, like us!"

"For Christ's sake, Antioch, lighten up—and watch your fucking language, you're supposed to be a religious network star and your reputation for holiness is what's paying the bills! I'm not in this for the millions it's going to end up costing me if you keep on emulating Tillman's manner of speech!"

"Look I'd love to go with you guys—!" I heard myself saying, suddenly breaking off, "but they're waiting for these groceries up at the villa, and besides nobody's told me what this is all about—"

"What this is all about—," Joe Stabat growled suddenly back in character as he snatched the plastic shopping bag of groceries out of my hand and lobbed it deftly into a nearby trash can. "It's only going to be a couple of days, a week or so at the most, and anyway your son says it's OK, your so-called housekeeper says it's OK, and that fucking mangy dog of yours almost bit my leg off says it's OK, so for Christ's sake everybody stop bellyaching and act like you appreciate what we're doing for you and get in the fucking limo, if there's anything I hate it's a worrywart!"

In the meantime Tillman had already been pushing me inside the Rolls-Royce's lush back seat and now got in beside me and slammed the door shut but then changed his mind and got into the front seat while the beautiful tall black girl came back to the rear seat to settle down beside me while Tillman got in on the driver's side of the front seat and slammed the door—

Then as in some nightmarish scene in a crime movie the stretch limousine, wheels spinning, brakes grinding and tires screeching backed wildly out of its narrow parking berth, then spun around in an elongated circle that just missed swiping the side of an empty police car parked nearby, then sped off wildly toward the highway as Little Antioch, for that was the gospel singer's name, moved very close to me on the back seat and, weeping uncontrollably (or at least that was my impression at the time), threw her arms around me and cuddled me like a mother cuddling a child, "I'm so sorry you lost your wife, but now you and I have found each other, you have no idea how long I've been dreaming of this moment—"

Joe Stabat, who'd been studying a road map, but now put the map down on his lap and twisted around to face me—

He was smiling but with a cynical pitying expression in his eyes as if (or so I imagined at the time) he had been forewarned about the sad emotional shape I was in since my wife's sudden death and was afraid I might do something crazy, like throw open the door and throw myself out in front of a speeding car—

"If it's your son you're worrying about—," he said, "stop worrying, at least someone in your Italian family's got their head screwed on right; no offense, but he's quite a guy; not a mealy-mouth worrywart like his old man, in fact he's the one got us the RAI-TV connection, turns out the vice president or some other big shot like that was a school buddy of his, and getting all the permits we needed to get our foot in the door was a piece of cake, so relax and enjoy the show—"

I was staring at him blankly as if (as indeed was the case) I hadn't the slightest idea what he was talking about until finally he grunted, made a nervous gesture of impatience, lit the cigar which he had already placed between his lips and blew out a dense cloud of smoke.

"As a matter of fact, the whole fucking country's getting excited about this show, and they're goddamned right, because there ain't been nothing like this in the whole fucking history of pop music and that includes Woodstock, and when you get right down to it, in the whole fucking history of the world, now whether or not these bozos are going to come up with the start-up money or not, we'll cross that bridge when we come to it—!"

4

Tillman first came into my life and I into his during World War II at the Fort Sill, Oklahoma, Army Reception Center where at the time of our meeting and along with some four thousand other Negro recruits in the segregated Army of those racially benighted days we new recruits were being "processed" in preparation for basic training—and inasmuch as a "short arm inspection" was an integral part of officially becoming a bona fide GI, Tillman (with whom as yet I hadn't exchanged so much as a single word) and I were buck naked and shuffling along with excruciating slowness in a long seemingly endless line of similarly buck naked and shivering black U.S. Army recruits that zig-zagged back and forth the entire length of the enormous and drafty Army warehouse hastily pressed into service to speed up the physical examination and registration process of the swarms of new recruits arriving in vast numbers at the reception centers every day as the war effort began to gain momentum, each of us with our genitals demurely covered with the folder containing our medical and enlistment records as the seemingly endless lines inched forward at a snail's pace toward a gaggle of wise-cracking all-white Medical Corps 2nd Lieutenants and Warrant Officers fresh out of med school, each attired in brand new officer pinks and armed with flashlights and wood "popsicle sticks" with which, after the recruit's mouth had been vigorously forced open, head forced violently back, the examining officer's flashlight beam would be aimed first inside his gaping jaws in a ruthless search for rotting teeth or sores, then down at the genitals for the Army's ill-famed and obsessional "short-arm" inspection—

On that day when the lanky disarticulated recruit in front of me (it was, of course, Tillman though neither of us had as yet spoken a single word to the other) finally reached the examination area he was suddenly and inexplicably rushed out of line while a bevy of highly agitated examining doctors came running up with towels and blankets to hide him from view—

What happened apparently was that moments before we reached the roped-off area where the physical examinations were being conducted behind some five or six folding screens Tillman had developed an enormous erection that not only refused to subside but became increasingly rampant as astonished recruits and medical examiners came pushing and shoving around the scene, some to gape and others to prudishly hide from view what was rapidly becoming on the part of the troops a riotous breaking of ranks and on the part of the examining doctors a medical nightmare—

At first mildly amused and having long since exhausted their repertoire of inane med school jokes, by the time I came running up to the roped-off inspection sites to see what was causing all the excitement, the cocky smiles had already vanished from the rookie doctors' faces and they were beginning to panic at the nightmarish sight of hundreds if not thousands of naked Negro recruits (incited by now by wild rumors as to what all the commotion was about, including a rumor that a black recruit had been maltreated by one of the doctors) converging wildly on the scene behind me, igniting the shimmering electricity of a race riot that could break out at any moment now—

In the meantime almost the entire staff of examining doctors had formed a pathetic phalanx around Tillman whose entire body in the meantime had been covered with a huge white sheet which revealed only his black feet and toes and beneath which he was prancing up and down and waving his arms around like a wind-up Halloween ghost—

Then just as the riot was about to get out of control and some of the more savvy recruits had even begun to raid the medicine cabinets stacked up high in the roped-off area where the physical examinations were taking place for narcotics, a platoon of military police came running into the warehouse blowing whistles and wielding police sticks and firing blanks in the air, until after a brief display of bulging eyed but flatfooted resistance the rebellious recruits quietly reformed the long medical inspection line and Tillman was unceremoniously led off to a private office where his short-arm inspection was carried out under the severe watchful eye of a full-colonel from Medical Corps headquarters who, when the inspection was completed, ordered Tillman to be sent back to his quarters and be given a one-day pass and a 12-pac carton of Babe Ruth bars for his trouble—

As if preordained Tillman and I became buddies and lifetime

friends and indeed that same evening after the riot when after a hasty meal of baloney sandwiches and tepid coffee he and I discovered that not only had we been assigned to the same outfit and room number, but that Tillman's bunk was the bunk on top of mine.

And in fact, as if to solemnize our new friendship, that same night, after lights out, and after we made sure the cranky sergeant had actually gone to bed and wasn't just pretending, Tillman put a towel over his flashlight beam, jumped down from his bunk and began rummaging in his footlocker for something which turned out to be one of his precious hoard of Babe Ruth bars which he deftly broke into two pieces and gave me half—

"Since it looks like you and me are destined to be good buddies I'm going to let you in on a family secret, a Tillman family secret—it may seem funny to you, you being from up North and all, but it ain't funny to us down here in the South— You listening to me?"

I could hear him in the darkness chomping down nervously on his share of the Babe Ruth bar and when the chomping sound subsided, he asked:

"Wanna hear something funny?"

And without waiting for me to answer either his first question or his second he began swallowing and clearing his throat noisily and then after a pause for dramatic effect he said—

"You probably won't believe it but you wanna know something, I'm not the first member of the Tillman family to have that little problem—"

"What little problem?" I asked, having all but forgotten the morning's wild events.

"Erectus superbus! You never heard of 'erectus superbus'?

Now I know you a college boy, but a lot of things happen down here in the South you never heard about up North, but back in slavery times 'erectus superbus' was a common occurrence and in fact so common the slave traders and the people used to hang out around the slave block where slaves were bought and sold, those people they knew all about it and even had this scientific name for it, 'erectus superbus,' and it was caused, so they say, by the fear of being sold down the river—"

When I remained shocked and silent, Tillman leaned down over the bunk to see if I was listening—

I was listening all right but I still couldn't make up my mind whether he was pulling my leg or telling me the truth—

"How it worked," he said, "there'd be all these sorry-looking black bucks chained together on the slave block waiting to be sold, naked as the day they was born except for maybe a towel or a rag around their waist, naked as the day they was born, then all of a sudden, like suppose you were there figgerin' to buy yoself a big black buck so your oxen wouldn't have to work so hard—suddenly you'd see them one by one—the bucks waiting to be sold—one after the other all of a sudden getting an enormous hard-on, and then start twisting and turning and trying to turn their backs to the slave-buying public so as to hide their shame for getting a hard-on like that in public—

"But for all those slave dealers, plantation owners and local yokels who used to hang out at the slave market looking for a bargain and a good time, 'erectus superbus' was the main event—

"So much so—," Tillman said, warming up to the dramatic potential of his tale while continuing to spy my reaction from over the edge of his bunk, "male slaves with a known 'erectus superbus' capability were much in demand because they offered a double advantage over the older male slaves who couldn't get it up in public like that—

"Advantage number one being that the 'erectus superbus' capability guaranteed the buyer that the slave up for sale was at least intelligent enough and still had enough freedom genes left in his balls to be scared of being sold down the river, but at the same time had the wherewithal to father a whole slew of little pickaninnies worth on the slave market of the day maybe a hundred bucks per pickaninny give or take ten bucks in today's currency—

"Not to mention advantage number two, which—especially if the master and his wife were in the early stages of their marriage—was that owning a young buck slave having the 'erectus superbus' tendency and capability was like having a sex toy there in the bedroom, to the extent that all young marster and missy'd have to do to get sexually aroused would be to have the wife come traipsing into the room where the young buck was maybe washing the windows or scrubbing the floors and she'd shake her booty at him causing the miracle of 'erectus superbus' to happen right before her eyes—

Tillman paused to wipe his forehead with the blue bandana that was always somewhere in reach and when he was finished he took his good time replacing it back under his pillow—

"At which time ol'marster, who'd been waiting outside the closed door all the while, he'd come bursting into the room pretending he'd just caught his wife alone in a room with a nigger slave with a hard-on, and right away he'd pull out his whip (in some versions of the story Tillman would say he'd rush into the room with his sword drawn) and start whipping poor 'erectus superbus' halfway to hell and back so that by the time he'd finished his young wife'd be all hot and wet and practically begging ol' marster to give-it-to-me-NOW! and before the poor terrified slave could figger out what he should do—run out of the room and save his ass or stay in the room and watch the show—ol'marster and his sexy wife would be rolling and rutting right there on the floor in front of the poor scared slave and dare him to look and be lynched for his trouble—!"

At the conclusion of this tale (which, as time went by, I was to discover there were countless variations and versions, invariably Tillman would let out a highpitched glory shout like a country preacher at the climax of a sermon: "Man, slavery was hell, worse than the U.S. Army!"

5

A few days after Tillman became an instant comic celebrity I was summoned to division headquarters where a young personable lieutenant in division personnel with refined features, perfectly manicured nails and a slightly European accent stopped leafing through my college records long enough to ask me pointblank if I wanted to become a psychiatrist's assistant at division headquarters for the duration of the war—

"I see you've taken courses in psychology, Psychology I and Psychology II, your first year in college," he began, arching his eyebrows graciously as if about to anoint me into a secret priesthood, "—so I'd like to preface my remarks by pointing out that what I am about to offer you is a wonderful and rare opportunity for a bright and talented young man like you to ride out the war in relative luxury and ease—"

He watched me closely and added:

"Unfortunately, given the abysmally low literacy rate of some of your more ethnic brethren in this quaint but completely superfluous horse cavalry unit, we've been having—as you can well imagine—a great deal of difficulty filling some of the more demanding slots so as to conform with the Division's manpower requirements—"

This time during his pause he offered me a flat oval-shaped cigarette in a flat black and gold box of some exotic Middle-Eastern brand, Syrian or Egyptian judging from the exaggerated "Orientalism" of the packaging.

And while he was lighting both our cigarettes, he sneaked a look at my hands as if to check for tobacco stains or to see if my fingernails were neatly trimmed and clean—

"I don't usually smoke—," I lied, hiding my free hand on my lap.

"Well good for you, it's a loathsome habit to say the least—"

And he crossed his legs and twirled around on his super-modern office chair and blew out a dainty cloud of oddly scented tobacco smoke and followed it with his eyes as it wafted toward the ceiling, then elegantly uncrossed his legs and suddenly spun around to face me.

"The reason is, I think—," he began, returning with Faustian elegance to what must have been a favorite topic if not an obsession, "—not only have your people, Negroes so to speak, no offense meant—not only have your people been disadvantaged by not having access to the finer universities, but those few of you who have achieved a university degree whatever its quality seem strangely uninterested in pursuing careers in the mental health sciences even though—both here and in Europe and eventually in both the Far East and the Near East—the mental health sciences will be the secret weapon so to speak in the what now appears inevitable restructuring of human society! Do you have any idea at all why this should be the case? Why your people seem so uninterested in pursuing careers in the exciting new mental health sciences?"

A hot anxious look had crept into his eyes and once again he seemed obsessed with my hands, indeed seemed to be caressing them with his eyes until, finally, I hid them on my lap again and realized for the first time there was no furniture in the room other than our two chairs, a wobbly table-desk and a cardboard box filled to overflowing with Army personnel files like the one spread out in front of him.

"What would my duties be?" I asked, hoping to deflect his interest away from my hands—

My question seemed to please him for almost involuntarily his body seemed to stretch out and relax—

"Forgive me," he said, "I was under the impression I'd already told you. Your starting rank would be Corporal First Class and your job description would be Field Assistant to the Division Psychiatrist, that's me of course, and, naturally, it goes without saying you would receive special training with credits leading to an academic degree—"

When he said that a tremendous sense of relief and accomplishment seemed to settle over him like a heavenly cloud—

He closed his eyes, then after a few moments of silence, he opened them again, and suddenly spinning around to face me and after snuffing out his cigarette in an empty glass of water and with a dreamy self-satisfied look of accomplishment in his eyes, he touched my knee with the briefest flick of a gesture and said in an almost brotherly tone of voice—

"In a way—assuming you accept, of course—you and I would be pioneers exploring the effects of this strangely racial war on your people who, in the opinion of many, and not only left-wing and right-wing radicals, would have every right to side with the enemy—"

A look of panic must have crept into my eyes for he quickly shifted gear—

"It's my understanding—," he began in a chirpy officiously condescending tone of voice, "—you published an article in *The Wayward Thinker*, a small Negro newspaper published irregularly during the Depression in a small office on the Northside of Pittsburgh entitled 'The Burden of Race,' and while you were junior editor of your high school newspaper, in an article published April 14, 1939, you insinuate that the war we are engaged in is less a war against Nazi Germany and Fascist Italy than a race war aimed at the ultimate subjugation of the colored peoples of the world—

"Would you care to comment?" he asked.

I was mortally embarrassed, not by the contents of the article but because the article had been written by my best friend and confidante, Abraham Stock, the son of a frustrated Jewish insurance salesman and a fairly recent emigrant from Vienna where he had worked as a photographer—

"I'm not in anyway suggesting you're disloyal, but to restate my offer in more simplistic terms, you would be my eyes and ears inside the Negro world, my private window into the hidden realities of Negro life so to speak, and as my precious assistant you would of course enjoy many special perks and privileges not to mention the power inherent in such a broadly defined military assignment, in brief, an opportunity that comes along but once in a lifetime—"

For the life of me I couldn't think of a thing to say, especially since he was staring at me intensely as if waiting for me to react, or was measuring the temperature of my thoughts, even observing the agitated throbbing of my pulse—

"Obviously I've learned a little about you from your records such as they are, that you are an avid if indiscriminate reader of books from the public library, that you voted socialist in your high school election, that in your freshman year in college you majored in psychology and minored in music, that in your sophomore year you wrote an essay entitled 'The Negro Race and Utopian Politics,' written for your history class but which you somehow managed to publish in a radical Negro magazine, not the one we mentioned before—"

For some reason I later regretted I felt it necessary to say something in defense of myself—

"My best friend at high school—his father was a socialist and a refugee from Fascist Europe and he got it published for me, not me!"

He smiled condescendingly at my outburst and continued without comment:

"I understand—but what do you really think about all this? All this ideological confusion? For example, it's my understanding many of your people are secretly sympathetic to the Japanese Fascist cause—"

"Only because the Japanese aren't white—," I blurted out without thinking.

"Then I suppose you are one of those who consider this a war for white supremacy—"

"Not really. I personally believe this is a just war, that it's being fought to save the world for democracy—I was referring to colored people all over the world who consider themselves unjustly oppressed, the colored masses who have been held down so long they consider the war a—"

My use of the word "masses" triggered a sudden epiphany of self-righteous excitement—

"—a world revolution for the liberation of blacks and coloreds? How does that make you feel as a Negro-American college student? Does it give you a feeling of manly pride? Does it give you an erection?"

Only then did it occur to me that for all practical purposes I was being psychoanalyzed and that my having been summoned to division headquarters had something to do with the Army's reaction to the near riot that Tillman's erection had provoked—and that upon how I reacted to the division psychiatrist's glib provocation would depend whether or not I would continue to be offered a cushy job at division headquarters or I would have to share the fate of an all-colored horse cavalry unit in a war as yet still undefined—

Suddenly I began to laugh, and the young officer stood up so suddenly he almost knocked over his chair.

"I don't think I'm the right man for the job," I said.

"And why not may I ask?"

He was livid and was furiously scanning my resume which suddenly now he held up triumphantly and pushed back his chair—

"It says here you are a member of the ROTC, that you're a volunteer, and that you're an Episcopalian—! Is that true?"

"I'm an Episcopalian and a volunteer but I'm still not the right man for this job!"

Even I was surprised by the harshness that had crept into my voice and apparently so was my would be employer—

"I just don't get it—," he whined, "—here I'm offering you a fabulous slot in the Army that all but guarantees you a privileged role in the postwar power structure and you turn it down even before you hear what the job description is and what's in it for you—"

"I'm happy where I am," I lied, rising and managing a fairly snappy salute. "I've always wanted to be a Buffalo trooper and, God willing, that's what I'm going to be—"

I felt foolish and terrified that I was making some horribly stupid adolescent mistake—

On the other hand there was no way in the world I could tell the lieutenant that what I really wanted was to stay with Tillman, become a black buck like him, wanted to be baptized in the holy pool of Tillman's family pride, ponder the solemn mystery and wisdom in Tillman's tribal memory and down home ways—

Instead I just stood there and said nothing until finally the frustrated young officer slammed shut my file and slid it across the table so violently it hit the wall and scattered all over the floor the futile papers of my Army life not to be—

"You may go now—," he said as, avoiding each other's eyes, we bent down in unison to gather up the papers scattered all over the floor, "—I still think you're the right man for the job, but the decision was yours to make, so goodbye and good luck—!"

6

The tension of that interview left me in a cranky, spooked out and agitated mood and as never before or since I needed Tillman's manic banter to explain what it all meant and cheer me up—

Instead when I got back to the barracks for a quick wash-up before dinner I found his bunk empty with all the sheets removed and his mattress rolled and there was a note pinned to my pillow—

"Dear D.," it read, "I hope you got the cushy job at headquarters with the shrink, because this Army is one screwed up operation and needs all the help it can get! (Just kidding, General, just kidding!) For example, dig this! This morning right after roll call and after you went off to division hq they sent me to personnel and sarge told me to pack my bags because since it said in my personnel file I had worked in a hamburger joint two summers in a row I was being transferred somewhere way out East to some Army Cooks School I can't remember the name right now but the sarge said I'd been sent to Fort Sill by mistake, probably because Lawton was my home town, so now it's so long sucker, just when we were getting acquainted, and who knows when we'll meet again, but I sure hope it's soon. In the meantime, you remember I told you I have an aunt lives right here in town in a big mansion that's been in our family for over a hundred years? Well when I told her I'd probably be coming over for Thanksgiving Dinner she told me I could bring somebody from camp, one of my buddies, if I wanted to. So when I told her about you being my bunk mate and that you were a college boy from up North she said bring you along but then I got my notice about being transferred to Army Cooks School and she said for you to come over for Thanksgiving Dinner anyway, so here's her address and telephone number and she'll be there expecting you on THANKSGIVING DAY, ANYTIME AFTER TWELVE O'CLOCK NOON! PS: THEY SERVE DINNER LATE SO YOU'LL PROBABLY NEED AN OVERNIGHT PASS!"

7

The house Tillman was referring to (a huge rambling Victorian mansion with towers and gables and stained glass windows that from a humpbacked tree-lined knoll presided haughtily but incongruously over the muddy Yellow River that cut the now bustling Army town in two) and, as I was soon to discover, had belonged to his family for over a hundred years and at one time, in the years preceding World War I, had been proudly described in the Ladies Improvement Society "Visitor's Guide Book" as one of the most historic houses in town. But now, except for the stained glass windows of the towers and gables which at sunset still glistened a fiery gold, the ancient but now rundown mansion's entrance could only be reached by taking a short cut through a briar patch and then down a winding trash-littered alleyway behind the red light district—

More than a mansion the house looked like a dismal orphanage, so much so and as I reluctantly pressed the doorbell only to realize it wasn't working and that I would have to bang the rusty iron knockers to signal my arrival, I was beginning to wish I had remained on the Army base for the Gala Thanksgiving Dinner and USO Show advertised on the mimeographed flyer neatly folded in my pocket as featuring a local rhythm and blues band with "high yallah" chorus girls and the legendary blues singer straight from Memphis, Big Daddy Doodle—and, in fact, appalled at the dismal rundown appearance of the building which as the sun set behind the hills looked more like some sad neglected orphanage than the elegantly austere mansion I had expected, I was just about to go look for a taxi that would take me back to camp when suddenly, from deep inside the hallway, I heard a muted titter of laughter and the sound of someone running down a flight of steps—

"Who is it?" a girlish voice called from within.

"Tillman sent me, I'm Tillman's buddy from the Army—," I yelled back.

"It's Tillman's buddy from the Army!" the girlish voice yelled to someone apparently upstairs.

"Well let him in and sit him down in the parlor—," a throaty older woman's voice yelled back, "I'll be down as soon as I get some clothes on!"

After which there came the sound of chains and latches and bolts being slid and finally the door swung open and a pretty light-skinned girl with large breasts and narrow hips, wrapped loosely in a purple silk kimono with an embroidered vaguely oriental flower design appeared in the doorway.

She couldn't have been more than fifteen years old and after a quick appraising glance stepped deferentially aside and then, with a charming toss of her pretty head, invited me inside—

"Miss Harriet says come on in—," she said, taking a quick peek behind my back as if to make sure I was alone before hastily slamming the door shut behind us.

Once inside I discovered the house was well maintained and meticulously neat and in spite of a pervasive steamy odor of collard greens cooking in a kitchen somewhere out of sight, the house looked to my surprise like the foyer of a public library.

"This way please—," the girl said, pulling open with both hands two double doors.

And waving me inside a musty parlour with ancient plush furniture vaguely reminiscent of a luxury Pullman car with spittoons filled with artificial roses in each corner, her breasts brushed against the sleeve of my khaki uniform and as I passed the tips of her fingers insistently touched my sleeve light as a feather duster, as if she was promising me something, or so I imagined—

But before I could thank her or engage her in conversation she made a vague curtsy, closed the double doors behind her, and suddenly I was alone, but not for long—

In about ten minutes or so a tall handsome brown-skinned vaguely American-Indian-looking woman with an elegant straight nose and an intimidating, somewhat disdainful look in her eyes came striding purposefully into the semi-darkness of the room in which two tiny boudoir lamps, tawdry souvenirs from some ancient state fair, were the only source of light—

"So you're the young college man from up North Tillman's been bragging about?!" she said, clamping a warm and powerful hand on my shoulder to keep me from rising—

"Please, no friend of Tillman's need stand on ceremony in

this house, I'm Tillman's Aunt Harriet, I've never married so it's 'Miss,' I'm so pleased you could drop by—"

And so saying she settled back in a red-plush throne-like chair facing the divan on which I was sitting and promptly lapsed into a trance-like silence while leisurely and with an odd dream-like intensity began to look me over—

I had time to count three showy diamond rings, two on her left hand and the other on her right hand before she broke her self-imposed silence:

"I'm so worried about Tillman," she said finally as I began to squirm. "I do hope he'll be all right, I've never heard of any Army Cooks School, he never said where it was—"

She was right, all Tillman had said while he frantically packed his gear was that it was somewhere out East, that he wasn't allowed to give the exact address, and that there was something hush-hush about the school, something he couldn't talk about—

"Well he does love cooking," she said, breaking the long silence, "that's for sure, always has—"

She was still studying me, still sizing me up—

"I could never understand why some men love to cook and some men can't even boil an egg—"

"In the note he left me—," I said, "—he said they told him the Army was going to need a whole lot of cooks, especially Negro cooks who could cook 'soul food,' whatever that is—"

She crossed her long legs as if to signal it was time to change the subject.

"In this town we've always been horse cavalry, did Tillman ever get around to telling you about our famous ancestor King Comus?"

And as if grateful to have found a subject that would take us off the subject of Tillman, she suddenly got up and went over to what must once have been a handsome sandstone fireplace with gothic carvings but which now was covered with a sheet of plywood to keep out the draft.

To one side of the mantelpiece which was elaborately decorated with hand-carved gothic designs there was a smelly kerosene stove while over the mantelpiece itself and inside a faded gilt frame almost two and a half feet high and covering almost the entire length of the mantelpiece was a jumble of yellowing photographs and time-faded tintypes of Negro men in pre–Civil War uniforms and a larger more formal tintype portrait of a brown-skinned man with a straight nose and a keen piercing gaze wearing the dress uniform of a U.S. Army Cavalry Bandmaster—

"That's King Comus, the founder of our family," she said in a quiet matter-of-fact tone of voice while briefly picking the framed tintype up so as to let me have a closer look but then quickly putting it back in place as if she had changed her mind—

I sat there politely waiting to hear more but she let out a sigh of impatience and sat back down on the divan—

"You're a college-educated modern young man," she said, "—and I don't want you to think Tillman's family has become a family of ghosts—

"The truth is—," she continued after another sigh and a pause for dramatic effect, "—the blood of this family is beginning to run very thin and as I say we're rapidly becoming a family of ghosts and ghosts can't pay off the mortgage—"

It seemed to me that for some reason she was becoming very nervous and distraught and in fact in a few moments she jumped up again as if she'd suddenly come to a decision—

"Come along, young man," she said, "in spite of Tillman's reputed enthusiasm for his new assignment that doesn't mean that all our young Negro men are born to be cooks now does it? For example what are you studying in college? Have you decided on a career?"

"Not yet—," I replied, "I haven't decided yet what I want to do in life—"

"I read somewhere the Army's going to train some of our colored young men to fly airplanes—"

I followed her out of the drawing room to the drafty hallway where she had already started up a steep and narrow winding staircase—

"We have horses—," I said limply, having not yet learned to ride.

"I'm not surprised—," she said smiling to herself, "—you 'Buffalo' soldiers have had horses for over a hundred years, ever since the Indian Wars, have they taught you to ride yet?"

The staircase was not only narrow but steep and I was already out of breath and waited until we reached the landing before answering—

I wanted to say we're not "Buffalo soldiers," we're the 9th Cavalry but somehow "Buffalo soldier" sounded a whole lot better—

"Well, not quite yet, we start out with regular basic training and then specialize—"

"Well I certainly hope they're training you for modern warfare not just to march in funerals and parades. From what I hear on the radio and see in those awful newsreels, horses are going to be no match for those Nazi panzer divisions—"

Saying that Tillman's worldly aunt's mood seemed to change and suddenly she became someone else, someone softer and saucier, now more a nightclub singer about to go on stage than a jaded social worker interviewing an alcoholic drifter trying to get on relief—

"You're a nice-looking young man, ripe to be plucked and sent to the market," she said over her shoulder as we headed down a long carpeted hallway—

"I hope you're not in a big hurry to get back to that awful camp!"

"I have a full one-day pass, which means I'm expected back in time for reveille tomorrow at dawn, so I guess I should be heading back to camp right after dinner—"

"Well we'll see," she said raising her voice as if to underline the fact that not only was I under her spell but under her command as well, "—I've got a room all fixed up for you in case you decide to stay over, and anyway, Tillman's uncle, Mr. Peebles, who you'll meet very shortly, is an old Buffalo trooper himself and knows all the tricks how to get you back inside the gate in time, no matter how late at night or early in the morning it is, so you just relax and take it easy and we'll see to it that this will be one Thanksgiving you'll never forget!"

For some reason the dining room was on the second floor and was every bit as spacious if no longer as elegant and glittery as the private dining room of a fancy hotel and just about as large.

Dominating the almost picturesque tableau of old time family life as Miss Harriet and I made our entrance through the double glass doors was a huge chandelier with clusters of dangling crystal doodads that sprinkled a muted light on the five very pretty and mostly light-skinned young ladies seated primly and expectantly around the table over which the shimmering cascade of sparkling light from above now cast a magic glow of theatrical expectancy—

"Girls, say hello to Mr. D., Tillman's friend from the Army," Miss Harriet said as she took her place at the head of the table while, at the same time, motioning me to sit down at her side—

I did so and smiled sheepishly around the table as each one of the pretty girls smiled back. All five were wearing flowered kimonos identical to the one worn by the young lady who had opened the front door and let me in and were sitting stiffly in their high-backed chairs like self-conscious schoolgirls at the first rehearsal of the annual school play—

In the meantime I could feel Miss Harriet's eyes on me, observing with obvious sly amusement every move I made—

"I'm sure you're wondering why these five attractive ladies are living in a spooky old mansion like this with your Army buddy's favorite old aunt—"

She must have been reading my thoughts and I was caught off guard as one by one the girls began to smile at the tortured look of embarrassment on my face, the expression of someone who has just in that moment caught on to the fact that he's fallen into a trap.

"Put your mind to rest, young man—," she was saying as if she'd been reading my mind, "I assure you there are no mysteries, no mystery at all—or rather whatever mysteries there are are far too deep for any one of us here at this table to fathom—

"You see, when my husband, who was Tillman's uncle—" (she had taken a compact out of a huge elegant purse on her lap and was nervously patting powder on her cheek), "—was shot to death at the Elks over how he had been keeping the books, the bank foreclosed the ancient mortgage on this ancient house and I had to find a solution very fast—"

"The solution I found was these bright and charming young ladies you see seated around this table—Amantha, Deidre, Simona, Elizabeth and Hopeful—my angels, my pupils, my soulmates and my disciples—without whose dedicated help this historic ghost-ridden house would have long-since ended up in the hands of those greedy harridans at the Ladies Historical Society who have been scheming to get their greedy clutches on it since way before the Civil War—"

As Miss Harriet spoke the girls kept their eyes lowered modestly while, at the same time, each was struggling to keep a straight face—

In the meantime an elderly but doggedly erect light-skinned dour-faced Negro wearing an old-fashioned Pullman porter's jacket with the logo of the Illinois Central RR embroidered over the breast pocket had come limping elegantly into the dining room from the adjacent kitchen pushing a hotel serving cart upon which a magnificent roast turkey was enthroned ready to be served upon a glistening white china serving platter and which immediately and expertly he began to carve while Miss Harriet began to gather up our plates—

"Buffalo soldier, huh?" he said grinning slyly and knowingly in my direction but without raising his eyes from his task, "I'm a Buffalo soldier, too, a veteran, and this is a Buffalo soldier town and around here they say when a Buffalo soldier dies and is about to be sent to Heaven he tells the angel if it's all the same to you, angel-sir, I'd rather stay around here at the Buffalo camp rather than go to Heaven because the women here in Lawton is so fine!"

The sly old man laughed and then started coughing a hacking cough but when no one else laughed with him because his face was almost buried in the turkey he quickly assumed a more dignified expression and started to fill the plates, one by one as Miss Harriet handed him the plates for him to fill—

White meat, dark meat, stuffing, green peas, candied yams, mashed white potatoes, boiled greens flavored with ham butt, cold slaw, assorted pickles—

When everybody had been served Miss Harriet turned to me and said:

"Would you honor us with the grace, Mr. D.—, Mr. Peebles usually says it but obviously this year he has other things on his mind like that half-pint of Southern Comfort he's got stashed away inside his jacket—!"

"We thank Thee O Lord for the Grace we are about to receive—," I began, struggling to remember the run-together words I'd heard my father mumble at Sunday dinner for as long as I could remember—

When I finished, Mr. Peebles (whose offended eyes had never left my usurper face as though he hoped I'd make a mistake) sat down directly opposite me and began staring at me challengingly as though I had suddenly become a dangerous rival in the house—

"College boy, educated up North, you say?" he said after a while, "You ain't afraid of ghosts by any chance, are you?"

Suddenly the table became very quiet—

"Now don't you start!" Miss Harriet said shrilly—

"And don't you start telling me what I've seen and what I haven't seen!" Mr. Peebles, his eyes ablaze, retorted—

Halfway through the dinner, which Miss Harriet fiddled with but barely touched, she glanced down at her watch and quietly got up from the table.

"I hope you'll forgive me," she said touching me lightly on the shoulder as she passed to keep me from rising, "—but I have a long-standing appointment with a dear friend I haven't seen for a very long time, so girls I want you to behave, I'm leaving Mr. D. in your hands and remember he's Tillman's honored guest—!"

In a moment she was gone leaving the whole table frozen in an attitude of intense listening as her footsteps echoed through the hall and down the staircase to the front door—

But the moment the front door slammed shut the atmosphere around the table immediately changed, immediately became rowdy—

In fact one of the girls (it must have been irrepressible, sloe-eyed Hopeful, but it's been so long I still get their names all mixed up, but I'm almost sure it was Hopeful) rushed to a corner of the dining room where a monumental crank-up Victrola shared the cramped space with an ornamental palm and quickly selected a record to put on the turntable from a stack in a cardboard box on the floor beneath the window sill.

Almost reverently she placed the record of her choice on the turntable, turned the crank vigorously a few times—and in a matter of moments the vigorous down home bluesy bounce of "Tuxedo Junction" began to transform the stodgy pseudo-neoclassic dining room into a dance hall.

Mr. Peebles was the first on the floor—cakewalking and "doing The Mooch" both at the same time as he came rushing back into the dining room from the bathroom still buttoning up his fly and pulled slender and slinky brown-skinned Deidre to her feet and held her so tight their bodies seemed glued together as they began the slow stop-time foot-dragging one-step called The Mooch—

In the meantime Samantha, the shy young lady who had opened the door when I arrived violently pushed her chair back and jumped up from the table and made a beeline to where I was sitting to the left of Miss Harriet's freshly vacated chair and jerked me to my feet and held me so close I could feel her heart pounding against my equally pounding heart as we moved to the center of the tiny dancing space in front of the Victrola and began our own private "desperate-lovers" version of The Mooch—

"Where'd Tillman's aunt go?" I asked huskily as my body temperature continued to rise precipitously—

"To the mayor's mansion, where else?" she said, her lips hot against my ear, "—poor man's wife hasn't been buried a week, so naturally Florence Nightingale feels it's her bounden duty to sashay over there to cook him his Thanksgiving Dinner which of course just the two of them will eat in the mayor's private dining room, that woman's too much, but then she and the mayor were high school cheerleaders together; and you just wait and see she and the mayor are going to end up running this town!"

In the meantime Hopeful, the only one not dancing, had started to clear off the table. But when the music stopped and I rushed over to the table to help, Mr. Peebles yanked the plates and silver out of my hand and unceremoniously dumped them on the serving cart while at the same time gently shoving me back toward the Victrola—

"Everybody in this house got a job to do according to their talents—," he said gruffly, "—and mine is doing what I'm doing right now and yours is being nice to the young ladies, now ain't that right, girls?"

"Yes, Mr. Peebles—!" the girls replied in chorus while shaking their pretty behinds.

Then suddenly the atmosphere in the room became very electric and quiet and continued to stay that way for almost a minute—

Until, suddenly, someone giggled and, eyes flashing wildly and still patting his back pocket with furious suspicion, Mr. Peebles swung around with the plate he had been scraping still in his hand—just in time to see Deidre smiling mischievously and holding up a ring of keys—

"Girl, those are Miss Harriet's keys, where'd you get those keys?!" he demanded, reaching out to snatch them out of her hand only to stumble over a chair and fall heavily to the floor—

As one, the girls rushed over to help the spry old gentleman to his feet and Hopeful began waving her hand in front of his face like she was fanning him to cool him off—

"Sweet-daddy, you're going to end up with a hernia and a heart attack you don't learn how to calm down and relax," Deidre said, surreptitiously slipping the keys to Hopeful who already had dropped them down her bosom.

"Those keys gonna get you girls in a mule's acre of grief!" Mr. Peebles grumbled as he scrambled unsteadily to his feet and, limping exaggeratedly, began to push and shove the serving cart and its precariously stacked load of dirty dishes through the swinging doors and into the adjacent kitchen—

But the moment he was out of hearing range and out of sight all attention converged on the precious bunch of keys—

"Where did you find them?" Samantha wanted to know, her eyes glowing with excitement.

"I was hemming the skirt on Miss Harriet's new suit from Saks Fifth Avenue in New York—," Hopeful said with obvious pride, "—and she laid them on the fold-up end of the sewing machine and evidently forgot to pick them up when she took the skirt back to her room to try on—"

"Lord almighty, girl, Miss Harriet never, and I mean NEVER lets those keys to her precious wine cellar out of her sight!" Samantha said breathlessly.

"Well she did this time," Hopeful said, frowning thoughtfully as if she were turning something over in her mind, "—what time she say she'll be coming back?"

"She didn't say, probably doesn't know herself, the funeral being so recent and all," Hopeful said thoughtfully as if arguing a case before a jury, "—this is just about the first time she and the mayor have had a chance to be alone like this since his wife had that stroke, and you know how long ago that was, I'd say she ain't coming back until tomorrow morning if then, the next day being a Saturday and with all the state offices closed for the holiday—"

She thought for a moment and everybody in the room began thinking fast and furiously with her until suddenly Hopeful let out a triumphant yell and everybody began to exchange excited glances and Deidre yelled and all joined in:

"Partee! Partee time, everybody! IT'S PARTEEE TIME DOWN SOUTH!"

Not more than an hour later I woke up to find myself totally naked and playfully tied up with bits of ribbon and silk scarves to the bedstead of a huge old-fashioned bed and with a blindfold tied tightly over my eyes.

My mouth was sour and fuzzy with the sticky resinous taste of a sweet California wine I remember drinking almost half a bottle of—

I remembered too dancing over and over again to the strains of "Tuxedo Junction" with Miss Harriet's mischievous handmaidens one after the other and over and over again until apparently I must have passed out and been put to bed—

Now I was awake and from somewhere outside the private darkness inside my head came the barely audible creaking sound of a door opening and then softly closing, followed by the sound of slipper-padded feet approaching the bed across the thick carpet, the silky rustling of some intimate garment being removed and falling to the floor, and a sudden heavy sinking of bedsprings accompanied by the moist weighty heat of bare female breasts hanging over my neck while furnace-hot thighs straddled me on either side and petroleum jelly-scented hair cascaded over my face and a cool slithery tongue began to flick frantically and lightly everywhere over the private universe of my body like the flittering flight of fireflies bringing an amazing light of revelation to the night—

By the time the flight of fireflies had reached my groin and I realized I was no longer alone the cigarette-and-wine-scented voice was saying or rather yelling in moist retreat—

"Ooooh-oooh-sheee-it! You better learn how to control yourself or you ain't never gonna be able to do a woman any good without her ending up with a house full of pickaninnies!"

It sounded like Hopeful but I couldn't be sure because she had already left me alone and tied to the bed while she rushed off to the bathroom and another girl was eagerly taking her place.

"Don't you worry about a thing—," this new warm cuddly presence whispered in my ear as she began to adjust the shape of her warm moist anatomy to mine, "—you just lay still and think of something pretty like Jesus smiling down on you from Heaven while you fall asleep between yo' mamma's sweet-smellin'-big-boobs—!"

The next thing I remember was waking up in the middle of the night with two girls cuddled up beside me, one on either side and a third girl stretched out across my feet but on top of the covers and wrapped in a man's bathrobe.

And I was no longer tied to the bed: the ropes were dangling loose from the rungs of the bedstead—

Of all the girls that night the one I have the most vivid memory of is Hopeful who in the heat of wildly aroused passion had climbed on top of me while I entered her and then, after a dazzling ecstasy of passion, collapsed on top of me and suddenly began to weep desperately on my chest—

Then apparently I must have fallen asleep in her arms with the artificial fur of the teddy bear she had been cuddling scratching my cheek—

But now suddenly the door to the master bedroom burst open with a smashing sound and a bang—

It was Mr. Peebles in his pajamas!

He was brandishing an old-fashioned Colt revolver and was crazy drunk.

"Boy!" he growled, pretending to be enraged, "—what you been doin' in here, in bed with all my womens, you been havin' some kind a orgy?"

By now all the girls were awake and preparing to jump ship—

"Oh please, Mr. Peebles—," they pleaded, cuddling up to the sly old fox with theatrical glee, "—please don't shoot that nice sweet college boy, it's not his fault!"

"Take your hands off me, you sinful bunch of Jezebel hoes!"

He pulled out his pistol and aimed it at Samantha who immediately ran behind my back to hide—

"We were only taking a nap—," she said, peeping out from behind my shoulder.

"With five womens! You call that a nap!"

The girls as one ran out of the bedroom and Mr. Peebles and I were now all alone.

"Did you enjoy yourself?" he asked, beaming from ear to ear.

"I guess maybe we had too much wine, I don't usually drink wine with my Thanksgiving dinner—"

"You might as well stay over and I'll drive you back to camp in the morning. You want some coffee or maybe a little taste of bourbon to rejuvenate your strength—"

"No thank you, sir, I'm not much of a drinker—"

"Well if you need anything you know where to find me—"

And with that I was suddenly alone and in a few minutes I was fast asleep.

Then suddenly I was awake and suddenly filled with terror

and the penetrating awareness that though the house was silent and dark somehow I was not alone—

At the same time I needed to pee and stealthily opened the bedroom door and tip-toed to the bathroom where I felt my way in the darkness to the toilet and relieved myself without turning on the light and was returning to my bedroom when suddenly out of the darkness of the hallway I saw it—

A ghost dressed in a tattered Army uniform from an earlier age and with a fiery otherworldly gleam in the sockets of its eyes—

For a few moments the ghost held its hand out to me and then mysteriously disappeared—

"So now you've seen him," Miss Harriet said quietly and in a matter-of-fact tone of voice as she climbed the steps to the second floor hallway still dressed in her fashionable street clothes but wearing dark sunglasses which she now took off and I could see that she had been crying as though her Thanksgiving with the mayor had not gone well—

"So now you've seen the family ghost—"

"At least I think I did—," I said hesitantly and somewhat ashamed, "I think I saw a ghost in an old-fashioned Army uniform with fire in his eyes—"

"King Comus' son—," she said, "—out looking for his father, still waiting for his father to come back from the Indian Wars, but forgive me, I'm too tired to talk, I'm sure one day Tillman himself will tell you all about King Comus and King Comus' son and about all the blessings and curses that come from having a celebrity ghost in the family—"

The next morning Mr. Peebles drove back with me to camp

in the rickety Buick jitney one of the girls had called from a pay phone just inside the mansion's main entrance—

"I'd give a thousand dollars to be your age again—," Mr. Peebles said as he began to cough noisily and at the same time shake his head solemnly like an undertaker unwilling to lower the price of a funeral. "I tell you this is going to be one helluva war over there, and believe me when it's over white folks is going to have to change their tune. You're a smart young man, I can tell that by the way you handled yourself with the ladies and the way you danced The Mooch, but Tillman's brash and rushes into situations without thinking about the consequences, and I want you to give me your promise you'll take care of him when he comes back to the outfit from Cooking School; I don't know whether I told you or not, but Tillman's the last one in the family with King Comus' blood running in his veins and the family sure as hell doesn't want to lose him, if you know what I mean!"

8

The following summer or, more precisely, the middle of August of that same chaotic war-haunted year, and together with over a hundred or so cocky and secretly scared Negro horse cavalry troopers of what remained of our by now decimated horse cavalry detachment, and after a numbing stop and go journey across the American hinterland on an overcrowded troop train that lingered long hours in almost every freight yard it passed through, I found myself off to war aboard an aging but once fashionable ocean liner, *The Cordelia*, newly commissioned as a troop transport and now embarked on its maiden voyage as part of a convoy of mostly Liberty ships spread like toys across a glassy picture-book sea, the tranquil beauty of which had after the first two uneventful weeks lulled us into imagining we were on a leisurely summer cruise—

Instead, only four days out of Hampton Roads, our port of embarkation, we ran smack into a freak summer hurricane that kept us confined below deck strapped to our bunks, praying and vomiting and cursing our fate as the creaking and aging former luxury liner tossed and pitched its way through mountainous seas and hideously shrieking headwinds toward a now delayed rendezvous, somewhere northwest of Nova Scotia, with what was rumored to be the largest troop convoy to cross the Atlantic since the war began—

On our fifth day at sea, about an hour before dawn, we were violently awakened and tumbled from our bunks by an enormous explosion that churned the sea around us and filled the waves with froth and seemed to seize our ship as if it were a toy and in one final gesture of contempt stand it on end.

Then—as in a desperate chaos I hope never to experience again, the lights went out and alarms began to sound and in the hellish din and in a collective orgy of fear we began to fight each other for the few rapidly disappearing life jackets remaining on their racks, all the while screaming names of buddies and obscenities while knocking each other over in a wild stampede for the exits—

When eventually the frightened babble and confusing orders began to subside and little by little we realized we were safe—that it wasn't our ship that had hit a mine or been struck by a torpedo but the Liberty ship just in front of us in the convoy and we were now allowed to grope our way through the darkness to the top deck where, in the eerie light of that arctic dawn, and as terrified and religiously chastened troopers began to mumble prayers (even today I remember the Negro farm boys from a cooperative farm in Southern Kansas who somehow had managed to form an impromptu quartet and were crooning a lugubrious version of "Swing Low Sweet Chariot, Coming For To

Carry Me Home—" in a pathetic and misguided effort to raise our spirits and take our minds off death) we looked out over the heaving stretch of angry sea and could see what looked like a vast abandoned picnic ground littered with rubbish and debris with here and there a dignified corpse afloat face down or, more rarely, given the cosmic violence of the explosion, a wildly gesticulating survivor—

By the time our mostly green merchant marine crew finally managed to turn *The Cordelia* around in a cumbersome U-turn maneuver and then return to the scene of the disaster, stop its engines and come to a silent halt, the torpedoed Liberty ship, its bow askew and almost close enough to touch, slowly began to sink beneath the surface leaving less than a hundred or so survivors bobbing up and down in the oily slick, all of them screaming up at us as we leaned over the rail to gape, "Please, please, for Christ's sake pull us out of this fucking shit—"

Incredibly one of the survivors was Tillman who I had assumed had remained behind at the Army Cooks School—

But no there he was standing on a huge pneumatic life raft with two other survivors, floating, oil and grease all over him like a tall skinny tar baby with a stocking cap on his head and a dull red slash running the length of his right arm where apparently the impact of the explosion had torn off the back of his fatigue jacket as well as the sleeve—

"Tillman, for Christ's sake!" I shouted hysterically, having ducked under the rope and pushed and shoved my way forward through the cordon of MPs, midshipmen and medics frantically at work assisting the survivors as one by one each stunned and frequently weeping GI was plucked from the water, loaded aboard rescue baskets and dropped aboard the top deck of our ship by the frantic cranes.

Apparently he had fainted and fallen off the life raft moments before the helicopter (one of those early gawky crane-like machines not the deadly earnest flying work-horses of today's war movies) had finished easing it to the deck, for now a nurse was helping him to his feet while a medic gave him an injection and wrapped a blanket around his shoulders to keep him warm and conscious while waiting for a medic to load him on another stretcher and be hustled below.

Incredibly and in spite of the noise and frantic confusion around him he looked my way and smiled—

"D. is that you? Then you must be dead like me—"

When he said that his manic smile froze on his lips and his eyes rolled upward and then he must have fainted and since casualty lists, even aboard ship, remained top secret until the notification of kin, I had no way of knowing whether Tillman was alive or Tillman was dead—

Until one balmy day a week or so later—shortly after our section of the troop convoy had split off from the other ships scheduled to continue on to northern European ports and was heading north through the Canary Islands toward Casablanca—I ran into him again this time presiding over one of two chow lines that stretched around the entire perimeter of the lifeboat deck, now dressed in neatly pressed fatigues but with a cook's bonnet perched jauntily on his head as he presided over an enormous steaming fifty-gallon pot of stew and splashed mashed potatoes and stew on our mess kits while carrying on a cheerful banter of obscenities and inane comments to entertain his captive audience until suddenly I was next in line—

"Well lookee here, Mr. D.—! Whatchu doin' in a lowly GI chow line like this? Shee-it, man, I'm afraid we're fresh out of caviar and pheasant's breast! All we got left for gentlemen folks like you is hog maws and black-eyed peas simmered five days and five nights in gorilla piss—!"

And right away, eyes bulging with laughter and love, he frantically began to overload my mess kit with triple portions of everything on the menu and in those precious few minutes of this our miraculous reunion somehow managed to tell me that starting the following day he'd been temporarily assigned to kitchen duty at the on-board so-called "officer's club" where, so he claimed, his job had been serving peanuts and beer to the officers and nurses while they watched dirty movies and got each other off—

But then in the organized chaos of that overloaded troop transport we lost track of each other until three days later, an hour before lights out, he showed up in our cramped quarters next to the engine room but so drunk and loud he tripped and fell into the permanent crap game at the bottom of the stairs—

"Hey, you sad-ass muthafuckers, you know who I am?" he yelled as he jumped to his feet and assumed a ready-for-the-bell Joe Louis boxing stance, "I'm the lucky nigger survived the enemy's latest model super-torpedo and assigned temporary duty at the officer's club! And you all want to know what I just found out from the horse's mouth or rather the blatherin' white-ass mouth of a drunk petty officer? Something ain't going to make y'all very happy, but there ain't no horses aboard this ship or any other ship in the whole fucking convoy! And without any horses Buffalo troopers ain't Buffalo troopers no more but pure and simple hired laborers—which if you ask me means that for the duration of the war the Emancipation Proclamation's been declared null and void and you-all so-called Buffalo troopers are going back to being what y'all do best, common ordinary handkerchief-headed ditchdiggers and mule-back stevedores, so what you got to say about that?"

Tillman was back in my life but even in those first few minutes of our reunion I could tell that the tragic sinking of the troop ship and the sudden vision of wartime death hadn't changed him one bit—

Which was why, some days later, after irritated and sleepy voices had begun to complain about Tillman's outrageous and by now futile efforts to draw attention to himself and his miraculous survival, I gently suggested he and I go out on the fantail of the ship which this time of night was deserted and where we could spend the rest of the night until dawn reminiscing and catching up on old times—

And it was then in the dazzling moonlight of the Gulf Stream and with our legs dangling over the side and our backs resting comfortably against a stack of life rafts and after I had given Tillman a sanitized and censored account of my Thanksgiving Day visit with his Aunt Harriet and the girls (but then had gone on to tell him what Mr. Peebles had said to me in the taxi on the way back to camp, that I should take care of Tillman because Tillman was the last one in the family with King Comus' blood in his veins) that Tillman finally got around to telling me who this mysterious King Comus was and why he had become not only a family legend but the Tillman family's founding myth, one of the strangest, most disturbing stories I have ever heard in my life—

"You're not listening, D.—," he began when I wondered aloud how King Comus had gotten such an odd name, "I said Comus was his slave name, he added King to it when he was already a handsome young man and an accomplished musician and his master had begun to hire him out to the Mississippi River steamboat companies as a band musician, which is another thing the family always mentioned about him—that because his master was himself an accomplished musician from Europe who had taught his slave to be a first-rate professional musician like himself, King Comus never developed what you might call a 'slave mentality' but in his heart and mind had always been free and intended to stay that way no matter what happened to him, not that he thought himself better than everybody else, but like it was as if he operated on a higher plane, as if the mere fact of his having been able to play so many musical instruments—play them like a pro—and read music like other people read detective stories and the Bible, and at such an early age, made him special the same way people who know how to read and speak Latin even if they never have to speak it except at Sunday mass consider themselves special, as if being a trained musician had somehow given him all the prerogatives of royalty and not necessarily African royalty but royalty along the lines of Prince Albert on the bright red pipe tobacco can, royalty with a top hat and cane and a long Chesterfield coat, that kind of royalty—

"And in fact that's the way he was talked about in the family, like some kind of royal presence that still existed, as if he hadn't been dead for over a century or so but was somewhere in exile and any moment might show up at a family reunion to dispense kingly wisdom to one and all and autograph the Family Bible—

"When my great-grandfather died in Oklahoma—I'm talking about King Comus' only child, the one he had with the Indian woman and who was almost a hundred years old when he died (I forget what year it was exactly but it was during the Depression, that much I remember) they came and got me out of school and took me to the big house some call a mansion overlooking the Yellow River, the same house where you had Thanksgiving Dinner, and on the night table in the piss-and-magnolia-smelling death room where great-granddaddy was laid out waiting for the undertaker to come, propped up on the bed table between a glass of pink denture water with his false teeth floating in it and a bowl of soggy cornflakes which I guess had been his last meal before he died there was this faded tintype of King Comus, the dead man's father, a haughty skinny-lookin' Negro dressed in the uniform of an eighteen-fifty-ish U.S. Army bandmaster with sleepy kinda eyes and a soft dreamy way of contemplating the world—

"But to get back to what happened in his youth, the defining event that made King Comus a legend not only in the family but all up and down the Mississippi River—to the days when his master, having taught his slave (who by now was—at least in his mind—his talented adopted son) how to play almost every instrument in the band and had even started to hire him out to the steamboats as a freelance band musician, sometimes the leader of a band—I once drew myself a little chart with all the dates known to the family as to what King Comus might have been doing at any given time of history and compared those dates with dates in my high school history books at school and very early in my life I came to the conclusion that King

Comus' famous leap into the Mississippi had to have taken place around 1837 or 1838 on a Christmas Day not too long after Old Hickory, as in those days they used to call Andrew Jackson, had signed the government decree that kicked the Cherokees out of Georgia and sent them on that long thousand-mile march across the country in the middle of a cold bitter winter with all their old folks and children and including their dogs and cattle and horses and meager belongings to seek a new homeland on the other side of the Mississippi—

"Now I grant you, how King Comus got mixed up in that terrible God-awful trek across the country is a story in itself, a story nobody knows too much about, but a story that has always stirred up a whole lot of controversy in our family, mainly because Indians were involved—and you know how skittish black folks are about anything having to do with the redskins—but also because it was a white girl, an emigrant German girl just arrived from Europe who was the real reason King Comus made his famous leap—

"As for the leap itself, for example when did it actually take place, I always figured it had to have been around 1837 or 1838 because that was when Andrew Jackson left office, sending some 80,000 Cherokee, Creek, Choctaw, Chickasaw and Seminole tribes west (I see that funny way you're looking at me D., but back home in Oklahoma where I come from black folks are more likely to get worked up about how much Indian blood you got running in your veins than whether your ancestors were 'house niggers' or 'field niggers' on some raggedy-ass cotton-picking plantation, the way it is up North, if y'know what I mean!)—

"Anyway, be that as it may, the day the 'leap' occurred, King Comus' famous leap into the Mississippi, it was dusk on the river and the brand new saloon steamer, the *Memphis Vanguard*, was on its maiden voyage, all lights burning, a big German-style Christmas tree with bright red and white tree streamers wrapped around it on the prow, smoke rising up out of its stack and a full load of passengers getting dressed for the pre-dinner band concert when suddenly the German bandmaster realizes King Comus, his ace trumpet player and substitute pianist hadn't showed up—

"Immediately smelling a rat the frantic bandmaster tells his first trumpet player to take over while he rushes off in a rage to the galley where the Negro cook tells him the last time he'd seen King Comus (you notice how everybody calls him 'King' Comus, ain't nobody, even back in those days, ever dared to call him just 'Comus,' at least to his face) anyway it must have been about half an hour or so before when King Comus had come down to the galley to fetch a deluxe tray with all the fixings for a five o'clock tea on it, especially those itty-bitty finger sandwiches which, so King Comus claimed, the bandmaster had ordered him to take to a supposedly sick passenger in a certain cabin on the saloon deck—

"The only trouble was that the only passenger on the saloon deck on that particular trip was the bandmaster's niece just arrived from Bremerhaven who was on her way to Memphis to be married to a banker who was the scion of one of that rapidly growing city's most prominent families—

"And since the bandmaster was no fool and had good reason not to trust a riverboat musician further than he could spit, and having already observed the way that buxom free-thinking Lutheran niece of his had been devouring his handsome Negro trumpet player with her big blue eyes, he made a beeline to the saloon cabin where—so one version of the story goes, the one strikes me as being the most plausible and the version I'm telling you now—he found the two young people on the bed in dulcet communion, if you know what I mean—

"So shrieking 'schwarzerschwein!' or words to that effect which to King Comus' ears must have sounded like a savage war cry the bandmaster pulled out the German luger he always carried in his pocket to defend himself from 'river pirates,' and then held it to King Comus' head—and was actually marching King Comus off to the brig—when suddenly King Comus made a break for it, started streaking off down that carpeted passageway to the door leading to a lifeboat station which he kicked open and then swan-dived over the rail—

"At least that's the version the men of the family used to tell at family reunions after the bourbon started to flow and King Comus' name would be brought up so as to start all the drinking and fun in good company—

"Another version, the version the womenfolk favored—you know how women like to nobilify the family name just like it really pissed them off when all the men would gather in a corner smoking cigars and drinking good bourbon and would slowly slowly start working their way to the annual discussion of King Comus' leap into the Mississippi—their version, the womenfolk's version, had it that King Comus was a petty thief caught stealing a silk shirt and a pair of gold cufflinks from the bandmeister's cabin where he'd been in bed with the bandmeister's niece who was on her way to Chicago to get married to the son of a big manufacturer, and that when the bandmeister caught him in the act King Comus made his famous dive into the Mississippi to avoid being locked up in some smalltime jail and sold down the river as a slave—

"In fact my great-grandmother, late in her life (like King Comus she was over a hundred years old when she died) and after she'd gotten a little dotty and started having visions of flaming chariots and angels carrying swords—one day after school she called me into her bedroom and even though I was only six or seven years old she warned me about 'trifling with a young lady's affections' and said I should always keep my 'thang' to myself until I was properly married otherwise I'd end up like King Comus who, so she claimed, had escaped being lynched by the skin of his teeth—

"Anyway," Tillman continued, "why he did it, jumped off a riverboat into the Mississippi River in the middle of the night, to my way of thinking has always seemed less important than that he actually did it, and many a night I've spent imagining how it felt and what it must have been like taking a leap like that into total darkness, the unknown—

"I mean, shit, you can imagine yourself how it must have been when he hit the stinking muddy water on a winter night, sinking into that slimy darkness, legs pumping, eyes focused inside his head toward the impenetrable foggy darkness of his lungs about to explode, praying for light but instead having to fight a battle royal with his fear of being sucked down forever down, down, down into that beckoning suffocating stinking nothingness that wants you to give up the ghost and bring your suffering to an end while at the same time he's twisting around and around like a spinning top, round and around in that crazy eddying current until suddenly, while you keep on sinking deeper and deeper into the darkness and silence of death, suddenly, like an answer to your prayers, you bump into something hard, round and slippery, something enormously and playfully alive like (and you think) a whale or an angel but which in reality is only a floating barrel around which, nevertheless, you throw your arms like it is your mammy, and you thank God for answering your prayers—'Thank you, Jesus, thank you, My Saviour!'

"But then the moment your head pops out of the filthy mess and you find yourself now spinning like a top, bobbing up and down like you've got an enormous fish on the line, suddenly you look around you across the violent cross currents of the Mississippi and what do you see?—you see far in the distance the *Memphis Vanguard* disappearing around a bend, that's what you see—

"But then you look in the opposite direction you see in the warm misty shininess of an early spring morning what appears to be a ghostly flotilla of rafts stretching all the way across the Mississippi, all of them, the rafts, loaded down with what in your feverish state of panic has got to be the souls of dead people, hundreds and thousands of dead souls being ferried across the River Styx but which instead are Cherokees, the Trail of Tears, those Cherokees, the ones Old Hickory has forced off their lands and rounded up like cattle into detention camps and then force marched a thousand miles west to the banks of the Mississippi—and here they are now, right there in front of King Comus' eyes, loaded with all their belongings and animals onto hundreds and hundreds of rafts with their wagons and carts and dogs and horses and mules, and now suddenly here comes popping up out of the muddy swift-flowing current a bedraggled and terrified King Comus, more dead than alive, bobbing up and down into their midst—

"Most likely they took him for some kind of evil spirit—a nappy-haired devil come to add even more torment and misery to their already miserable lives and probably started hitting him on his head with their oars hoping he would sink out of sight and return to the world of evil spirits from which he came—

"Except for a young Indian maiden (and no use pretending she was beautiful because in all likelihood even then she was fat and ugly as sin but to King Comus in those moments of hallucination and dream she must have seemed as gorgeous and ethereal as the Virgin Mary, and on the part of that Indian maiden she must have taken an instant and hysterical liking to him and decided right then and there whatever he was she had to have him), who while everyone else was doing their best to batter him out of sight with their oars, sticks and anything else they could get their hands on, reached down and grabbed him under his jaws and yanked him determinedly up onto her raft and, since she was a close relative of the chief, she got her way and claimed him as her own—

"What happened next," Tillman said, spitting out the pit of one of the dried prunes he had begun snacking on as a remedy for shipboard constipation, "—from when the Cherokee woman fished King Comus out of the Mississippi and loaded him more dead than alive aboard her raft until the time some seven or eight years later when he showed up in the frontier Army town of what is now Lawton, Oklahoma, looking for work and a brand new start in life has remained and always will remain one of those argument-starting mysteries nobody, at least nobody in my family, wants to talk about anymore, mainly because of the uneasiness we American Negroes feel about having so much unauthorized and unaccounted for Indian blood in our veins—

"White blood, even low-life redneck blood or even the blood of one of those indigestible genetic concoctions we call 'Creole' blood your average middle-class colored family is willing to admit, but Indian blood, forget it!

"Not to mention the fact that, according to a story my grandmother told me as a child, a story she claims King Comus' son told her about and which all these years she'd kept to herself, to the effect that after King Comus' Indian wife died of tuberculosis and had been buried in the tribal burial ground and King Comus was left all alone to raise their son, because the son was mostly black and not a full-blooded Indian, the other women in the tribe turned their backs on him and refused to sleep with him or work the vegetable garden all the tribal women had behind their cabin, or wash his son's clothes—

"Now if it were me I'd be prouder of my Indian blood than my African blood, but things were different in those days and for me the story always rang true since the one thing everybody seems to be sure of is that sometime around the 1840s King Comus, then a young man still in his twenties, showed up in Lawton looking for work and a new life for himself after first dropping his son off at a mission convent school run by the Ursuline Sisters—

"As for Emmagold Maynard who just the day before had

received from a U.S. Army notary the deed to the late general's mansion which then was the biggest and showiest house in town, which now made her the mansion's legal owner, King Comus' skinny good looks, gentlemanly manners and cultivated European way of speaking must have made him seem the perfect accoutrement (and don't ask me where I learned that word) to her new status in life, the answer to a dream come true—

"In fact, at the time King Comus showed up at her door (I'm not going to get into the exact dates everything happened because I've never been sure of the exact dates myself) she was still a good-looking woman in her early forties with a buxom figure and a handsome head of auburn hair.

"But she'd spent almost her entire life taking care of white people, first in Boston where at the age of five she'd become a live-in servant and playmate for the abolitionist family's only child, even though it was taboo in the family to admit she was the family's legal slave, and later on in life as a grown woman, and after her young master had graduated from West Point and left for the Oklahoma frontier town of Lawton, smack in the middle of Indian Territory, to begin what turned out to be a mostly comfortable and uneventful military career, which career had now just come to an end with his untimely death from typhoid fever, and his burial (with full military honors) in the cemetery up at the fort having taken place only two weeks before King Comus knocked at her door looking for work—

"Anyway to make a long story short, as soon as King Comus was hired and without changing out of his best and only suit, he spent all that first day rubbing beeswax and linseed oil on the floors or—propped precariously on top of a stepladder, sweeping cobwebs and hornets nests from the dark corners of the plaster lattice work of the ceilings—as he cheerfully went about his work, frowning in that elegant, concentrated, concertmeister manner typical of a highly trained musician, which in reality he was, Emmagold couldn't stop stealing admiring glances at him and every so often their eyes would meet—

"That first day near quitting time and while Emmagold was busy in the kitchen fixing him a slice of pie and a cup of coffee, King Comus quietly slid open the sliding doors of the drawing room and sat himself down at the grand piano the general had never learned how to play, lifted the cover, dusted off the keys with his sweaty bandana and began to play the Haydn 'Clavier Concerto' the master he'd run away from so many years before had taught him to play—

"And when King Comus finished playing and was sitting there with his head bowed like he was praying and with his long elegant fingers resting on his knees, Emmagold came tipping up behind him—

"'Where did you learn to play like that?' she asked as tears began to well up in her eyes—

"It was then King Comus told her as much as he dared about his Austrian-born benefactor and master, and when she seemed eager to listen he told her some of the stories the baron had told him as a child, fairytale-like stories about how the young Mozart had astonished the local princes and dukes with his precocious talent and about the quaint villages where king and poets and happy peasants frolicked together in blue-eyed rosey-cheeked harmony in a picture-book land where art and music and refinement were the stuff of everyday life, a far cry from the muddy wagon trails and smelly horses and nasty spittoons of the wild frontier towns of the Oklahoma Indian Territory—

"And by the time King Comus had finished his inspired epiphany of story-telling, Emmagold's eyes had become misty with nostalgia and hope—

"How can it be—, she asked herself, —that in the person of this artistic and yet hardworking Negro handyman she had found the answer to her most intimate, secret and romantic dreams: a strong sensitive young lover to calm the appalling emptiness of the life that now almost certainly awaited her in that lonely and death-haunted mansion?

"And recklessly she invited him to come the next day for tea—

"The following day King Comus arrived the moment the grandfather clock stopped chiming at three o'clock, wearing a clean white shirt and a neatly-tied black tie he'd fashioned out of a snippet of black velvet filched from his landlady's sewing basket—

"And perfectly aware of the dramatic change in her new handyman's status this her genteel invitation to tea had implied, Emmagold invited him inside and with a nervous little flutter of her hand invited King Comus to have a seat in the armchair facing her stiff-backed knitting chair—

"And hardly before he had time to get settled she came right out and suggested (though in a strangely squeaky tone of voice that surprised even her it sounded so silly and schoolgirlish) they get married, the two of them, as soon as she could get them the proper papers from Mr. Herbert Justine, the notary up at the fort—

"And then, when King Comus just sat there staring at her

blankly but said nothing, Emmagold got up and smoothed her skirt and then went to the mantelpiece and carefully selected a cigar from a box that had been the general's favorite brand and then handed the box to King Comus as though she were handing him the keys to the house—

"And this time King Comus understood what she was trying to tell him and it almost brought him to tears but instead he forced himself to remain silent and instead began to roll the fragrant cigar she had just given him between the palms of his hands then put the cigar between his teeth and bit off the end and then slowly got up and went to the fireplace and spit the tiny nub of tobacco into the coals and when he came back and sat back down in his easy chair she smiled and got up and carefully chose a small chunk of glowing charred wood and with it carefully lit his cigar—

"And then, now standing with her back to the fireplace but looking him boldly in the eye, she nervously cleared her throat and asked if by chance he was already married—

"'Yes mam, in a way I suppose I am—,' King Comus replied, but quickly went on to explain what he'd already told her, that he'd been living on the reservation with an Indian woman, a Cherokee, but she'd died of consumption and left him with a seven-year-old boy to raise before they'd been able to get around to having a proper Christian marriage, which in any case her tribe would have scoffed at because, from their point of view, a 'white man's treaty wasn't worth a cripple sparrow's turd—'

"To Emmagold's credit she didn't bat an eye nor did she say another word one way or the other, nor show any emotion.

"All she did was push her chair back as a signal their little tea party had come to an end without either one of them having enjoyed so much as a sip of the by now cold tea—

"But then, lo and behold, a week or so after that aborted tea party, Emmagold woke up with a start from a damp feverish sleep and saw a flickering red glow dancing around on the wallpaper above her bed and heard screams and confused shouting coming from the street in front of her yard—

"And when she rushed to the window, pulled the curtains aside and looked down on the street she saw a rapidly growing crowd of soldiers and townspeople, some of them still in their nightclothes, all of them running toward the footbridge leading to Sweeney's Tavern on the other side of the creek which was where the flickering red glow was coming from—

"Usually Emmagold wouldn't be caught dead on the street not properly dressed but now she put on a robe and without even bothering to lace up her boots ran down the steps and out the front door toward the bridge and on her way asked a stableboy what all the excitement was about—

"And when the stableboy yelled over his shoulder as he too raced toward the footbridge that Sweeny's Tavern was on fire she stopped in her tracks and stood there a moment feeling all shivery and cold and numb all over, then rushed back into the mansion, put on her everyday dress and a shawl, and rushed back to the scene of the fire where without a moment's hesitation she joined the frantic line of roustabouts, loiterers, drunks, Negro and half-breed laborers and Indians and just ordinary everyday citizens of the town including the preacher and the deacon of the church, all passing buckets of river water from one hand to the other in a futile attempt to extinguish the by now roaring and leaping flames—

"Moments later she heard someone near the head of the line remark that the nigger piano player was inside trapped under the bar—

"What happened next you can believe it or not believe—because there was no way in the world Emmagold could have known for sure that the nigger piano player was King Comus—

"But she seemed to know or at least acted like she knew. Because just as the beams supporting the roof of the tavern started to creak and buckle and then the roof itself caved in in a huge shower of sparks, suddenly there she was pushing and shoving her way through the panic-stricken crowd of people running to get away from the inferno and the next thing anybody knew she had run into the tavern through a side door nobody else seemed to know was there—

"Minutes later, the folds of her skirt so charred you could see her pink underwear underneath, she suddenly appeared from out of a ballooning cloud of black smoke, dragging an unconscious and badly burned King Comus by his boots—

"Back in those days there were few medical facilities worthy of the name outside of the fort, just a tiny unsanitary so-called 'infirmary' in the back room of a blacksmith shop that, among other things, sold patent medicines and so-called apothecary supplies, which, if you didn't want to get sicker than you already were, you'd be better off doin' without—which is why Emmagold, without thinking twice about it, had two white soldiers from the fort load King Comus onto a handcart which she herself pushed across the swinging bridge and up the hill to what had once been the general's mansion but which now was known as the house where that former nigger housekeeper of his lived—

"Once there and ignoring the leering scandalized looks on the faces of the ever-growing crowd gathering on the sidewalk outside the mansion entrance to see what the uppity colored maid from up North in Boston was going to do with this new nigger piano player Sweeney had just recently hired (and which customers of the bar were saying was 'pretty damn good for a jigaboo' without any training), she ordered the only two white soldiers present to carry the still unconscious King Comus through the front door of the mansion and up the elegant carpeted staircase to the big room at the end of the hallway that had the general's enormous brass bed—

"No one more than Emmagold understood the cosmic significance of what on the surface had been a simple act of mercy, but which now had become the most important decision of her life—

"And tight as she was with money, she gave each of the soldiers who had just witnessed the deposition of King Comus' body on the general's bed one of the newly minted 'federal' dollar bills which she fetched from the general's safe and which, it must be pointed out, was a handsome sum of money in those days.

"And after the soldiers left, bowing and scraping their gratitude but obviously impatient to spread the news all over town, Emmagold closed the shutters and drew the curtains tight—and in the intense silence that was descending over that huge lonely mansion, she undressed King Comus just as not too long before she had undressed the stricken general the night he had suffered the violent stroke that had so suddenly taken him from her and then, ever so gently, began to rub ointment on King Comus' burned and blackened skin—

"All that week and the week after Emmagold nursed her handsome black prince back to health the same way she had nursed every single one in the general's numerous family back to health when every fall and winter each would get sick in turn just so they could be spoiled by Auntie Emmagold's loving ministrations—

"And when, after fifteen days had passed, and King Comus' burns and bruises had healed and he was able to sit up in bed and eat, she repeated her offer of marriage and invited King Comus to stay—

"And finally he accepted and less than three months after the fire Emmagold and King Comus were married in the vestry of St. Thomas Episcopal Mission by a certain Major Glisson who had been one of the general's roommates at Yale and two classes ahead of him at West Point and who, after retirement chose to remain in the Indian Territory as a kind of lay missionary and who, as part of his self-defined mission, occasionally officiated at marriage ceremonies of dubious legality, usually marriages involving white and Negro enlisted men and non-commissioned officers and Indian women of mixed Indian and Negro blood—

"But as Emmagold was soon to discover, circumventing the indecipherable slave codes to make sure their marriage was legal was the easy part, the hard part was what went on in the bedroom after they had been finally declared husband and wife.

"Remember King Comus was seven or eight years younger than the widow and for most of those years with the Indians he had known no other woman than the Cherokee maiden who had plucked him out of the Mississippi—

"For her part Emmagold had grown into womanhood in a puritanical white household where sex was never mentioned and seldom practiced, unless you want to count those sweaty little games of Little Miss Muffet she and the general used to play as children when nobody else was around and which they kept on playing as adults—

"'I hope you'll find it possible in your heart to be patient with me,' she said one night after yet another futile bout of groping and fumbling had left both of them disgruntled and out of breath—

"'I've been a lonely woman so long that sleeping with a strong healthy man like you doesn't come easy for me, but if you're willing to accept my love for what it is, even if it isn't the kind of love you found with the Indian woman you've been living with all these years, there's no reason in the world we can't live in peace and harmony and holy matrimony too, and just be grateful we found each other and that I have a house to offer you and money enough to make sure the two of us will never have to worry about where the next meal is coming from—'

"Unfortunately King Comus was no saint and when Emmagold finished the speech she felt in all honesty it had been her duty to make King Comus rolled over on his side with his back to her and in the deep silence and funk that he sensed was beginning to settle over their marriage he asked his bride of two weeks if she had any objections to his riding over to the mission the next day to fetch his son and bring him back to the mansion to live."

9

"You remember, D., the week we were out on the artillery range on maneuvers and I told you I wanted to show you something from my childhood, and Sarge gave us a three-hour pass one Sunday if we promised to be back at the bivouac by sunset—?

"I know you remember because it was just after you'd learned how to ride and you were nervous about getting saddle sores—

"Anyway remember after riding about six miles out of camp toward the foothills we came to a spooky clump of trees at the top of a bluff overlooking a valley and then dismounted and walked our horses a hundred yards or so until we came to the end of an abandoned wagon trail and almost got lost in a huge patch of thorn bushes trying to find what we were looking for—an old ruin of a building with the roof caved in and all grown over with poison ivy and you tripped and fell into an abandoned cesspool stank to high heaven must have been choked with a thousand years' worth of rotting leaves?

"You remember that day? Well that old ruin I showed you

used to be the mission school run by the Ursuline nuns where, after his Indian wife died and the women of the tribe wouldn't support him anymore and after eight years with the Indians, King Comus dropped off his son to be educated properly and then showed up in Lawton looking for work—

"What I'm getting at is that now that he and Emmagold had decided to set up housekeeping I guess they reasoned having a son to raise together would help hold their marriage together. But sometimes the way the women in my family told the story you'd think the nuns had kidnapped the boy and were trying to turn him into a Catholic nun and that the real reason King Comus showed up at the mission that day was to rescue the boy from some kind of evil Catholic plot to keep the boy from his rightful father, which of course was nonsense and far from the truth—

"Anyway, to make a long story short, around mid-afternoon and just before vespers, here comes King Comus riding into the compound on the buckboard the saloon keeper loaned him for a couple of days in exchange for the back pay the saloon keeper still owed him from before the saloon burned down—

"He could have taken the general's spiffy calash but Emmagold was reluctant to loan it to him because the roads that far out of town were too rocky and anyway King Comus had qualms about being seen riding through the town on property belonging to the general, because he still wasn't sure where he stood with those rowdy soldiers up at the fort and they might get it into their heads that he stole it—

"Be that as it may, in those days the mission consisted of about half a dozen or so log cabins and timber sheds surrounding what once had been a good-sized two-story frontier Army post barracks. The post was abandoned when the regiment was transferred west for wagon train duty, and when the nuns took it over the first thing they did was add a twenty-foot stone bell tower which they built stone by stone all by themselves and then added that enormous cross they had dragged all the way from their convent way back East which now in that flat landscape could be seen from over a mile away—

"But that morning, as King Comus tied the hinny's reins to a tree and it became so quiet all of a sudden he could hear the kids singing inside, he suddenly had misgivings about whether he was doing the right thing removing the boy from this holy tranquil setting where the big gold cross and the holiness of the nuns protected him from the violence and hatred of that rowdy frontier town—

"But before he could run very far with those troubling doubts jiggling around in his head, a spry hardboiled nun came running out to the veranda as if to see who had the temerity to be disturbing their prayers when, in reality, she had been skulking behind the door, waiting to pounce on King Comus the moment he arrived—

"In fact the nuns had already heard the news about the former slave of uncertain status, a piano player who played sinful jimbo-jumbo music at the Irishman's saloon which, by the Grace of God, had burned to the ground, and who'd had the temerity to marry the general's housekeeper, she too a colored of uncertain status especially now that the general, her master, had passed away. And that the two of them were living in that big house as if he was a white man and the general's equal, which was why the nuns couldn't wait to get a look at what they'd heard was a handsome Negro young man with good manners and a refined way of speaking but who seemed to walk the earth as if he owned it and in a perpetual state of grace—

"So while King Comus is finishing tying up the reins to the post in front of the convent entrance here comes another nun out on the veranda to have a look, an old nun looks like a mummy a couple hundred years old who grabs hold of the big crucifix dangling from her neck as if she's about to give King Comus a good spanking with it, but then, the moment he comes stomping up the steps she scurries back inside the mission which in the meantime has become so quiet King Comus can hear the wind whistling through the birches a hundred yards away—

"By now King Comus is beginning to get nervous, like maybe it ain't such a good idea to take his son back to town after all, or maybe even the nuns have changed their minds about letting the boy go—

"—until suddenly the door opens again and another nun, this one young and pretty but kind of sickly with watery eyes like she's got some kind of fever won't go away, comes out on the veranda leading a slim copper-complected little boy with shiny black hair like a Chinaman and a darting scared fox-in-a-trap look in his eyes like he's already trying to figure out what this is all about and how he can make his getaway—

"And in fact the moment the boy sees King Comus all dressed up in a black homespun suit and a white shirt and wearing a tie coming his way, he hides behind the young sickly-looking nun's skirt, all the while kicking out at his daddy's shins as King Comus cautiously approaches like a cowhand approaching a skittish colt, and when King Comus reaches out to take his hand the little devil starts yelling at the top of his voice, 'I don't want to go with him, he's not my father, he's in league with the devil and tainted with sin, I want to stay here at the mission and become a nun—!'

"By now King Comus doesn't know what to think and he takes a second look at that hysterical little rascal as if he's having trouble recognizing that peevish whining little voice as belonging to his son—

"In the meantime here comes still another nun out on the veranda, this one plump and jolly and carrying the register for King Comus to sign. 'Now there what's all this fuss about?' she wants to know in a sarcastic tone of voice, patting the boy while she herself cops a sly glance at King Comus' visible and invisible measurements, '—this handsome young man is your father and I understand he's just moved into the fanciest house in town with a nice Christian mulatto lady who's going to be your new mother—'

"As she is saying all this in a kind of nasty hypocritical tone of voice she opens the big ledger in her hands and places it on a table and opens it and runs her finger down a column of writing where King Comus has to sign while another nun comes out the door with an ink well and a heavy pewter pen which she holds gingerly out to him and asks in some kind of thick foreign accent: 'Can you write your name, if not just make an X—'

"Then, while King Comus ignores all the sarcasm coming his way he concentrates instead on dipping the pen in the ink well so it doesn't drip and then starts to sign his name with a big flourish like as if he's signing the 'Declaration of Independence,'

'King Comus,' the same name he'd signed on the marriage certificate only this time he underlined the name twice and added an extra decorative flourish for good measure—

"'And is that going to be the boy's name too, King Comus—?' the plump nun wants to know as she fans the page with her hand so the ink will hurry up and dry.

"It's not that King Comus doesn't know the nuns are making fun of him, it's just that long ago he'd learned how to hold his feelings in check when he's around white people by sniffing in on his nostril so he couldn't breathe, a trick he'd learned on the riverboats when drunk passengers would stuff worthless paper money down the front of his shirt and tell him to play some of that jimbo-jumbo music he was famous for instead of all those waltzes and mazurkas the ladies preferred—

"Anyway, by then all King Comus wants from the nuns is to get away from there so he can head back to town before it gets too dark to see the trail. And as he wipes the ink off his fingers with the big blue bandana he keeps stuffed in his back pocket still another nun comes out on the veranda to see his son off, this one young and pretty and judging from the broad forehead, high cheek bones and glittering wild animal eyes, she's got to be a full-blooded Cherokee—

"Anyway, she's brought the boy a couple of goodbye presents, a penknife and a freshly baked corncake wrapped in a muslin napkin. And while she slips the penknife into the boy's shirt pocket and gently closes his fingers around the muslin packet with the cake inside she contrives to twist her head around long enough to give King Comus a sly sizing-him-up-as-a-man kind of look. After which, blushing like a maiden in love, she hugs the boy to her breast like in reality it was King Comus she was hugging, and rocks him back and forth rhythmically while crooning a mysterious lament-like melody in his ear—

"'You should be proud you've got a daddy who's come back to fetch you,' she whispers in his ear, '—we thought he'd gone off to California to look for gold and instead he's come back to take you back to town with him to start a new life in a big mansion a rich man built—'

"Then suddenly she straightens up and grabs hold of King Comus' fingers with one hand and the boy's hand with the other and is about to join their hands together when the boy starts bucking and kicking and screaming again while pitifully looking back over his shoulder at the nuns lined up there on the veranda like black-clad prison guards blocking the doorway in case the boy tries to bolt past them and make it back inside the mission—

"'I don't want to go with him, I want to stay here and be a nun!' the boy whines—

"And that's when King Comus seizes the boy by the collar, hoists him off his feet and gives him a good whack across the head and sure enough, having long since become accustomed to the rough handling Indian kids get from their elders, or perhaps taken aback by the sudden ring of white man authority in King Comus' voice, the boy quickly quiets down and lets King Comus lift him in his arms and carry him off to where the wagon and the hinny are waiting under the birch trees—

"Impatient to get started, King Comus plops his son down on the high driver's seat and climbs up himself on the driver's side, gathers up the reins and is about to drive off when the spry old nun comes scurrying down the steps of the veranda with the corncake wrapped in muslin which in all the confusion of saying goodbye they'd left behind on the table—

"'Don't forget your cake!' she yells hurrying to catch up with the wagon as it rolls through the gate and is about to make a right turn onto the trail leading back to town—

"And when King Comus, frowning with exasperation for all these delays, pulls on the reins and the wagon stops and all out of breath the old weather-beaten nun catches up to them, she reaches into her sleeve and pulls out what at first looks like one of those magic Tarot cards but instead is a garish red, gold and blue image of Our Lady of Guadalupe—

"'May this protect you from the temptations of the Hoofed One,' she says in that hollow airless way of talking nuns have, all the while slipping the religious card into one of the pockets on the boy's homespun jacket, and finally they were on their way—

"For a long time King Comus and his now sad and quiet son didn't have a whole lot to say to each other, and anyway the trail was gutted with deep ruts hidden by prairie grass and King Comus had his hands full trying to avoid breaking an axle—

"And for a long time he kept wondering why it was he hadn't stood up to the nuns, why he had just stood there and let them make fun of him like that, why he'd felt so intimidated by their quiet self-assurance and calm independence from the world of angry boastful white men he used to think he understood—

"But having long ago and indecorously abandoned the glamorous world of the Mississippi steamboats for the suffocating security of a backwoods Indian tribe and having now entered into a kind of informal marriage agreement with an older woman whose outlook and background he never in a thousand years could expect to understand, he felt buffeted by awesome winds of cosmic change—the same mysterious but suffocating sense of foreboding he first experienced the day his child-like Indian wife died and the other women of the tribe turned their backs on him, though for a while he could always count on one or the other of them to slip into his cabin after dark to bring him a hunk of bread or an apple or a cut of smoked meat wrapped in leaves, small offerings like that proffered without artifice after having spent the night with him under his blankets and disappear at first dawn—

"But with the nuns it was like they were always trying to teach him a lesson, like it was their holy right to mock him and make him feel small and useless just because sometime somewhere someone in his past had added 'King' to his name—

"And the boy, sensing his father's turmoil, now moved closer to him and snuggled up against his father's brave warmth and, almost tearful with gratitude, King Comus tried desperately to think of something appropriate to say—

" 'You know something, boy?' he began as the sun began to melt into the foothills, 'I had a dream about your mother last night and she had a crown on her head and was wearing a long white robe like an angel and asked me how you were getting along—'

"The dream he'd really had was of his young Indian wife kneeling nakedly on top of him and riding his hard-on like a war pony for all it was worth and then screaming long and wild—

"But then, stealing a quick look at the boy as if the boy had heard his dead mother's scream, he said, '—and she looked very happy when I told her I was going out to the nuns to bring you home with me and, in fact, it was your mother wanted me to take you to the mission in the first place, she was always saying how it wasn't an Indian's world anymore, that you needed book learning and money if you wanted white people to respect you, and she didn't want you to grow up on the reservation and be made fun of because your father wasn't an Indian—'

"And suddenly, no sooner were the words out of his mouth, all the horror and boredom of his life with the Indians came back to him, the miserable, grubby ghostliness of a way of life lived outside of time, the young bucks preening and sashaying around the witch doctors like hustlers on the make, the endless squabbling among the women about acorns and morsels of rancid meat, the older men laying around scratching their asses, smoking weed and getting high while watching the stallions fuck the mares, while in King Comus the fear of dying and rotting away on that alien planet before he had made his mark was slowly driving him mad—

"And while thoughts like that were distracting him and increasingly making him nervous, about halfway back to town a puny little deer came streaking across their path followed moments later by a pack of wild dogs barking and biting at the deer's legs as it tried to escape—

"All that racket so suddenly crossing its path frightened the elegant half-breed pony, causing it to stop and rear up on its hind legs which in turn caused the wagon's brakes to lock and wrench the axle out of its socket so that before they even realized what was happening King Comus and the boy were tossed headlong into a ravine with the wrecked wagon minus a wheel bouncing down the ravine behind them—

"To make a long story short King Comus ended up having to shoot the crippled hinny, abandon Sweeney's wrecked wagon in the ditch and hike back into town with the boy and then come back the next day with another horse and a blacksmith to get the wagon moving again—

"But they hadn't gone very far from that ravine when King Comus' son realized he'd lost the penknife the nuns had given him and the saint's card with the picture of Our Lady of Guadalupe on it which the boy was secretly counting on to help him remember some of the pleasanter things about his brief stay with the nuns.

"But by then, as it turns out, it would take them the better part of the night to hike the fourteen miles into town and by the time they finally got to the footbridge in front of Sweeney's Tavern and started up the grassy hill to the general's palatial mansion, the sun was coming up over the Yellow River and you could hear the muted bugles sounding reveille over at the fort—

"It was then from the corner of his eye King Comus caught sight of the two shadowy figures slipping out from under a trellis to one side of the entrance to the tavern and then standing there in the shadows pretending they were picking their teeth and scratching their behinds like as if they'd just got out of bed.

"But by then King Comus was too worn out from the long hike into town to pay them more than a passing glance, and besides the boy was plodding along doggedly half a step behind and more asleep than awake—

"Any other time the sight of two strangers heading purposefully his way in the misty semi-darkness of early dawn when there was nobody else on the streets would have set off alarm bells ringing in his head—but by then Emmagold had already opened the door for him and was saying in a distraught tremulous tone of voice, 'Oh my Lord, just look at that poor boy! How come you two are walking, what happened to the wagon and the horse—?'

"But suddenly she broke off and the muscles of her face stiffened with alarm: 'Oh no! No—!' she gasped in one long desperate sigh—

"King Comus too had been about to turn around and look, but now at the last moment he changed his mind but by then it was too late and suddenly he felt the barrel of a shotgun poking him in the small of his back—

" 'Just put yore hands up, niggah, so we won't have to fill that high-priced asshole a' yores with lead!' the first man, a buck-toothed youth wearing a floppy hat two sizes too big that kept falling over his eyes said gleefully like he was having the time of his life—

"His companion, an older man with bushy eyebrows and a square pox-marked jaw was about to shove the boy out of the way when Emmagold, her eyes flashing, finally managed to scoop the sleepy child up and hug him tight against her ample breasts—

" 'What's this all about?' she demanded in that crisp New England voice of command she'd learned from the general and which up to that moment had sufficed to cower any frontier bully who'd had the temerity to offend her dignity. 'This man is my lawfully wedded husband, what do you want with him?'

"But by then it was all too obvious to both King Comus and Emmagold who the two men were, bounty hunters—

" 'Legally married my ass!' the older bounty hunter snorted,

'—this here nigger's a runaway slave and about as legally married to you as a monkey is to an organ grinder's cage!'

"While the older bounty hunter was still laughing at his would-be joke there came a flourish of drums and the piercing clarity of a bugle call, and at the same time the gate of the fort swung open and a mounted patrol came riding out smartly and headed their way, its yellow and black company flag fluttering proudly in the morning breeze.

" 'Shee-it! We better get in off the street' the buck-toothed bounty hunter whispered all the while pulling and yanking King Comus up the steps of the mansion's porch where, since the front door was still ajar, he shoved King Comus inside—

" 'You too, alla you get inside, quick!' he said to Emmagold and the boy, using the butt of his rifle as a prod—

"When he said that the older bounty hunter piously stood at attention with his hat over his heart while the mounted patrol rode by in a stately clatter of hoofs.

"And then, with all of them bunched together on the carpet just inside the mansion's partly closed front door and at least for the time being it was beginning to look like no one knew what to do next, the older bounty hunter, a heavy-set Irishman with a drinker's flushed red face, wandered off down the elegant carpeted hallway like a tourist visiting a historic site, first sticking his nose into the dark elegantly furnished parlour, then down the long carpeted hallway to inspect the huge spotlessly white kitchen, and finally back to where the others were still bunched motionless in the hallway waiting fearfully for what would happen next—

" 'Mighty fancy house for a couple a niggah newlyweds livin' in sin!' he said, shaking his head with wonder and mock approbation.

"'But you know something? I know a couple Cherokee whores could make a whole lot better use of a highfalutin' residence like this, could make me rich overnight!'

"Then he farted and the stench settled over that stuffy room like a poisonous fog—

"'Excuse me mam, no offense meant,' he said facetiously, getting up to stretch and go into the parlour where he flopped down on the plush sofa, resting his muddy boots on the exquisite tea table on which Emmagold had served King Comus tea—

"Then, twisting his head around so he could watch Emmagold's expression change the older of the two bounty hunters assumed an expression of baleful politeness and asked Emmagold, 'Excuse me again, mam, but think I could trouble you fo' some of that good whisky I see over there in the cupboard?' adding as Emmagold walked over to the antique armoire and reluctantly fetched the general's cut glass decanter of bourbon and two glasses, '—you do understand don't you, mam, how us pore country bumpkins what has to do Uncle Sam's dirty work and wait all night out in the cold for you-all recalcitrants to show up feel? I tell you it's no work for a good Christian but someone has to do it, hun, and as the old saying goes, the better and older the whisky the better it takes off the chill—!'

"'What are you going to do with my pa?' the boy wanted to know, sidling up to King Comus and taking him by the hand—

"At once King Comus put his arm around the boy's shoulder as if to show the boy he appreciated the boy's innocent tone of protectiveness and he drew his son close—

" 'What we're going to do with yore pa,' the younger bounty hunter said, imitating the boy's whining tone of voice, '—is put his stuck-up black ass back into bondage where he belongs, then collect the money owed us for all the time and trouble it took to find him and go somewhere and get drunk! Now does that answer your smart-ass question?'

"By then the two bounty hunters had finished off their first round of drinks and were about to help themselves to a second round—

" 'Now don't get us wrong,' the older bounty hunter was saying while playfully poking the barrel of his shotgun in King Comus' face, 'I personally ain't got nothing against niggahs, and I sure would hate to have to blow that smug look off that sissified niggah of yours face, especially now that a certain foreign gentleman from way back when your nigger friend used to play piano on the riverboats who—if his word is as good as his money—will have no trouble at all identifying your so-called husband as the long lost runaway niggah he's been lookin' for for years—'

"When he said that the man rose lazily to his feet and moseyed over to where the younger bounty hunter was guarding King Comus—

" 'Take off yore shirt!' he ordered all of a sudden—

" 'Take off my shirt for what?' King Comus retorted.

"In reply the bounty hunter rammed the butt of his shotgun into King Comus' gut, knocking the wind out of him and causing him to sink to his knees so that for just an instant he looked like a pitiful Negro praying for his life—

"Instead and letting out a terrifying cry of rage King Comus sprang to his feet and sent the bounty hunter reeling with a blow so violent and precise, blood spurted out of the bounty hunter's nose—

"'You fuckin' shitty-ass-nigger sonofabitch!' the bounty hunter shrieked while snatching up his shotgun from where it had fallen under a chair and now was ready to shoot—

"And in fact he'd already cocked the trigger and was about to fire when the younger bounty hunter leaped forward and knocked the shotgun out of the older man's hand—

"'Are you crazy? We been looking for this niggah for close onto five months,' the younger bounty hunter yelled, pinning King Comus' arms behind his back while his chastened partner yanked off King Comus' jacket and then pulled his shirt over his head—

"And while King Comus stood there completely immobilized and unable to budge, the older bounty hunter began to sniff under King Comus' armpits like he was sniffing for body odor but instead what he was looking for was a tiny tattoo which he had been told he would find there, and which would positively identify King Comus as being who he was supposed to be—

"And in fact in a few minutes the older bounty hunter let out a yell—

"'Here it is, I found it! A tattoo!' he said, wrinkling his nose with feigned disgust, '—the Jerusalem Cross it's supposed to be, but, shee-it! Whoo-ee! I just can't stand nigger stink!'

"Right away he put on his coat and headed for the door—

"'You stay here and make the nigger halfway presentable while I go across the street and fetch our benefactor—,' the older bounty hunter said as he bubbled over with newfound energy.

"Not five minutes later the bounty hunter reappeared on the garden path in front of the mansion entrance pushing a hand-cart containing a human figure rolled up in a ball like a hibernating spider.

"In the meantime it had started to snow and when finally Emmagold reluctantly had no choice but to open the door in response to the insistent knocking, King Comus turned just in time to see over her shoulder a tall ghostly figure materialize out of the sudden almost blinding whiteness."

10

“The first thing King Comus noticed, it having been over eight long years since he had last laid eyes on his master, was the man’s feverishly possessive gaze set deep inside the twin-shadowed craters of his long emaciated face. Still courtly of manner and elegant of dress in spite of the frontier clothes he now preferred (only his polished riding boots with an embossed border at the top stamped him as being a foreigner to these parts), the baron let himself be helped down from the cart and tottered and almost fell—

“Only then did King Comus realize his master was not well and to the contrary seemed blotched and consumed by some dreadful disease.

“Nevertheless and without thinking about what he was about to do, moved perhaps by some distant melting sorrow for his long forgotten slave mother, King Comus pushed past Emma-gold and gently took the ailing and fragile white man out of the bounty hunter’s grasp and carried him inside the mansion to the drawing room where delicately he propped him up on the divan and placed a cushion behind his drooping head—

"'I trust you're well,' King Comus said in a tone of cool formality dictated more by the fact their reunion was taking place in the drawing room of a general of the U.S. Army than by any identifiable emotion he was feeling for the man—

"But even so, the baron seemed gratified, even deeply moved and reached out haltingly to take King Comus' hand in his and hold it briefly to his lips—

"'At last I've found you, dear boy,' the baron said, tears overflowing his eyes and trickling down his cheeks, '—I was afraid, dear boy, I'd lost you forever—'

"And after paying the two bounty hunters almost twice the amount of money he owed them, and after double checking twice the soiled and wrinkled indemnification papers the bounty hunters insisted the baron sign before they would hand over King Comus' semi-official release papers, the baron let out a long sigh of relief and then, rising unsteadily to his feet, he turned toward Emmagold and gracefully bowed, clicking his heels together in the style of the German aristocracy he so admired and then took her hand and gallantly kissed it twice and accepted her invitation to dinner—

"But more than dinner what Emmagold finally prepared became all at once a homecoming banquet for both King Comus' son and King Comus' master and a wedding feast in celebration of his marriage to the new owner of that palatial mansion none of them as yet had had the time to enjoy—

"Halfway through the meal, after Emmagold had collected all the plates and taken them to the kitchen to be washed and then brought back to the dining room along with a baking pan of peach cobbler for dessert, the baron daintily wiped the dried gravy from the wispy mustache he now affected and pushed his chair back and rose unsteadily to his feet to make a speech—

" 'Dearly beloved,' he began, looking around the table at each bewildered expression in turn, '—as if by Divine Fiat I at last sit here among you in a state of grace and domestic bliss—'

"By then it was crystal clear to everyone that the baron was drunk from the bourbon whisky Emmagold had left on the table beside the divan after she had given him a tumbler full to take the chill from his bones—

"And, in fact, when after his speech he pushed back his chair so he could go relieve himself he teetered and wobbled and finally fell to the floor with a violent crash that scared everybody half to death—

"In the general consternation that followed, Emmagold and King Comus exchanged alarmed looks as if they were interrogating each other as to whose responsibility it was to do something—

"In the end it was King Comus who, fully aware that what he did next could bind him to his master for all eternity, yet again took the baron in his arms and carried him upstairs to one of the general's guest rooms where he undressed him and then pulled over the baron's nodding head one of the general's fine freshly laundered linen nightshirts Emmagold silently handed him after she quietly slipped into the room—

"Then, without either saying a word or exhibiting a shadow of doubt, they both put the baron to bed and closed the shutters and snuffed out the candle and tip-toed out of the guest room and closed the door—

"Later that night, after she had put the boy to bed and then put a pot of milk and honey and a slice of cake on a tray which she took to the guest bedroom where the baron was fast asleep and snoring with a contented smile on his face, Emmagold came back to the master bedroom and as she had done so many times before undressed behind the folded screen and slipped into the huge master bed alongside King Comus who, even before she could turn over on her side, took her tremulously in his arms—

"When they finished making love and their breathing had returned to normal Emmagold reached over to the bed lamp and turned up the flame so she could look into King Comus' eyes and study his reaction to what she was about to say—

"'I should have told you long before—,' she began in a serious Boston-flavored voice but now a voice tinged with sadness and regret, '—but now's about as good a time as any to tell you I can't have any children of my own, the general's mother saw to that when her son got me pregnant when I was little more than a child myself—'

"'You're a good man, King Comus,' she continued after a pause and after King Comus remained silent and she began to realize his pain, '—and I'm mighty grateful to you for bringing that boy of yours here to live with us, and I give you my word I'll be a good mother to him and a good wife to you, but as far as what goes on here in this bedroom, no matter how hard we try there won't be any babies—'

"As for the baron, for the rest of that week his fever raged and wracked his body, and every night and all night long he coughed and spat and wept and called out in German for King Comus to come and comfort him, and several times during the night he would struggle to his feet and come banging on the master bedroom door for attention—

"Then, just when it seemed certain the baron was about to die and they would have to face the unexpected expense of giving him a proper burial, he suddenly became well and hearty, jumped out of bed one sunny morning, washed and shaved and put on the neatly ironed shirt Emmagold had hung in his closet soon after he'd arrived and came downstairs to the dining room where the table was already set for King Comus' breakfast and quite cheerfully sat himself down in King Comus' place at the head of the table where, knife and fork in hand, he waited for someone to serve him—

"A little while later King Comus came out of the kitchen carrying a platter of hot buttered biscuits and a pitcher of corn syrup which he placed in front of his master next to the steaming pot of coffee and then stood very quiet, almost at attention, as if waiting and watching to see what would happen next—

"What happened next was almost an anti-climax—

" 'I have great plans for us, dear boy!' the baron said quietly—

" 'You got plans?' King Comus asked, 'What kinda plans you got—?'

"The baron smiled dreamily and turned around to face his slave—

" 'A finishing school where along with the rudiments of music, Old World culture and manners would be taught—'

"And all the while spying King Comus' reaction he added—

" 'Yes, yes—I truly believe we have found the New Jerusalem, and we shall make a marvelous family, the four of us, and become, God-willing, a beacon of light in a world of darkness and deceit—'

"It was then King Comus slipped up behind his master and put both his hands around the baron's neck and began to squeeze, tighter and tighter until when the baron slumped to the floor unconscious he was sure he had gotten rid of his master once and for all—

"Instead the baron sat up on the floor and held up a hand so King Comus could help him to his feet.

" 'We're both too old to do what we think both God and the Devil expect us to do—,' the baron said to his slave.

"That night King Comus got out of bed and went downstairs to the drawing room and opened up the grand piano and, in the silence that had fallen over the slumbering mansion, began to play the Haydn 'Clavier Concerto'—

"And in the abrupt silence that fell when he suddenly stopped playing and slammed the piano shut, he slipped out the back door and went to the stable and saddled up the hinny and rode twenty miles to the fort where that same morning he signed up with a new regiment being formed to carry out warfare against the Indians attacking the wagon trains headed west, and was never heard from again until one rainy spring day, many, many years later."

Part II

1

And now, in one of those mysterious though no doubt commonplace displacements of memory and time I am seated in almost papal comfort on the back seat of what surely must be the longest, most decadently luxurious Rolls-Royce stretch limousine the world has ever seen, wondering less what I am doing here than why I am adjusting so quickly to this affront to my once cherished sense of propriety and good taste but which now, in any case, seems finally to be bringing to an end my self-indulgent and self-destructive binge of prolonged two-year mourning my wife Lucia's untimely death—

And in fact, snuggled against the soft white leather cushions of this king-size back seat, speeding south from our villa toward the sizzling commercialism of a media-crazed Rome I never knew existed, growing increasingly comfortable as the truth sinks in that this improbable visitation of my old World War II Army buddies is not only real but is rapidly accomplishing for me what apparently I had not been capable of accomplishing on my own—overcoming that paralyzing fear of a life without Lucia at my side which fear had already begun to short circuit that mysterious and always tenuous balance between sanity and the loss thereof—

So in a very private way, therefore, I am not surprised that, yes, they are here, and in fact Joe Stabat, the commanding officer of my World War II Trucking Battalion is sitting in the front seat next to the driver, a very pretty (the awareness has come only gradually) indeed strangely beautiful, brown-skinned young black woman, a gospel singer I have just been told, whose name, at once poetic and enigmatic, is "Little Antioch," and who, I understand, is related not only to Tillman, our company cook and my Army buddy of those almost forgotten days of World War II but that (and for me this is the most unsettling realization of all) the four of us, all living ghosts from each other's past, are actually here inside this glistening white behemoth of a Rolls-Royce stretch limousine, speeding down a narrow two-lane, poplar tree-lined country road just outside the town of Pontassieve on a fantastic mission that will eventually take us, so Tillman has just told me, to a place not far from our first World War II campsite in Italy, a place called Campo di Constantino—

But why we are going there and why I am being dragged along with them has just been explained to me in great detail by Joe Stabat himself who like all of us looks older, flabbier and more vulnerable though everyone, everyone except me, is dressed snappily in what appears to be some fashion designer's concept of a futuristic military-inspired unisex uniform in shiny lavender and black gabardine with the insignia STABAT .COM tastefully embroidered above the breast pocket—

But most unnerving of all, at least for me, is how little Joe Stabat and Tillman have changed from the last time I remember seeing them, the two of them driving off somewhere in the front seat of a jeep loaded down with duffle bags filled with stolen art objects and other contraband—

Joe Stabat, who seems to have changed least now has a slight middle-age bulge and deeper worry lines on his face but also that secret weapon of his, a childish expression of helpless vulnerability which apparently is still capable of changing in a matter of moments to one of flashing rage, still looks sun-tanned and fit and very much still in the game, especially now as I watch him place a possessive arm around the young gospel singer, Little Antioch (who every time our eyes meet in the rear mirror seems dying to tell me something only to signal me with her eyes to be patient and wait until the moment is right) who for nearly an hour now has been driving this our outlandish and outsized chariot with the easy nonchalance of one who has been driving Rolls-Royces all her life—

Right on cue Joe Stabat senses my frantic musings about the young lady seated beside him and now turns around to face me and says in that gruff snarling voice that has always been his trademark, "Come on, man, I know you've heard about Little Antioch, what kinda padded cell you been hiding out in? This young lady here just happens to be the hottest thing in gospel, number one on the charts and one of the 100 Most Recognizable Celebrities on the planet as listed in *Planet Celebrity Review*, and don't tell me you don't read *Planet Celebrity Review*, Oprah reads it, Larry King reads it and even Henry Louis Gates who I'm sure you know because he's a college teacher and a snob just like you and teaches slobs like me how to be cultured and smart like you, only a little hipper, hipper and younger, not that you look like an old guy, you could still be in your thirties, no more than your fifties, your early sixties maybe, but you got to do something about that mousy tweed jacket, shit, man, you gonna be hanging out with the likes of us, you gotta look like the future to be the future, which is to say that by the time we go worldwide, Campo di Constantino is going to look like some kinda futuristic Garden of Eden, all silver and gold and lavender and white, glistening in the night like a beacon of hope and salvation for a world gone sour and just about ready to vomit its fear and violence all over the fucking universe, isn't that right Angie?"

Little Antioch winces, but moments later smiles that late-blooming teenager smile of hers which in my furtive, love-starved-widower state of mind makes her seem wild, savvy, and conscious of the power she wields over her captive audience of older men—

(But now on closer scrutiny, observing the homely curlers and pigtails beneath the Gucci scarf that covers her head I decide Little Antioch must be well over thirty years old and, I naively decide, has to be one of those knowing professional women who cunningly reinvent their beauty over and over again according to whatever new histrionic challenge life has thrown their way, so that even now hunched over the wheel like a racing car driver and driving at an outrageous speed down this narrow ancient road once travelled by chariots and carts, her eyes sparkle with teenage risk-taking glee, a wild child out on a Saturday night date—)

But my old Army buddy Tillman can tell I'm still not impressed and apparently it's beginning to get on his nerves—

"Man, I don't know where you've been all these years, or what you've been doing beside writing books nobody wants to buy, but you've got to have heard about the scandal that happened when Joe Stabat bought out Little Antioch's contract with the Living God Religious Publishing Company of Nashville, Tennessee, the outfit signed her on the spot the same night she won that *Gospel Time* talent show, used to be on once a week way back when and long before big time shows like *American Idol* ran itty-bitty talent shows like that off the air, wanted to give her a measly fifteen-percent share in the label, and that was way back in the nineties when the white boys were just discovering the big-bucks potential of gospel and were robbing some of those down-home gospel singers right and left, shit, man, it was all over the newspapers, even *Variety* ran a piece about it—and can you believe it!—that same year she became the hottest thing in gospel, three platinum albums in a row, not including her latest ten million copy album and worldwide hit, 'Lord, Lordy Lord, I Need an Explanation—' "

Suddenly I wanted to turn back and go home to the villa and my son because, frankly, I was already bored and very much over my head and moreover all this frenetic immersion into gospel lore and gospel greed was beginning to make me feel stupid and trapped as though the measured cultural life Lucia and I had shared for so many years was being purposely defiled, demolished, and condemned as elitist and effete—and that, in fact, by getting into Joe Stabat and Tillman's improbable white Rolls-Royce stretch limousine I had fallen (albeit involuntarily) into some kind of metaphysical trap on wheels, a wild rollercoaster ride leading nowhere but to the metaphysical amusement park exit—

"But then she had that horrible accident made headlines all over the world!"

"Who? What horrible accident? Luminella, Joe Stabat's wife—?"

"No, man, Angie! Little Antioch! If she'd known Joe Stabat when it happened Joe Stabat's lawyers would've sued the dentist whose drill perforated her vocal chords for a billion dollars, but unfortunately Joe Stabat wasn't in the picture then—but now that his wife has disappeared and he's managing Angie's career full time, things are definitely looking better, and you wait and see this Gospel Summit of ours is what's going to put her back on top!"

I was staring at Tillman with suspicion and shock and he jabbed me playfully in the ribs—

"Hey, old buddy, cheer-up! This is good news I'm giving you, not a death sentence, and from what I hear, especially now you've lost your beloved Italian wife, right?—you could use some good news, which reminds me, I've been meaning to ask you this for years and never did get around to it: you remember that Thanksgiving 1942 or maybe it was 1943, anyway that Thanksgiving just before we were shipped overseas, and I was away at cooking school, and I had my Aunt Harriet invite you to the big house in Lawton for Thanksgiving Dinner, and you went and in fact—or so my aunt told me—what I heard was, the girls gave you a REALLY good time, in fact the way my aunt described it to me, you-all horny teenagers had like a one-man, five-girl orgy in bed, you remember that? Well what I want to know is just one thing, something's been keeping me awake at night all these years, what I'm asking you now is was the girl you finally got it on with that Thanksgiving Day orgy so to speak, was her name Hopeful by any chance?"

Almost immediately I was shaken by a major tremor of memory, a flash memory of a battered Christmas package I received the same year the war ended with a mistaken APO address on it and inside a canned Thanksgiving Dinner with all the trimmings but with no name or address on the package inside or out, only a Kodak snapshot of a cute brown-skinned baby girl and on the back of the photograph the inscription: "Guess who's the daddy!!!"

Seldom have I felt as trapped as I felt in that moment!

Fortunately in that very moment Joe Stabat who I thought had been napping was suddenly and vociferously awake and wildly yanking on Little Antioch's arm for her to stop—

"Stop, Angie, goddamit to hell, didn't you hear me tell you to stop?"

"How could I hear anything with you snoring right in my ear!"

"Well, damn it, if it would please your fucking highness would you mind pulling off the road into that vineyard there, I've got an urgent call of nature, RIGHT NOW! I should've known better than eat mussels this far from the sea—"

And still grumbling to himself he flung the door open and jumped to the ground paratrooper style just moments before Little Antioch was able to brake the Rolls-Royce to a gentle halt on the edge of a rather large vertically tiered and walled vineyard whose finicky rows of grapevines crisscrossed the softly rolling hillside as far as the eye could see—

Then as we all watched while pretending not to, Joe Stabat first pretends he is admiring the elegant symmetry of row after row of grapevines rising toward the distant summit of the hills, then suddenly turns to the left and trots off spryly toward a secluded spot behind a disintegrating stone wall where now, only partially out of sight, he frantically lowers his trousers and hunkers down to do whatever it is he has to do—

In the meantime Little Antioch was already reaching inside her oversize brocade and leather travel bag to pull out a roll of extra-soft (the words were emblazoned in English just above the label) toilet paper, causing me to speculate whether they had brought toilet paper all the way from New York; while in the meantime Joe Stabat was squatting down in plain view and apparently just in time to catch the roll of deluxe toilet paper Little Antioch had just run over to toss him—and apparently at the precise moment he needs it most—

"Man calls himself one of the twelve most richest men in the business," Tillman says snickering (but with his hand cautiously covering his mouth while at the same time he is nudging me in the side), "—and the biggest thrill he can come up with is taking a crap in the middle of a stoney-ass Italian vineyard!"

But now Joe Stabat's head has already reappeared over the top of the crumbling stone wall and then the boss himself—taking deep breaths and jerking his arms up and down and backwards and forward in a pitiful imitation of U.S. Army calisthenics—comes swaggering back toward the Rolls and I can't help but admire how quick Tillman jumps out of the stretch limousine to hold the door open for him and how elegant and well preserved and even boyish-looking my old Army buddies look as they perform their comedy routine of noblesse oblige—

In fact, with the exception of the almost theatrical whiteness of Joe Stabat's full head of hair, the shrewd wrinkles around his eyes and the self-satisfied bulge of his stomach that no amount of expensive tailoring can hide, our old legendary company commander appears to have aged very little since the day he first showed up at our camp—

Especially now as in an almost frightening moment of déjà vu, he suddenly stops in his tracks as if he has just remembered something, drops to his knees at the edge of a row of grapevines and begins digging furiously into the soft black soil with both hands, like a dog digging for a bone, then stops digging long enough to pull a penknife out of his pocket which he quickly opens and then starts hacking away at the grapevine's roots which he has just uncovered with his hands—

When after what seems an eternity he finally comes back to the limousine while he gets in the back with me—

Then, as soon as he has slammed the door shut, he hands me the moist grapevine root he has dug up just a few moments before and, with a sly look of amusement in his eyes, asks gruffly—

"Soldier, do you remember what this is?"

"A root, sir—a grapevine root!"

"Then run your finger over it!" he orders in a credible imitation of a commanding officer's tone of voice—

Obediently I take the grapevine root out of his hand, run my finger over its moist nubby surface, and then hand it back—

"You feel all that suffering and pain, soldier—?" Joe Stabat asks sternly.

"YessSIR!" I reply, involuntarily snapping to attention as suddenly I remembered that strange wartime ritual he'd imposed on us that wartime day in Italy he showed up unannounced at our camp to become our new commanding officer—

But then, almost as if the memory of those days is too painful to make fun of, he lets out a deep sigh, takes the grapevine root out of my hand and almost angrily tosses it out the window and then settles down in the back seat beside me—

"You make any money writing books?"

I laughed nervously and looked away without answering—

"That bad, huh?"

In that same moment Little Antioch swerves recklessly onto the superhighway access lane—

"Goddamit to hell, Angie! Slow down, for Chrissake!—you trying to get us killed before we even get there?"

Then, turning back to me and taking up where he left off, "—well don't let it bother you, money's only part of what it's all about, I suppose you heard about my wife—?"

(For a fleeting moment a tenuous image of her cool aristocratic beauty floated into focus but just as quickly floated away.)

"No, was there something I was supposed to have heard about?"

"I didn't mean to imply she died—and my condolences about you losing your wife—but as far as anybody knows she's still alive somewhere—we'd been living separated inside the same big house for more years than I care to remember, I remember she read one of your books and wanted to write you but never got around to it, and now I guess it's too late—

"But then again she was a rebel, always was and always will be a rebel, she got it from her father, a professor like you, you remember the story, don't you? Christ, we all knew, must have heard it a million times, how the fucking Fascists arrested her father and locked him up in a prison for the criminally insane just because the old fart—actually he wasn't all that old—got it into his head to protest those idiotic so-called Racial Laws Mussolini dreamed up, the one fucking thing me and the countess had in common, keeping one step ahead of those fucking Fascist Police—I'm talking about her crazy father, the nutty professor—he and his nutty students wearing huge Star of Davids pinned on their supposed-to-be biblical robes and, can you imagine?!—on Mussolini's birthday, parading back and forth in front of Fascist Party headquarters while another nut in a black uniform and boots walks behind them with a whip, pretending to be scourging them, and none of them were Jews, just a bunch of smart-ass radicals, probably rich kids didn't have anything better to do with their time, what happened was, they put her father, the nutty professor, in one of those dismal hospitals for the criminally insane where they must have done something to him, something to his mind, because he never got his memory back, and though she never said anything to me about it until much later, you remember that first day the countess showed up at our camp? We didn't know it then but that was the day her father, the nutty professor died—"

In the meantime two deep furrows have appeared on Joe Stabat's forehead and I notice his lower lip has become limp and dry and is trembling angrily until finally he starts sucking it in while he tosses his cigar out the window and reaches in his breast pocket for another cigar which he sticks between his lips and takes a deep breath like he's trying to get hold of himself—

"That's the trouble with people like that," he says finally, fumbling for matches or a lighter, "—those so-called aristocrats, they always go to extremes!"

And when he realizes that by our silence everybody in the stretch limousine is embarrassed because he himself is embarrassed, he forces a laugh and says in a bright, “Who cares?” tone of voice:

“You know what she always used to say, my late wife, the countess, what she’d say when she wanted to get my goat? That I’d lost touch with my agrarian gods.”

2

They met, Joe Stabat and Luminella di Constantino, his aristocratic Italian wife to be, shortly after our by then decimated and demoralized and all-Negro horse cavalry battalion had finally arrived in the Italian Peninsula War Zone—but without officers, without our horses, and without an official mission, but with our status as an historical horse cavalry battalion under serious reexamination by Army headquarters, and therefore without any clearly identifiable mission and suddenly up for grabs—

So that when after nearly a month at sea our troop ship finally was allowed to drop anchor in the Bay of Naples, Naples had just experienced one of its worse bombings of the war and the port area was almost totally in ruins so that in order to disembark from the rickety troop transport that had brought us from Oran in North Africa to this suffering, shell-shocked city, each soldier coming ashore had to juggle an overstuffed barracks bag on his shoulder while tip-toeing precariously over a floating walkway of narrow planks precariously tied onto a pathway of wildly bobbing pontoons—

And yet and in spite of the tragic devastation all around us and the scary reminders of wartime danger and death we were still the same motley assemblage of cocky black horse cavalry GIs who had embarked from Hampton Roads, Virginia, some six or seven weeks before whose morale therefore was still unrealistically high, mostly because of a certain persistent rumor concerning our wartime destiny that for the last week or so had been spreading through our ranks like wildfire, a rumor which to this day no one knows for sure how it got started but which had actually convinced us that as soon as our ship landed on Italian soil, and on special orders from the White House and Franklin D. Roosevelt himself, our legendary and historic Negro horse cavalry battalion was going to be issued brand new 19th-century horse cavalry uniforms, theatrical costumes but authentic in every detail from the wardrobe stocks of Italy's famous Cinecittà film studios in Rome along with thoroughbred horses from the Royal Stables just outside Rome so that, the moment the 5th Army broke out of Anzio and was ready to march north to liberate Rome, we Negro troopers of a glorious Indian fighting tradition were to be invited to ride at the head of the 5th Army's armored column as it made its triumphant entry into Rome—

"You know how Italians love those John Wayne movies where the horse cavalry arrives just in the nick of time!" Tillman, the main purveyor of this highly suspicious scenario crowed, always adding with a knowing nod of his head, "At least that's the PR image they'd be trying to convey—"

The truth was, true or not, we really wanted to believe that ridiculous rumor, mainly because all during basic training we had been encouraged to wear our yellow and black horse cavalry shoulder patch with exaggerated pride—

For that reason our sudden transformation from romantic Indian-fighting cavalryman to your everyday average truck driver was a letdown almost too great to endure—

Which is why, the very morning our outfit received orders straight from Theatre headquarters to change the name and designation of our horse cavalry detachment to the 3824th Quartermaster Truck Battalion, a grinning and demoniacally cheerful Tillman was right there on hand to rub it in—

"Well what'd you-all chumps expect?" he teased, "Jim Crow is Jim Crow in the Army or out of the Army and I KNOW all you bona fide country Negroes ain't forgotten my man Jim Crow, so what I'm hearing on the grapevine is that since Jim Crow's always been the boss man in Rome, Georgia, now that you're in Italy—what did y'all chumps expect?"

And in fact no more than three weeks later what was left of our glorious horse cavalry battalion did indeed make its entry into Rome, but not at the head of a triumphant 5th Army armored column hosanna-ed by pretty girls tossing flowers and kisses, but in the dead of night and only long enough to unload our trucks of their cargo of countless sacks of flour—with the inscription "GIFT OF THE AMERICAN PEOPLE" stamped on each sack in green ink—into various dismal warehouses behind the Central Railroad Station of Rome but in the middle of the night while the city slept, and then proceeded with our trucks unloaded to a point on a map some twenty or thirty miles north of Rome across the Milvio Bridge toward a site some historians claim was the hallowed ground where Constantine I experienced his "Vision of the Cross"—

Which is why dawn of the second day of our chaotic arrival in Italy found us curled up asleep in the cramped front seats of brand new GM 6x6 trucks (now parked in the middle of a vineyard just outside the walls of a tiny medieval town dominated by a somber ancient church which other than its graceful bell tower was hidden from our view by an incredible jumble of ancient stone dwellings which from a distance seemed to be spilling into a distant calm blue sea)—

Five hours later and after a fitful sleep had partially calmed our surly put-upon mood, and just moments before a dazzling burst of sunlight exploded over the horizon like a splattered egg, we sleepless, quarrelsome and unfed Negro GIs ("A long way from home—") many of us growing increasingly belligerent and drunk from frequent trips to a huge demijohn of purple wine a stocky farm woman had given us in exchange for a carton of Lucky Strike cigarettes, suddenly out of nowhere a seemingly out-of-control jeep driven by a stocky officer dressed in what appeared to be brand new officer's pinks came careening into our midst raising a huge cloud of vineyard dust and sending us racing for cover while yelling obscenities and curses over our shoulders before finally coming to a screeching anticlimactical halt—

And while the dust settled enough for us to see who if anyone was driving the apparently out-of-control vehicle, a swarthy, stocky, tangle-haired young officer with bushy black eyebrows and a cocky street-smart look in his eyes, took his good old time first getting out of the jeep and then climbing up on the hood to ask loudly and in a—for us—unusual variation of a New York or New Jersey accent, "Who the hell's in charge here?"

It was Tillman who, having just completed cook's school and thus almost automatically been promoted to the rank of staff-sergeant, promptly (some said too promptly there having been little or no discussion among us as to who really was in charge of what remained of our now decimated and horseless 9th cavalry horse cavalry battalion—) raised his hand and then snapped smartly to attention and saluted in the direction of the stocky white newcomer who with equal finesse saluted him in return, clicked the heels of his boots and saluted once again for good measure, and then ordered Tillman to have the men line up for formation while in the meantime he himself got out from behind the wheel and awkwardly got up on top of the brand new jeep's hood—

"Form ranks!" Tillman shouted—

And while all this manic hustle and bustle was going on, and an extremely bright summer sun was beginning to rise over the distant horizon, I glanced at my wristwatch and made note of the time which was 5:45 in the morning and for us, at long last, World War II was about to begin.

3

When finally we had lined up, our new commander looked down at us and—so Tillman claimed—involuntarily winced and swallowed but then quickly got himself together and in a surprisingly deep but foreign-accented tone of voice said quietly, "All right, you guys, the party's over and we've got a war to win, for your information my name is Joe Stabat, Captain Joseph Stabat, and I am your new commanding officer, any questions?"

Obviously there were none, only bewildered looks—but then, having said that and without waiting for a reply he seemed momentarily confused as if already he had forgotten what he was doing there standing on the hood of a jeep in front of a bunch of surly undisciplined Negroes and instead began looking around until something in the direction of the vineyard had apparently attracted his attention—

In fact and as we began to exchange puzzled looks with each other, the burly young officer with a tough-guy New York accent promptly jumped to the ground, marched stiffly toward a row of grapevines where he immediately got down on his knees and with a penknife he pulled out of his pocket began to hack away at something in the moist soil, something he was having a hard time hacking loose—

But when finally he straightened up from his labors and came back to the jeep with whatever it was he had been hacking away at (now wrapped in a handkerchief pulled out of his back pocket) he climbed back up on the hood of the jeep and held up something for all of us to see—

"How many a you guys know what this is I'm holding in my hand?" he asked in that gruff urban-ethnic accent most of us had heard only in the movies—

By now the whole scene had become so unexpected and theatrical no one seemed inclined to answer, so I spoke up—

"A root, sir, a grapevine root!"

"What's your name, corporal?" our new leader asked, gratitude written all over his swarthy-complected face— "I'm glad we have at least one smart soldier among you, your answer is exactly right, a grapevine root! And as a reward for your acumen and expertise, you're entitled to a one-day pass to Rome as soon as we set up camp and get settled—"

So saying he then jumped down from the jeep, motioned for me to step forward and when I had done so he placed the severed grapevine root in my hand, closed my fingers around it and ordered me to pass it on—

"Pass it around! I want each of you to feel it!"

And while our new commanding officer began parading back and forth in front of us while keeping one eye peeled on what we were doing the grapevine root began to be passed gingerly from one hand to the other—

Then suddenly he stopped and raised himself on his toes—

"Now then, men, pay attention! As each of you soldiers passes this sacred grapevine root to the man next to you I want each of you soldiers to run your fingers over all those bumps and nubs and experience all the pain and suffering my people felt tilling it on those rocky ancient fields—"

By then we were all hypnotized by what we were being asked to do until finally the root found its way back to the front of the formation and it became Tillman's turn and then mine—

Instead I didn't wait for Tillman to hand it to me but snatched it out of his hand and, breaking ranks, gingerly tossed the root back to the captain who, after giving me a smart salute, ceremoniously and like a priest serving mass, pulled a huge handkerchief from his back pocket which he painstakingly wrapped around the root like a shroud, then stuffed the unwieldy bundle into an unbuttoned breast pocket of his shirt, and in a hoarse stagy voice yelled smartly:

"At ease, men! Did everybody feel the pain and suffering?"

"Yessir!" came the reply in chorus—

"—the agony and suffering of all we hard-working, God-fearing peasants who in imitation of the Holy Christ have watched over that root through the darkness of the ages—?"

"Yessir!"

"Now how many of you soldiers know what a peasant is?"

You could hear the sound of shuffling feet but no answer was forthcoming—

"Well I can understand your puzzlement—but what I want you men to keep in mind and never forget is that by virtue of this uniform and the two gold bars on my collar your commanding officer is both and at the same time a peasant AND a gentleman and therefore I don't want to hear a lot of whining about cotton fields and slavery, because all of us are here in Italy for one reason and one reason only and that is to win this fucking war for Uncle Sam! Have I made myself clear?"

"YESSIR!" came the resounding reply.

"Attention!"

We snapped smartly to attention—

"Sergeant, have the men stand at parade rest!" our new captain ordered, having forgotten we were already standing at parade rest—

"Parade rest!" Tillman yelled smartly before executing a near perfect about face to stand at parade rest himself—

And it was then our new captain, Joe Stabat, began that strange introductory speech of his which for some inscrutable reason to this day I have never forgotten.

"My name is Joe Stabat!" he began, "Stabat, S-T-A-B-A-T, Stabat as in 'Stabat Mater' except the first name is 'Joe' not 'Joseph—!' "

And then as our new captain, bushy eyebrows arched challengingly, beady-eyed gaze roving wildly over the three rows of black GIs as if out of some desperate compulsion to impress each of us in turn, take possession of our souls so to speak, we did indeed become a military unit but a military unit with a pagan priest as its leader and given our isolation from the front lines and division headquarters there was nothing we could do but submit to this madman's vision of himself and to his manic self-serving will—

"No doubt you're asking yourself who the fuck's this crazy white man shows up out of nowhere and claims to be your new company commander, and if I were in your shoes, believe me, I'd be asking the same questions, because in wartime the commanding officer is sometimes like God but more often he has to act like the Devil because of the control he has over not only your life but also what you think your wartime mission is, so what we're talking about now is not the Boy Scouts of America, but the big bad United States of America getting the job done and don't bother us with the details!

"Which leads me to the next point I wanna make—

"By now a lotta you colored boys are beginning to notice only now that I speak with some kinda foreign accent, and you're asking yourself, 'Jeezus, what kinda fucking accent is that,' right—?

"Well, I can tell you right now you're wasting your time because nobody knows what kinda accent this is, and the reason nobody knows what kinda accent this is is because where my family originally came from nobody knows where we came from or how we got here—

"Because by the time we had gotten to where we were our tribe had completely dropped out of history—

"The truth is my family comes from some kind of ancient Italian tribe so ancient history has forgotten all about it, and there ain't a soul anywhere on the face of the earth who remembers where our tribe came from or why it ended up in that dark forsaken valley in the foothills of the Italian Alps—

"So why am I telling you this? Because when I started high school in New Jersey—which is where my piss-poor family ended up when we were forced to pack up and emigrate to America—all you smart-ass colored guys in the schools I eventually ended up attending had an attitude like as if your people had the world monopoly on suffering and hard times because your not-so-long-ago ancestors had allegedly been kidnapped from the jungles of Africa by ruthless Moslem warriors to be marched off to the coastal seaports to be sold as cotton-picking slaves, right? Is that your story?

"Well I got news for you, you colored people ain't got no world monopoly on this kinda so-called ethnic suffering, and for starters what about if I told you I grew up in a cave?"

He paused, his bushy-eyed gaze swept over us like the cracking of a whip—

"That's right, you heard me, a CAVE! Three big rooms took Mother Nature a million years to carve out of the side of the mountain where we lived, stalactites hanging from the ceiling like chandeliers, stalagmites all over the floor which, just in case you're interested, was as big as two or three basketball courts in a row—

"So that living inside that fucking cave along with the rabbits and the goats and the rats there was my crippled father who was a veteran of World War I where at the time he was discharged at the age of nineteen and after a whole fucking year of unmitigated hell in the freezing fucking trenches of the Argonne Forest he—now I'm talking about my father when he was you guys' age, and was in the Italian Army in those cold fucking trenches in the Argonne Forest, and unfortunately ended up with his lungs eaten out by poison gas and his toes having to be amputated because of frost bite and gangrene, and where, you better believe it, he was lucky to come out alive—

"And as if that wasn't enough grief for one young guy your age that last horrible winter in the trenches he'd had to eat his dead buddy's typhoid-infected flesh just to stay alive—"

Even now I can remember the ghostly silence that suddenly fell over our ranks as Captain Stabat paused to wipe the perspiration off his face before he continued—

"Most normal kids—," he resumed, putting his cap back on lopsidedly, in what obviously he intended to be a more quiet and reassuring tone of voice, "—which, thank God, I was not—usually when you're growing up you've got either a grandmother or a grandfather or an uncle or an aunt who tells you fairytales before you go to bed or these days you hear them on the radio or see them on TV—

"But growing up in that cave we were too poor to have a radio or a phonograph or story books or even old newspapers or magazines to leaf through before we fell asleep at night, but almost every fucking night, all through my childhood, and at the end of every evening meal—such as it was, usually some warmed over pasta with a single egg beaten up in it for all of us to share, my crippled father would light his pipe from the candle in the middle of the dining room table, pour himself another glass of that bitter purple wine our meager vineyards produced—or very rarely a cheap poisonous grappa, or occasionally one of those cheap cigarettes smelled like the inside of a mattress burning, which for a crippled veteran on a nonexistent pension were about the only luxuries he could afford—then, like someone about to start picking at a favorite scab, he'd settle back in his broken-down armchair and begin telling us—over and over again, every night those same gruesome war stories of his, stories of the first World War which in comparison, I'm not proud to admit, make this war we call ourselves fighting a Sunday School picnic—"

At which point our new enigmatic captain excused himself to go behind the headquarters tent to pee since as yet there hadn't been time to construct a proper officer's latrine—

When he came back, and moments before we were about to break out in wild irreverent comments, our new commanding officer had found a folding-chair to sit down on while he lit himself a cigarette—

"Anyway, to make a long story short and so that you-all colored boys don't miss the point I'm trying to make and think I'm trying to set myself up as some kind of superior example of suffering for you colored guys to imitate, which I'm definitely not—

"That poor shell-shocked father of mine, just when he was about to throw in the towel and send me off to an orphanage run by the nuns so he could mourn my mother's death and drink himself to death in peace, one of his old Army buddies from World War I and the freezing trenches of the Argonne Forest, an educated young man if you will, son of a schoolteacher who'd been studying for the priesthood but gave it up to join Mussolini's new hotshot Fascist Party and now had just been appointed the local agricultural labor boss as a reward for having taken part in Mussolini's March on Rome, this Fascist-True Believer—a real asshole, believe me—somehow managed to convince my father to apply for one of those special land grants the Fascist Party was offering veterans to grow grapes on unused land where no grapes had ever been grown before—

"And you know what? Lo and behold that miserable so-called vineyard ended up becoming the sensation of the valley, a sensational success beyond our wildest dreams—

"Because as it turns out there was a hot spring under that

rocky two acres of land, an underground thermal spring nobody dreamed was there—

"And in fact, once the grapevines were planted and had started to sprout up and grow, those roots began to act like they were somewhere in sunny Greece, and every morning before the sun came up my crippled father and my Uncle Pippo and me, we'd be out there hacking and harrowing the soil and covering the rows with hay to keep in the heat and moisture, and every single day before quitting time we'd spray insecticides on the ground to keep the bugs under control because the bugs loved that heat from the hot springs every bit as much as we did, and remember this is the freezing fucking Alps—!

"In other words for the bad luck family I come from those were the glory days and I tell you, sometimes we worked without stopping twelve hours a day, eating two meals a day out in the field, so that by the third year there were so many grapes to harvest we had to truck them all the way to a Swiss wine maker and bottler who lived on the other side of the mountain—

"All this history I'm going into is for a specific purpose and must've took place in 1936, 1937, 1938, what with all the crap going on in the world who can remember all the dates? But my point is simply this, that after word started to get around we were having these huge prosperous crops of grapes and were even thinking about going into the big time wine producing business, you know with gold on the label and fancy bottles, you can well imagine why there was so much poisonous envy going around, and in fact it wasn't long before other poor bastards just as poor or even poorer than we had been started thinking maybe they had a right to strike it rich too—

"Which now that I think about it is probably the reason my father's old World War I Army buddy, who now had become the local Fascist Party hotshot, comes moseying around one evening and after a big dinner of spaghetti and roast rabbit suggests my father make a patriotic contribution to Mussolini's war effort, something like a fifth of the proceeds from that year's boomer crop—

"Only this time my father, who as usual that time of day was drunk, laughed in the Fascist Party guy's face and says he doesn't give a fuck about Mussolini's war effort because he'd been vaccinated once and for all against war and so-called wartime patriotism in the fucking trenches of World War I where the only time you saw an officer was when the Red Cross ladies showed up to hand out cigarettes and chocolate bars—

"But don't get me wrong! I'm not saying there was a direct connection between what my father said about Patriotism and Fascists and what happened a few hours later in the middle of the night, but there's no denying that smack in the middle of the longest stretch of good luck anyone in that bad luck family of mine could remember, suddenly—just like that!—the good luck comes to an end and we're up to our necks in shit again—

"In other words and to make a long story short, one minute we're all sitting around the table singing 'Happy Days Are Here Again!' each in turn telling the others what he's going to buy with all the money we're going to make, when all of a sudden my father holds his hand up for silence, cocks his head and listens a while, then holds his hands up for silence like he's just heard something spooky and unusual going on out there in the vineyard—

"And sure enough, after sitting there with his head cocked like he's listening for ghosts, suddenly and without saying a word he jumps to his feet, kicks the door open and before we can figure out what the hell is going on that put such a wild and crazy look in my father's usually grave and serious eyes, he jumps to his feet and bolts out the door—

"The next thing we know there my father is, down on his knees in the vineyard with the lantern he snatched off the table at his side, frantically digging into the soil with both hands like a dog digging for a bone, until all of a sudden he lets out a scream you could hear all through the valley—

"There are people still alive who remember that scream, the Devil's Scream they call it, because what it was caused my father to scream like that was something so unexpected and tiny but something that ended any further possibility of growing grapes and making wine in that cursed valley of ours—tiny little grapevine-root mites, so tiny you wonder how they could do the damage they do, itty-bitty flea-like little gnat bastards you can barely see with the naked eye, millions and millions of them, sticking their tiny itty-bitty proboscises into the inner tissues of the grapevine roots, and hardly before you know what hit you, the whole fucking vineyard starts to experience a slow agonizing death nothing in Heaven or Hell can be done to stop it—

"Anyway, now here comes my Uncle Pippo running out of the house to the vineyard and now he too gets down on his knees and starts digging with two hands like a dog digging for a bone. And when he too is finally convinced the vineyard mites have taken over the vineyard, thriving in the warmth of the hidden hot springs like rich tourists in some fancy summer resort, probably the reason since ancient times nobody ever bothered to grow grapes in that cursed valley before we tried our luck and miraculously succeeded—but now here comes my father back into the house only now he just sits there without saying anything to anybody and then starts drinking one glass of wine after the other until suddenly there comes this loud knock on the door—

"Who it is is the same town clerk who'd been in the trenches with my father and who now is the highest ranking member of the new Fascist Party, which makes him the biggest big shot in the valley—

"Right away his sly greedy eyes take in the scene like he's surprised us partaking in some secret satanic rites. But at the same time he's smiling like a bishop and makes a motion with his head for my father to join him out in the yard for a quiet talk—

"We could tell it was serious because of the low grumbling sing-song drone of their conversation, which at a certain point grew angry and jaggedy until suddenly I hear my father yelling at the top of his voice—

" 'But we're not Jews!'

"It was then everything became quiet outside and you could hear a dog barking far off somewhere way down the valley—

"Anyway, to make a long story short, when my father came back into the house he was pale as a ghost and in a quiet urgent tone of voice, almost a whisper, he tells us to start packing, we've got to leave—

"No use me boring you horse cavalry guys describing how it felt and what it was like climbing up that mountain on a dark moonless night, each of us lugging a heavy suitcase filled with the useless junk each of us thought we wouldn't be able to live without—

"So to make a long story short we finally made it to the top of the mountain, and then after sliding down the other side of the mountain just as dawn is breaking and then crawling through a field of barbed wire into a tiny cemetery with a nice white neat fence around it and then out into the spotlessly clean picture-book world like Switzerland was in those days and where, at least in theory, we would be safe but in reality were in more danger than when we set out, mainly because in those pre-World War II days all those quaint border towns were teeming with spies, paid killers, bounty hunters, and hustlers of all description just like the wild west, everybody trying to enrich themselves off the suffering of desperate refugees trying to escape the death camps—

"And, in fact, it wasn't long before my father and my uncle were stopped on the street and were about to be taken away in a fake bakery truck belonging to the police when a Swiss lady came by on a bicycle and, after whispering something to the policeman who had stopped us and now miraculously was giving the driver of the truck directions how to get to a certain slaughterhouse on the outskirts of town where, though now we were relatively safe, we ended up having to hide in an airless room smelled like a cesspool with slippery innards scattered all over the floor, until finally at last a mysterious man looked like a stuffy Protestant preacher but who spoke Italian with a Neapolitan accent suddenly appeared out of nowhere and gave us money, passports and train tickets which he assured us would get us to Cherbourg where, after a short wait that might turn out to be as long as several weeks, we would be given tickets and provided with more money and clothing to board the once fancy-dancy cruise liner that would take us to New York and what for us was freedom—"

To this day I still remember how moved we all were by the tale our new captain, Joe Stabat, had just told us, and for a long time nobody said anything because nobody could think of anything to say—

In fact there was something almost Biblical in the story he told us and, looking around I could see that all our eyes were damp, some of us were on the verge of tears—

Most remarkable of all was the dramatic change in the way we felt about our new commanding officer, a feeling best expressed by Tillman who when Joe Stabat finished his tale said loud enough for the whole outfit to hear, "That's some bad shit he been telling us, the man's got guts and He's the Man!"

It was then and at the very moment Tillman said that that a shot rang out and at once everybody ducked and ran for cover—

Including Captain Stabat who had just pulled out a fresh pack of Lucky Strike cigarettes which now he held squeezed tight in his left hand while his right hand was reaching for his revolver—

"Stay calm, men!" he yelled, holding up his hand, still clenched tightly around the pack of Luckies—

Tillman, just recently appointed company cook, and I, just recently appointed temporary company clerk, had as per regulation been standing on either side of our commanding officer, but now both of us were racing each other around the back side of the headquarters tent, and had already reached the mess hall tent on the other side and had begun to peek cautiously around the tent pole in the direction from which the shots had come, just in time to see Private Dudley (a quiet lanky farm boy from Arkansas) standing astride a very pretty and well-dressed but politely outraged Italian young lady who, if not a member of the nearby town's fashionable upper classes in no way could have been one of those camp-following whores or, for that matter, not even a stolid peasant girl canvassing the camp for laundry to wash but whoever and whatever she was, she was now sprawled indecorously at Private Dudley's feet, the barrel of his rifle shakily aimed at her delicately sculpted head, the head of a young Ingrid Bergman in the role of Joan of Arc—

But suddenly here comes Captain Stabat his jaw jutting out and his revolver cocked and ready to shoot; but then he takes a good look at her—

"Who is she?" he asks, shamelessly blushing (a fact confirmed that very evening when Tillman and I were amusing each other with comic recreations of the scene)—

And when no answer came forth Joe Stabat, our new commanding officer, gallantly offered the young lady his hand which the young lady proudly disdained and instead sprang gracefully to her feet like a ballet dancer and then just stood there, elegant and boldly unafraid—

"She speak English?" Captain Stabat asked in what came out as an unnatural hoarse whisper—

"A whole lot better than me!" said Private Dudley with a big happy smile on his face, adding for good measure, "Still, I didn't want to take no chances so I unshouldered my rifle and asked the young lady—the prisoner—what she was doing digging in our garbage can, but instead of giving me a straight answer, she tried to grab the rifle out of my hands, and that's when the shot went off!"

Captain Stabat shook his head disapprovingly—

"Anybody know who she is?"

And when there was no reply, Captain Stabat blushed and then just stood there shifting his weight from one foot to the other, until finally he turned around and shouted loud enough for everyone within earshot to hear:

"All right, men, the show's over! Tillman, get the men back in formation and have this young lady report to my office for interrogation! Pronto!"

"I keep forgetting—," Tillman said, slapping me on the knee, "—shit, you were there like we all were there and you experienced what we all experienced and so it goes without saying, you saw trouble coming like we all saw trouble coming, especially at that so-called trial—"

And no later than half an hour after we all heard the shot the trial that brought Joe Stabat together with his future wife was now about to begin—

"Prisoner present and ready for interrogation, sir!" I intoned in my new role as de facto company clerk—

"Does the prisoner speak English?"

"A lot better than I do, sir!" Private Dudley replied—

But Captain Stabat was ill at ease and was still nervously arranging and rearranging over the top of the folding desk all the necessary forms that would eventually have to be filled out—

As an ex-college student I had been summarily appointed court clerk and was therefore seated on a folding chair on the other side of the camp table facing the very pretty plaintiff—

Who suddenly now let out a piercing scream—

"Such a good man! You have no right to do this! My father meant no harm to anyone! He was a saint, and they crucified him, crucified him!"

Tears streaming down her cheeks and eyes wild and histrionic, she jumped to her feet and now seemed about to bolt past the enlisted men guards on either side of her and attempt an escape—

Instead the captain reached out and gently pulled her back onto her folding-chair seat—

"Crucified who?" he asked politely, "I thought they didn't crucify people anymore—"

Instead she collapsed into his arms and as she did so we watched his fingers slide ever so surreptitiously over the prisoner's elegant and perky breasts—

"God-damn-it-to-hell!" the captain was yelling, "don't just stand there, somebody get a medic!"

And in that precise moment every one present realized our new commanding officer had fallen head over heels in love—

"Signorina, your name please, what is your name?" the captain asked in a simpering fatherly tone of voice—

"Luminella—"

"Luminella di Constantino—," she repeated, adding, "—shall I spell it for you?"

"No-no, Luminella—"

Captain Stabat repeated the names and began scribbling.

When he finished he folded his hands and crossed his knees and looked over at the countess with fatherly concern—

"Now would you tell us please, Signorina Luminella—write this down, Corporal, this will constitute the prisoner's official deposition—exactly what happened—"

"Excuse me, Captain, but I haven't finished writing down all the names yet—"

The captain nodded impatiently in my direction but then decided to take advantage of the momentary recess to move his chair closer to the prisoner's and whisper something in her ear—

"I hope you understand—," he was saying, "—all this is just a formality, Army regulations require that we make a report on any infraction of the rules on the part of civilians, therefore—Signorina Luminella di Constantino—do I have the name and title correct?—are there any other titles or professional designations I should add?"

"Countess di Constantino—!" the girl said ruefully, but immediately after broke out in a fetching smile and added: "But only if you insist, for legal reasons, to me it makes no difference, but for better or worse I happen by birth to be a countess—"

"A countess? Very good. Congratulations! Now if you don't mind, countess, 'contessa'—did I pronounce it right?—would you be so kind as to explain to the court—to us—for the record and in your own words—exactly what you were doing fishing, so to speak, in the camp's garbage can, giving us the impression, as stated in the verbatim, Private Dudley had become suspicious—and rightfully so—you were about to place a bomb!"

From the countess' direction came neither a reply nor a comment—

Instead with tragic grace she lowered her head and buried her face in her hands and began quietly to sob—

The captain seemed mesmerized by the performance—

Eyebrows arched philosophically he said—, "Have Private Dudley brought in—"

As if by magic Private Dudley's head came poking through

the tent flap and then Private Dudley himself entered and paused a moment to get his bearings, took one step forward, saluted briskly and, without waiting to be told, began what apparently was his carefully memorized deposition—

"I was making my rounds when I felt a call of nature and retired briefly to the officer's latrine which was closer to my post than the enlisted men's latrine—"

"You know the officer's latrine is off-limits to enlisted men!" Captain Stabat said quietly, his face red as a beet—

"Yessir, but the call was very urgent, a number two, sir!"

"Watch your language soldier, there's a lady present! Now continue your report!"

"Well, when I returned to my post I saw the prisoner, this signorina here, poking in the garbage can with something that was smoking—"

"Something that was smoking?"

"Yessir, something that was smoking. I thought it might be a bomb and that she was trying to blow up the camp! In fact, the night before, if you remember, some of the guys sneaking back into camp from a three-hour pass said they'd heard there were Fascists holed up in caves at the top of the mountain who came down every now and then to make raids on the houses of people who'd turned against Mussolini—!"

When he heard that all the fun and games drained out of Captain Stabat's expression—

"Nobody asked you to make a speech, private! Stick to the facts!"

Nevertheless the captain spun around on his chair to face the countess and asked:

"You heard anything like that?"

"Of course not, that's ridiculous!" she said in fairly confident English, "Up there in the hills the partisans are in complete control and have been so for months!"

"Then why don't you tell us your version of what happened—"

"My family—," the countess began with a haughty toss of her head, "—we're not Fascists, we're free thinkers, in fact I'm studying for a degree in the political thought of the Danish Protestant philosopher Kierkegaard who in his early writings first theorized—"

The captain frantically raised his hand for silence and completely ignoring the fact that he was the only one with a stack of pencils and several yellow pads in front of him, began yelling loud enough for everyone in the outfit to hear:

"Goddamit to hell! Is anybody writing this down?"

When nobody answered he turned to the girl and gave her an encouraging smile—

"Please continue—," he said, adding protectively, almost vehemently, "—no one on my watch is accusing you of anything, and if they do they'll have me to answer to!"

"Well, as you know I do charity work—and though I am a university student the women of my family, the Di Constantino family, have traditionally felt it their responsibility to take care of the poor—as you know my name is Luminella di Constantino and I am a university student and I have a dear friend who I am completely devoted to, a nun at the local convent, whose name is Sister Agnes and we do charitable work together—

"On this particular morning, I am telling you about, because my professor was sick with the flu and I had no classes at the university I decided to make my rounds among the poor today instead of Friday and while doing so I noticed for the first time your camp which seemingly had sprung up overnight, and I was very curious about your garbage can because it had been told to me by the Mother Superior that what the American soldiers throw away in one meal would feed the poor of this town for a week, and I wanted to see for myself—

"Unfortunately, your garbage cans are so tall and deep, not at all like our inferior dumpy little Italian garbage cans, I was having a difficult time examining the quality of the food your men had thrown away because it was so dark inside the can, and therefore I rolled up a sheet of an old newspaper I had in my bag and lit a match to it so that at last I could see for myself and judge the quality of the garbage you Americans produce which, as I said, I had heard was often better than the food served in our wartime restaurants—

"However, as fortune would have it, just as the newspaper torch I had made began to die out, my wristwatch became loose and fell off my wrist into the garbage can and I was busy lighting yet another newspaper torch so I could find my wristwatch—which by the way had belonged to my great aunt, the duchess, when suddenly the soldier on guard, whom I had already noticed from the corner of my eye, for no reason at all began to fire his rifle in the air and then, before I knew what was happening, he appeared out of nowhere and began to wrestle me to the ground!"

"Hold it right there, signorina!" Captain Stabat shouted, jumping to his feet to raise his hand to silence the hubbub of comments that had begun to rise from the twenty or so soldiers crowded inside the headquarters tent, "Before we go any further, did anyone find this young lady's watch?"

Private Dudley stepped forward and saluted smartly—

"Yessir, Captain-Sir, I did, sir—"

And so saying he began rummaging in the back pocket of his pants until he found what he was looking for: a delicate ladies watch which now he proudly handed to Captain Stabat who in turn, a glowing smile on his face, handed to Luminella—

"As you see—," he said, "—murder will out!"

4

By the time Captain's inane homily had died out in my mind I was solidly back in the stretch limousine which was speeding past a double-decker auto-transport loaded with tiny Fiat 500s in every color of the rainbow—

In the meantime I had turned around to face Tillman and was asking: "If that's how Joe Stabat met the countess how did he meet that bastard brother of hers who I thought you said was up in the mountains with the partisans?"

In reply Tillman nodded his head toward the front seat where through the glass partition we could see Joe Stabat fast asleep and snoring noisily with his head resting heavily on Little Antioch's shoulder—

"Next thing we know she'll be taking out her tit to give him his midday fix of mother's milk," Tillman whispered, adding—

"I think it must a been at that public funeral they had for her father, you remember how, a week or so after that wristwatch trial we had at the camp, we got an official invitation from the mayor of the town to send an honor guard from the camp to his funeral but some asshole at headquarters telephoned at the last minute to say we shouldn't get involved in whatever shit was behind his death, that there was some dark political business connected with the old guy's death and being this close to the front showing up for the funeral with a U.S. Army Honor Guard could be interpreted that our outfit and the U.S. Army in particular sympathized with one political faction over another, which was not the message the big guys wanted to convey, especially not that Commy-loving Christian-Democrat faction the old guy was so tight with; and besides as an all-Negro outfit, headquarters wanted us to appear neutral so the Communists couldn't claim we were Communist-sympathizers like 'Old Man River' Paul Robeson, especially now that both the King and Mussolini were on the lam and the new government was up for grabs—

"On the other hand—," Tillman was saying, "—when you think back to those screwy days, it had to have been right after her father's spooky public funeral that she started showing up at the camp almost every day, supposedly to supervise the collection of our leftovers to feed the hungry with, but mostly I suppose because that freaky go-for-broke love affair of hers with Joe Stabat was already starting to boil over and was getting out of control—

"In fact, as I remember it, it was about that time she started showing up at the camp every evening, always a little later in the day than the day before, until finally she was showing up right after evening chow at which time she would park her bike behind the headquarters tent—you remember that?—where it wouldn't be so noticeable to the men going on guard duty—

"And you remember how, right after—or, as often as not, the

very moment the sun was about to sink into the distant sea, she'd come pushing her bike up the trail, then the moment the sun actually sank into the sea and shadows suddenly wrapped themselves around everything in sight, including the entrance to the captain's tent, there she'd be sneaking inside through the flap and in twenty minutes or so you'd hear the captain yelling for me to come drive him (he never said them) on an inspection tour of the town, which inevitably and always ended up on that secluded beach road where they'd get out of the jeep and while I made a big show of pretending I needed a quick snooze behind the wheel, the two love-bugs would get out and stroll down the warm sandy beach out of sight where they'd stay doing whatever it was they did until way after dark when finally the moon came out, at which time I'd turn my headlights on and flash them two or three times as a signal I was ready to pick them up and drive them back to camp where the countess (which is what Joe Stabat told us we should call her because that was what she was, a real life Italian countess), she'd pick up her bike and pedal her ass back to that big villa on the side of the hill she'd lived in all her pampered life—

"Which you can imagine was about as nearly perfect a set-up for a wartime romance as they come and, I don't mind admitting, I was as sentimentally involved as the captain and the countess, which is to say I remained a willing cupid so to speak until one night I was driving the two lovebirds back to camp to a certain spot to one side of the latrine where she always parked her bike when suddenly this tall arrogant guy in a gray-green uniform and a hunting hat with a feather on it on his head and a rifle strapped across his shoulder materializes out of the shadows of the wire-trellised grapevines that marked the eastern boundary of the camp and stands there in the glow of the headlights of our jeep like a traffic officer, frantically waving for us to halt—

"'Riccardo!' the girl exclaims in a little whimper of surprise—

"Oh, oh!" I am saying to myself, "I smell trouble—what's her brother doing popping up out of the bushes like this? And at this time of night and while his sister is out on a hot date with a captain of the U.S. Army of Occupation—?

"But Captain Stabat stays cool as a cucumber and in fact seems anything but surprised—takes his good old time popping a Lucky Strike between his lips, takes his good time lighting it, takes his good time getting out of the jeep and takes his good time walking over to where the tall Italian soldier with a feather in his hat is waiting in the shadows, and takes him gently by the arm and finally without either of them so far having said a word, they stroll off across the road to a secluded spot behind some hedges, well out of earshot of our jeep, where they stop and light each other's cigarettes after which I can hear them talking quietly, sometimes in English, sometimes in Italian, always in a quiet harmonious tone of voice like old buddies meeting to go hunting or look for mushrooms or—as it turns out later (and something tells me this ain't going to surprise you!), partners in a murky hardcore criminal enterprise who trust each other enough to keep each other's secrets to themselves) in other words good old buddies who've known each other long enough to be up to their chins in each other's shit—

"Which leaves me and the countess alone in the captain's jeep holding the bag so to speak because as it later turns out, at this point in their romance she acted as if she hadn't a clue what was going on behind her back, and as far as she was concerned the tall guy in the green uniform even if he was her brother was also and for the record a partisan hiding out in the mountain who every now and then came down to visit and discuss politics and military strategy with her U.S. Army captain fiancé—

"At this point it's legitimate to ask how much of what was going on was true and how much was play-acting. As it turned out, the part where she says her brother was hanging out up in the mountains is true enough but in no way was he a partisan or, for that matter, a Fascist deserter. What he was in reality was a corrupt and ruthless member of a Mafia-type criminal organization that had penetrated the Italian Army at the precise moment it became clear the regime was about to fall apart, whose sole mission was to corner the market for priceless art objects illegally dug up out of the countless Etruscan tombs scattered all over the neighborhood and for which that part of Italy was famous, while at the same time organizing and policing every step of the secret route by which this priceless loot stolen from the Etruscan tombs which already even before the war ended had become a multi-billion dollar enterprise—

"How come I never told you this before? Because Joe Stabat made me promise on a stack of Bibles and threat of castration by blowtorch that anything that happened on those so-called 'inspection trips' of ours was to be kept 'top secret' or bye-bye any further promotions, special privileges, or recreational leaves—

"And in fact, when after a while Joe Stabat figured he could trust me, he changed his story and hinted that in reality he was an undercover agent for the U.S. Department of the Treasury investigating Mafia penetration of the old historical gravedigger gangs the 'tomberoli' and that if I could manage to keep my mouth shut and if I remained loyal to him and proved to be one hundred percent reliable he'd eventually establish a secret Swiss bank account in my name which, he guaranteed, would make me rich, but that for the time being everything going on now had to remain hush-hush government business and if I so much as hinted to anybody, in or out of the Army, any part of what he'd just told me he'd have me transferred to a front line outfit in Cassino and make sure I ended up freezing my balls off in a foxhole where I'd have to melt frozen icicles in my helmet to wash my ass and shave—

"Now don't think—smartass that you are—I can't hear you screaming to yourself—'How could an asshole featherweight like Joe Stabat gain entrance to an outrageous level of crime like that?'

"Fair question, but your chickenshit analysis suffers from a common assumption we black people have about the white man—that the white man remains on top because he deserves to be on top, and he deserves to be on top because he's white! White is Right, right? Wrong! And if you're still having difficulty believing the shit I'm telling you is credible, how about this?—

"Something that happened Christmas Eve, 1943, 1944, or maybe 1945, my mind's too fucked up by Social Security to remember exact dates when things happened anymore—

"Let's just say it was either the first or second Christmas Eve after the captain and the Countess Luminella started getting it on, but before they got married and I cooked them a Plantation Dinner as a wedding present, at least that much you remember—

"Anyway muthafucker comes storming into the mess tent

where I'd started sleeping to wake me up and then after I finally wake up and want to know what the fuck's going on, he holds a finger to his lips so I'll be quiet and not wake up anybody else, and after I put on my heavy jacket and boots because it was cold out there, he leads me on tip-toes to the motor pool where he whispers in my ear, we've got to go off camp on an urgent mission, just the two of us, because (same old line he always uses when he's about to do some underhanded shit) I'm the only one in the whole goddamn outfit he can trust—

"And without another word of explanation he tells me to drive out of camp with the headlights off and then proceed southeast on the state highway to the abandoned railroad station at San Giovanni in Basso and, when we get there, park out of sight behind an old storage shed alongside the tracks which I was familiar with and been told it'd been out of use for years, maybe twenty years, but that when war broke out some generals thought it might be useful one day as a temporary storage for durable food supplies and ammunition in case the front moved south as far as Grosseto—

"Anyway, when we got there the captain seemed to relax a bit, he was less hyper, and for an hour or so we just sat there smoking cigarettes from a fresh pack from the cartons of Pall Malls the captain got from the officers' PX and since he didn't seem to feel much like talking I let myself doze off to sleep. But after a while—like suddenly he was hit by some worrisome thought—he started jabbing me in the ribs to wake me up and when finally I woke up he started asking me a whole lot of questions about where I came from, what my father did for a living, how much schooling I'd had—dumb questions like that.

"But then, exactly 1:28 in the morning—I remember the time

because I'd just looked at my watch—out from one of those low clinging dense fogs swirling around us like in a horror movie, all of a sudden, here comes one of those small dinky old-fashioned steam locomotives chugging around the bend without any lights on and pulling only one car, a passenger car but with bars on its windows like on a mail train—

"So far it was like, 'Hey, look at that cute dinky-ass train!'—but then, the moment the train is halfway around the bend, the captain, who in the meantime has taken over the wheel, starts up the engine, frantically flashes his headlights like he's signaling somebody on the train and what d'ya know, the train slows down, and barely moving, continues coming around the bend—

"Now, remember, so far Stabat hasn't given me a word of explanation what this shit is all about, just calmly gets out of the jeep (and for the first time I notice he's wearing his webbed combat gun belt and regulation revolver, not the flashy pearl-handled cowboy pistol he usually swaggers around in) and I also see, and say to myself, Christ, this nut's got a fucking hunting knife stuck in his belt—

"Still and I can't emphasize it too much, neither the revolver nor the hunting knife are enough to arouse my suspicions because if you remember those days, all of us, from the lowest flunkified enlisted man to the highest-ranking officer, we all strutted around wearing all kinda knives, guns, hand grenades—you name it—to impress each other and impress the local 'signorine' always hanging around the camp that we were the real thing, tough hardcore combat soldiers like in the movies when in reality there wasn't a single one of us who'd ever been closer to the front lines than a hundred and fifty miles—

"Anyway, by the time this dinky slow-moving train has almost slowed down to a stop, Captain Stabat—who in the meantime has gotten out of the jeep and is standing alongside the tracks waiting for the locomotive to get to where he's standing—jumps up on the rear platform of the tail-end coach which has bars on its windows, kicks open the rear door, and the first thing I know he's disappeared inside—

"A few minutes later he appears in the doorway at the front end of the coach (remember I'm in the jeep riding alongside the tracks, moving just slightly faster than the train), wrestling what looks like an enormous barracks bag stuffed with hard-edged jingly stuff, because you could hear whatever it was was jingly inside when, as delicately as he could manage, he lets the overloaded barracks bag slip gently out of his arms onto the siding, then as the train begins to pick up speed and finally disappears around the bend he jumps down himself and almost falls on his fucking face—

"By then I'd parked the jeep and gotten out to help the captain load the overstuffed barracks bag into the back seat of the jeep, and while the train vanished around the bend the captain asks me casually if I knew the way to Livorno, a seaport and naval command not far from where we had stopped and goes on to explain that our next job is to make sure the barracks bag gets aboard a certain freighter due to ship out in a convoy the following day—

"Now I can't truly say that I knew for sure what was in that barracks bag and to be honest, at the time I didn't want to know—but what I could feel while I was carrying the overstuffed barracks bag to the jeep was priceless art objects dug up out of those ancient Etruscan tombs scattered all over the landscape around our camp, art objects worth billions if not trillions of dollars that Joe Stabat as the founding father and boss of a huge new Brooklyn-based gang of smugglers so powerful and above the law—both Italian law and U.S. Customs law—they were able to operate far into the postwar period without ever once being investigated or ever getting caught—

"So there you got it, the Joe Stabat Story, how he got his start—smuggling priceless art antiquities during the war, then oil, then stock manipulation, whatever that is, and now the biggest racket of all, STABAT.COM—

"Without any doubt the man's got to be one of the richest men in the world, bar none, and yet nobody really knows how rich he is, or even if he is rich, least of all me, I'm only his cook—

"But getting back to this one particular hustle of his, the one I know something about because I was there, normally the drive to Livorno should have taken a little over two hours or so, but this time the captain insisted we keep to the back roads, probably to avoid the military road blocks—so it wasn't before dawn on Christmas Day 1944 or 1945 (I can't keep these fucking dates straight in my mind) before we got to the Graves Registration Depot where (to be honest it took me several trips before I figured out how they did it), after we dropped off the barracks bag filled with precious black market antiquities stolen from Etruscan graves, actually it wasn't a barracks bag but an oversized body bag, the kind they shipped corpses in, the body bag filled with precious antiquities would be stuffed inside a casket with a fake name and serial number on it to be shipped off to the States, as often as not to the port of Brooklyn, New York, closest to Staten Island, where whoever they were working with at the time would recognize the fake body bag and see that it got to the right people—

"And whoever those right people were they sure must have had what it took because every time I drove Joe Stabat up to that Army road block at the entry to the port area in Livorno and Joe Stabat would pull out that handwritten pass he carried around with him in his breast pocket, the one bearing the seal of Army headquarters and the name of a major general whose name was an illegible scrawl, the guards first would take a first, second and sometimes even a third suspicious look at that official pass, then snap to attention with a smart salute, a smart click of the heels, and this last time I'm telling you about, a sickeningly sincere 'Merry Christmas, sir!' all the while staring at Joe Stabat as if instead of our sweaty hotshot leader he was God Almighty and nervously wave us through—

"When the war was over how did I start working for him again?

"How did we meet again after the war and why did I start working for him again? How much time do we got? This is getting pretty damn close to my life history—

"Actually the war was long over—," Tillman began in a somewhat shamed, chastened, almost secretive tone of voice, "—and under the pressure of a whole slew of personal problems I don't want to get into now, I'd just about forgotten all about our outfit and the war—

"Remember this was the 1970s, or maybe coming into the 1980s, you know how forgetful I've always been about dates and exactly when certain things in the past happened, but it musta been the 1980s 'cause *Roots* was all over TV and the talk shows were beginning to get worked up about slavery again like as if slavery had suddenly become the nation's number one social problem again, that much I remember because I was watching it on a big brand new TV set back home in Lawton where I still called myself 'taking care of business' as first my Aunt Harriet and then Mr. Peebles—you remember him, the old horny Buffalo Trooper always seeing the son of King Comus' ghost wandering around the house—well first he finally died over a hundred years old, then my Aunt Harriet died, and suddenly I knew I better damn well get my ass out of that spooky old King Comus–haunted mansion before I became a ghost myself and anyway the mansion itself was on its last legs and had already started lop-siding itself into the river, which was the main reason why when out of the blue I got this call from Joe Stabat to come work for him in New York (and don't ask me how he found my phone number because you know as well as I know if Joe Stabat isn't the Devil himself he must be the Devil's apprentice and always gets what he wants when he wants it and what he wanted then, which was right now, was me) so taking his call like a one-time reprieve from what destiny had in store for me if I stayed on in that sinking mansion, probably ending up a ghost, I went to the local pawnshop and pawned a gold ring with a pure blood ruby in it which I kept under a plank in the bathroom for just such an occasion and bought me a round-trip ticket to New York just in case the sneaky old bastard's phone call was some bullshit hoax or something—

"Instead what I got was an apron because the moment I arrived at Joe Stabat's sumptuous mansion which was set smack in the middle of a private forest in the boondocks of Staten

Island, hardly before I had time to take my hat and coat off, our commander-in-chief—looking exactly the same except he's more puffy and nasty around the jowls and makes jerky movements with his arms and hands when he moves around like he could use a stronger tranquilizer, informs me in no uncertain terms—like we were still in the Army and the war was still on and it was up to him and me to win it—that I was going to have to start cooking right away because in less than three hours from then some of his closest business associates and their wives were coming over to eat collard greens, yams and smothered chicken with Alabama potato salad on the side, washed down with some of the finest bourbon on the market to cut the grease and facilitate digestion; that's right, you guessed it—a rehash of that Plantation Dinner you and I put together and served during the war when Joe Stabat and the countess got married, a dinner apparently neither Joe Stabat nor the countess had ever forgotten and which now, along with my new role as his new hotshot personal cook I would be responsible for recreating and serving during a fancy formal dinner the purpose of which (this I later figured out for myself) was to hide the fact that his family life and marriage was desperately on the rocks and he and Luminella were one step from breaking up, a nightmare Joe Stabat was desperately incapable of facing because (no surprise to me) he had once again become totally dependent (in the hardcore Mafia definition of the word) on the largesse of a consortium of cut-throat Italian bankers and local private banking interests known informally as 'The Mod Squad' but known formally as 'The Alpha Consortium' because of the enormous amounts of money they could amass on a moment's notice to take advantage of even a minor fluctuation of the market and still make a killing, in other words a jolly band of pirates his brother-in-law, Riccardo, had put him in contact with and to whom Joe Stabat was over his head in hock—

"Anyway, so as not to stretch the preamble of this story beyond the number of days you and I have upon this earth, it must've been around three o'clock in the afternoon when I arrived at that horror-movie mansion of his stuck in the middle of the woods—"

(And it was then, suddenly, I began to cough and steal nervous glances toward the front seat where Joe Stabat himself, the bête-noire of all our Army nightmares, was curled up into himself, apparently still fast asleep in an alcoholic snooze after a lunch stop break we had just taken in a tiny restaurant a travel book entitled *Tuscany's Hidden Treasures* had enthusiastically recommended and where all of us, with the exception of Little Antioch who religiously doesn't drink, had had too much wine with our predominately fettuccine meal—)

(And it was Tillman, no doubt interpreting the wild look of embarrassment in my eyes as fear our flamboyant former company commander could overhear our conversation especially when I began to point insistently at the Rolls-Royce stretch limousine's rolled down, bullet-proof glass partition that physically and psychologically separated Tillman and me and Joe Stabat and Little Antioch from each other while preventing what was being said in either sound-isolated area to hear what the others were saying—)

"From the gate to the mansion proper was almost half a mile of tree-lined driveway," Tillman chortled (continuing and savoring his description of this, his postwar reunion with Captain Stabat)

"—and the mansion itself looked to be about one and a half

times the size of the White House but with the original white paint painted over a pinkish gray lavender color you'd expect on something called 'The Flamingo Motel'—

"But Joe Stabat himself looked real enough, bastard never changes, same-old, same-old Captain except maybe that slight bulge he had during the war had just about become Teddy Roosevelt size when I arrived, and his hair as you can see is gray but dyed that freaky-deaky blonde color you see a lot of on the heads of fashion execs and funeral directors, otherwise the guy seemed to be in pretty good shape and—don't ask me how he does it because I don't know and if I did know I'd have bought a couple of bottles of what he takes for myself—the guy doesn't look a day older than the last time we saw him—which as you must well remember was standing on his jeep parked on the just-that-week newly-repaired docks in Naples with that inseparable cigar in his mouth, waving goodbye to his 'boys' as the troop transport *Pres. Woodrow Wilson* pulled away from its berth with you, me and about 3000 other GIs aboard, happy as hell to be still alive and kicking and at long last headed home from that chickenshit of a bullshit war—

"Anyway, even before the cab pulls up to the porch, there he is banging on the window of the front seat of the cab where I was sitting next to the driver, yelling at me, 'Don't pay the fucking driver nothing, he works for me, just get your ass out of there and follow me in the house someone will come out to pick up your luggage in case the driver thinks he's too good to carry the suitcase of one our heroic black GIs' (and when I get out he suddenly breaks out in tears and throws his arms around me), 'Christ old buddy, I'm so glad to see you, am I ever glad to see you, you look great Tillman, you look really really great, I can't tell you how happy and grateful I am you and I are together again—!'

"Now I can say it, can say it to you, but at the time I didn't know what to say, the muthafucker was so goddamned hyper, in fact looked and sounded to me, naturally my first impression, acted like he wasn't all there, had maybe lost his marbles and become a fairy queen—

"But don't get me wrong, old buddy, in no way do I want to give the impression he was actually falling apart or that he had changed his denomination, if you know what I mean—

"To tell you the truth he looked pretty good for his age which had to have been at least eight or ten years older than we were, but no way as good as you look! Shit, D., look at you! But then you probably been living in the lap of luxury all these years, eating that good Italian food and getting all that good Italian pussy and living the good life in a villa, and even so, look at you! You haven't put on any weight hardly at all, like you're still in your fucking twenties, your late thirties, early forties, early fifties, no more than fifty, shit, look at you, you're a fucking young man still: one thing you still have, and maybe it's because you've become a writer, you still have that sneaky baby-faced priestly look about you—

"As for me, I've long since given up trying to keep track of the years as they go by, so fucking fast I don't care no more, just don't turn me into no ghost, when I'm dead I want to stay dead and not be resurrected or artificially brought back to life and have to live this shit over and over and over again like the Buddhist people do, until I get it right—

"But getting back to our lord and master Captain Joe Stabat—how long after the war was it before I heard from him again? And how did he know how to find you?

"I'm sorry, old buddy, I thought I already told you, I was living in limbo at the time, and for that matter, still am—

"So let's just say I know it had to be out of the sixties and into the seventies, late seventies, maybe, but not yet the eighties (and please bear with me) because the morning I arrived—and I already told you what that was like—right off the bat he tells me I've got to start cooking, not a couple of hours from now, not a few minutes from now, but right now, because that same night, about three hours from whatever time it was I arrived, some of his closest business associates and their wives were coming over to watch—what's that famous black writer's name?—Alex Haley—they were coming over to watch Alex Haley's *Roots* on TV while they stuffed themselves on collard greens, yams, smothered chicken and Georgia potato salad and peach cobbler a-la-mode! Sound familiar—?

"Well it damn sure ought to be because that 'Plantation Dinner' was a wedding feast to celebrate the marriage between Joe Stabat and the countess was your idea in the first place, nobody but a bookworm like you could have come up with an idea like that—give the natives a taste of real Southern cooking and black folks' culture, something the local Italian gentry could not only appreciate intellectually but could get their teeth into, so to speak, and, in fact, remember, *Yank Magazine* even sent a photographer, but the bastards never published the pictures and never explained why, remember?—each black soldier in the unit furnishing the recipe for his favorite down-home dish—

I know you remember that, you were the major instigator, and the wedding itself took place at the outdoor Catholic chapel they set up at the entrance to our camp, and after the wedding ceremony, THE Social Event of the Year, I think we even sang spirituals—a genuine Plantation Dinner cooked and served and offered by our former and ever famous 9th Cavalry All-Negro Horse Cavalry Troop—

"But unfortunately at the time I arrived at the mansion Joe Stabat's marriage to Luminella, the bride, was already beginning to come apart at the seams and, as usual, the man who always did think I was some kind of a witchdoctor who could work my magic on anything and everything thought just my being there could save his marriage at least until the loan sharks got off his ass—

"And of course the magic bullet was going to be this new and improved version of the Plantation Dinner of World War II fame which, however—typical Joe Stabat bullshit—I had less than three hours to cook! And apparently the way he was going to make it happen was to stage this new version of our old 'Plantation Dinner' for his Mafia lenders to whom he was in hock up to his neck, and their wives and to add to the flavor, so to speak, after dinner they would watch Alex Haley's *Roots* on TV—

"In the meantime Joe Stabat continues looking at his wristwatch (obviously worrying about his falling apart business affairs) while at the same time yelling over the intercom for Mrs. Meany to get her ass down here as quick as she can because he, Joe Stabat, has a meeting with some bankers at Rockefeller Center in half an hour and with a pat on the back and a wave of his cigar, the clown disappears through the swinging doors of the kitchen and leaves me standing there in the kitchen like an idiot, wondering what the hell I'd let myself in for, until this Mrs. Meany, his tough Irish housekeeper but naturally with a heart of gold, the one I just mentioned, pops up out of nowhere, and a few minutes later here come the Countess Luminella and Little Constantine, their dwarf child who I haven't mentioned yet because, in a way, this little kid of theirs, fruit of their wartime love affair, is the key not only to understanding everything I've been telling you about but everything that happened afterwards which includes why you and me are sitting in this stretch Rolls-Royce limousine talking about our wartime experiences with Joe Stabat and headed for who knows what and for what reason, something only Joe Stabat and God seem to know, and that includes his perky little girlfriend, Little Antioch, about which we will have a lot to say in just a little while but not too big a little while, because this is one of those stories that feeds upon itself and therefore seems never to end—

"Does any of this make sense? Of course it doesn't. Because as you know and I know nothing involving Joe Stabat ever makes sense! But don't let that bother you because, make no bones about it, what you and I are involved in now is really big time shit, bigger than you or I could ever imagine we'd be involved in, but for now relax, I don't want you to worry about a thing, because I guarantee that if and when we get to where we're headed and what is in the books to happen actually starts to happen not only will it all make sense but you'll get down on your knees and thank the Living God that you were there when it happened, no matter how all this looks to you now!

"But getting back to this Mrs. Meany you just heard me talking about a few minutes ago, the kinda woman the moment you lay eyes on her you know she's a different kind of beast, a dumpy mean-looking and mean-spirited but ferociously devoutly religious and evil-eyed Irish-Catholic-looking old woman, the kinda woman God uses to do his heavy-duty dirty work who must've been at least seventy years old but no doubt is a lot older and is definitely still interested in what we men have swinging between our legs—

"A fiercely loyal woman who became Joe Stabat's more or less permanently ensconced housekeeper as part of the deal when he bought the mansion with some of the 'war profits' he'd earned shipping dug-up art objects to various phony addresses in the U.S during the war, which pot of gold Joe Stabat and his merry band of thieves invested on Wall Street with the insider information they got from a group of Wall Street insiders called 'The Alpha Consortium' (which I think I mentioned before but you've probably forgot, mainly because you probably don't go to crime movies) and with breathtaking success—

"But scrolling back to when I was meeting up with this Mrs. Meany for the first time and couldn't help but notice how timid and squeaky our tough company commander's voice became in her presence, for the life of me I couldn't figure out why a tough guy like Joe Stabat was so afraid of an old woman who besides being a glorified maid was, after all, just another household employee—until almost as an afterthought and while he was on his way out the door to his important meeting with his hotshot money-men up at Rockefeller Plaza he comes back into the kitchen, takes off his hat and puts his arm around Mrs. Meany and says like I was a little boy he was leaving with a trouble-making old aunt, 'Now listen, you two, I want both of you to understand this is an equal opportunity operation I run here, which means that inasmuch as my old Army buddy Tillman is a bona fide veteran of the United States Army as am I there is to be no racial prejudice and no discrimination on the basis of color, race or creed in this house, is that clear? Any questions? Unfortunately I'm late for my appointment and Mrs. Meany will show you where everything is and give you your chef's uniform; from then on, you're in charge of the kitchen; all the rest including the menu is up to you, you'll find all the ingredients in the pantry and in the refrigerators, and we're all looking forward to this famous 'Plantation Dinner' of yours I've been bragging about to everyone ever since I got out of the Army—

" 'And as for how we run things around here—Tillman, you'll be in charge of the kitchen and Mrs. Meany, she's in charge of the rest of the house, so for Christ's sake, you two, try to get along, and any problems come up, come to me first instead of trying to fight it out between yourselves, because if Tillman and I learned anything in the Army (and with your permission, Mrs. Meany, this is for you) what we learned was that common sense and a healthy dose of self interest and greed can go a long way toward eradicating the disharmony that exists between the white ruling class and our Negro friends—'

"But then, while Joe Stabat is saying this, who should come pussyfooting into the kitchen like a ghost from the distant past than the Countess Luminella di Constantino (I used to love pronouncing that name and never forgot how to do it) who I never would have recognized if it wasn't for the outfit she was wearing, you know, navy blue dress, sometimes a navy blue suit, but always with a white collar made her look like a nun, not only that first time she showed up at the camp to scrounge around for leftovers from the mess hall to distribute to the local poor, but every other time we saw her, including her wedding day—

"The only difference now was her hair had turned gray and stringy and she's thinner and has no bosom and her eyes, now they're kind of wild and restless and dart back and forth as if she's looking for something she lost but has forgotten what it is—

"Her voice, though, her voice is just the same, but quieter now, distant and kind of hollow and with some kind of spooky ring of holy authority to it, but as soon as she sees me and remembers who I am her face lights up and she gives me a balsam wood hug like if I squeeze too hard everything's going to fall apart—

"'Tillman, how wonderful of you to come to make a Plantation Dinner for us again!' she says like it's been maybe a couple of months we haven't seen each other—

"And when I took her hand to shake, it was as dry and light as a dead leaf and felt just as fragile—and when after standing there like that for a while with neither one of us being able to think of anything else to say and so we've started to avoid each other's eyes—this Mrs. Meany, she breaks in impatiently and says in that he-man Irish voice of hers that maybe she better start showing me around the kitchen otherwise I'll never finish the Plantation Dinner in time—

"When I look up, Joe Stabat's already halfway out the door—

"'Good seeing you, Tillman—,' the old bastard says, 'good seeing you and remember, my life's in your hands!'

"No truer words have ever been said, and he winks and comes back to give me a reassuring slap on the back and makes a beeline for the front door—

"And when a few minutes after Joe Stabat finally left and Mrs. Meany was leading me off toward the enormous range that occupies the center of the enormous kitchen which, incidentally, I see now is presided over by one of the biggest, fanciest and most modern cooking stoves I'd ever seen in all my years of cooking around, including the Plaza in Oklahoma City—something tells me to glance over my shoulder which I do, just in time to see the Countess Luminella still standing there but with her eyes closed and with her lips moving silently like maybe she was saying a prayer—

"It was then in that moment when I'd started back to where she was standing, trying to think up something nice to say to her like maybe, 'How nice to see you again,' or 'How great you look,' something cordial and polite like that, something wouldn't provoke any gushiness or tears, when suddenly I see this little dwarf come skipping into the huge kitchen, dressed in what looked like to me one of those 'Little Lord Fauntleroy' schoolboy uniforms, you know—nice crisp white collar, and one of those sweet little schoolboy looks in his eyes—until suddenly I realize the sweet little schoolboy looks like maybe he's a hundred years old, and has that same sly heavy-lidded sleepy look in his eyes and the same puffiness in his little nose, kind of reminds you how Joe Stabat might've looked when and if he'd ever been a little boy—

"'Oh there you are, Constantine dear,' the countess says, stooping down to scoop the cute little dwarf up in her arms, then cuddling him close as if she was about to nurse a baby, 'Say hello to Mr. Tillman, he's daddy's friend from the Army and—aren't you excited?—he's going to live with us and be our cook just like when he and daddy were in the Army, and—just you wait and see, I bet he'll make you some really lovely home-made cookies a whole lot healthier than those horrible Twinkies you've become so fond of lately, so shake hands with our dear old friend from the Army, Mr. Sergeant Tillman, you see I remember your name and everything about you—!'

"But my first real hint of the weird nuthouse atmosphere that reigned in that ridiculous nuthouse of a mansion came when I held out my hand for Little Constantine to shake and the cute little devil grabbed hold of three of my fingers and began twisting them in a professional wrestler's vise-like grip so painful it was all I could do to keep from whacking him one across the head—

"And you know something? That little bastard continued to hold on to my fingers, painfully twisting them back for at least three full minutes, until the little bastard was sure I'd gotten the message as to which of us was the strongest before he finally let go and then reared back with an idiotic grin on his face, but watching me with sly shrewd eyes like I was some new toy for him to play with—

"Which is when I began to notice the wrinkles on the dwarf's neck and on his little hands and the clouded old man look of his gaze, which finally woke me up to think 'Christ! Stabat Junior the little bastard could be maybe fifty years old!' though after quickly doing the arithmetic in my head I realized that from when Joe Stabat and Luminella first met that day she called herself collecting leftovers from our battalion garbage can to feed the local poor to when she and Captain Stabat had that all-night fling on the beach which common wisdom had it was when she got pregnant and lost no time in breaking the news to Captain Stabat they were going to have to get married or else the wrath of her entire aristocratic clan would be unleashed on him and the whole United States Army if the knot wasn't tied before their love-child was born, the little dwarf they named Little Constantine had to have been at least thirty-two, thirty-three, couldn't have been more than maybe thirty-five years old at the most, but to me that morning I'm telling you about he looked to be fifty, maybe sixty years old—

"But that morning, there in Joe Stabat's immense hotel-like kitchen, you'd think Mrs. Meany and the dwarf were acting in one of those corny sugar-sweet shredded wheat commercials—

" 'Come on Constantine, dear—,' Mrs. Meany cooed patiently while at the same time reaching out to take the dwarf out of the countess' arms, '—it's time for your vitamin candy and oatmeal and a nice glass of milk, and then maybe we'll watch *Howdy Doody* on Daddy's brand new giant TV—'

"It was in that moment she said that that a bell started to ring insistently—

"At which time Mrs. Meany looked down at her watch, looked back at me, and winked slyly.

" 'What do you bet, mark my word, she'll be here in exactly four minutes flat on the nose!'

"There was no time to ask who because exactly four minutes later a towering figure of a woman dressed all in black and about as big and tall as Primo Carnera but dressed in a flowing robe of black velvet and with a jewelry store window full of diamond rings on her withered fingers came sweeping into the kitchen like the wrath of God—

"'I've been ring-ring-ring for half hour more but nobody pay attention what my needs are!' she said in a furious rasping voice and in some incomprehensible foreign accent—

"Then the black-clad tower of wrath caught sight of me and, making no attempt to hide her contempt, said—

"'And I suppose you another of my son's nigro mens troopers from war days in Italy, I keep tell him over over again, to be success he must forget war and nigro soldiers no good for success—'

"'But this is Sergeant Tillman, your son's cook in the Army,' Mrs. Meany said trying to put a good face on the situation, 'Mr. Tillman has come to work for Mr. Stabat and I understand he's a very good cook and in fact is going to prepare a 'Plantation Dinner' tonight for your son's important business associates who'll be coming to dinner to watch that TV show, *Roots*, everybody's talking about, they tell me it's about slavery—'

"But by then the Tower of Wrath had swept out of the kitchen as silently as she'd entered, but leaving behind her a strong scent of impending disaster—

"And in fact, a few hours later, the Plantation Dinner all cooked and ready to serve and less than an hour before Joe Stabat's cosmically important dinner guests were scheduled to arrive, I was still trying to fit myself into the brand new but three-sizes-too-small white jacket with gray and red piping on the cuffs and collar which Joe Stabat had bought for me to wear for the gala occasion, when the Countess Luminella, Joe Stabat's wife, came slipping into the kitchen, obviously anxious to get something off her mind before the dinner guests arrived—

"'What people don't understand—,' she said, sitting down at the huge kitchen table already loaded with some of the just-out-of-the oven goodies for that night's gala dinner, '—he'll always be the baby I dreamed about the night before he was born, a child bearing the proud name of the Roman emperor who brought Christianity into our world, a holy royal baby who no matter what happens in his life spent on this earth will never have to worry about being something different than what his mother is and was, but at the same time will never have to become what his father is and was and might now very well become, a normal baby—he really is quite normal no matter what you might think and he can talk though for the time being he won't talk with anybody else but me, but, you know, I've always had the feeling he might talk with you, I can tell he liked you by the way he was looking at you, God speaks to us in such mysterious ways, I sometimes wish my son and I could live in a nice quiet convent with prayers and soft bells and strict silence beginning with the setting of the sun—'

"I smiled politely and nodded my head but there wasn't a damn thing I could comfortably say, but take my word for it, what she said made a deep impression on me, hit me in the gut and hit me in the heart—especially in light of what happened the next day after that disastrous so-called Plantation Dinner, but right then and there I couldn't think of a damn thing in the world to say, I was that moved, and a feeling of dread and inevitability was coming over me—

"Fortunately it was time to set up the bar, and after about

another five or ten minutes of silence during which the Countess Luminella, holding Little Constantine the dwarf by his tiny little fingers, and I just stood there, the countess and I smiling at each other like thieves planning a secret heist, until finally I had to excuse myself and after she and Little Constantine had at last disappeared through the swinging doors, I went off to the pantry where Joe Stabat kept his booze under lock and key and only then, realizing I didn't have the key, called Mrs. Meany on the intercom to tell her I needed her help quick—

"As for Joe Stabat's 'Plantation Dinner Number Two' the dinner itself went well enough in spite of a lively but increasingly nasty conversation about the merits of Southern Negro cuisine compared with Southern Italian cuisine which started out well enough but began to unravel when Joe Stabat, who had had one glass of wine too many, suggested Southern Italians lived in a far worse state of oppression than did the slaves in the American South because the 'fucking Negro slaves were so expensive to buy, nobody could afford a slave unless they were filthy rich and thus upper class—!' a topic which everybody around the table felt it their responsibility to add their two-bits to and which was rapidly becoming a rowdy shouting match that almost certainly would have gotten entirely out of control had it not been interrupted by that night's episode of Alex Haley's *Roots* just then beginning on the giant screen of Joe Stabat's brand new, just arrived that day TV console—

"As for me, I was watching the whole scene from a chair I had placed just inside the swinging doors that opened onto Joe Stabat's royal living room. Nobody knew I was there, but there I was, still dressed in my white cook's uniform and white cook's hat, but with a half glass of some of the best bourbon in the world in my hand and my gaze fixed entranced on that giant TV screen, and the beauty of it all was that not a soul in the world knew I was there—

"To be truthful and to my great surprise up to then Joe Stabat's upscale 'Plantation Dinner Number Two' was going better than expected, the conversation was gentle and reserved and altogether it was becoming quite a nice evening—there had been no complaints about the Southern cooking and just about everybody had asked for seconds of just about everything on the menu including the collard greens, but now that the eating part of the evening was over and the heavy drinking and slavery part of the evening was about to condition the jolly mood which up to then had characterized the evening, a mood of resentful bad-tempered hilarity began to take over the conversation and suddenly all hell broke loose—

"The fracas characterized by hoots of irreverent laughter and ribald comments began during the scene when suddenly we see Kunta Kinte along with a hundred or so other newly captured slaves chained to one another in the bowels of a slave ship about to set sail for America, at which moment one of Joe Stabat's business cronies began to snicker out of control and then say, barely able to control his drunken mirth, 'Can you imagine the smell, all those horny niggers piled up against each other in chains and having to fart in each other's face, I remember reading somewhere each of those African tribes has a separate and distinct smell, not to mention all those jigaboo hard-ons, imagine what that must have been like, all chained up like that and not being able to get off, Jeezus, makes you want to vomit just to think about it, that god-awful stench and all those foul gassy farts down in the cramped bowels—get it?'

"To her everlasting credit, you should have seen the expression of shock, shame and rage on the countess' face as she hugged Little Constantine—who a few minutes before had awakened and was crying for attention and whom she had gone to fetch and bring back to the huge living-room-salon where the guests were now seated in comfortable armchairs around the expensive new TV set with drinks in their hands, 'How dare you speak about those poor Negro slaves like that! Whatever else this house may have been in the past I'll have you know it is now a Christian house and don't any of you dare forget it!'

"So saying, she plopped little Constantine down in an empty easy chair and rushed to the enormous TV set, turned it off, scooped Little Constantine up in her arms and stormed out of the room without explanation or even saying 'goodnight'—

"You can imagine Joe Stabat's embarrassment! Remember, these were his closest business associates, the ones with access to unlimited credit and whom Joe Stabat was counting on to bail him out of his desperate financial situation, and now his wife had just offended his cronies to the core like that, and in the name of what? Civil Rights?—

"Man, you could cut the tension with a cheese knife as for a long, long time Joe Stabat just sat there, slumped in his oversized armchair looking like he was trying to disappear—

"And remember his guests that evening were some of the toughest and most ruthless Italian businessmen in the country and the core providers of Joe Stabat's wealth, power and prestige—

"So if he didn't do something quick to reinstate his authority, something that'd make it look like he was still one of the boys in spite of the unforgivable outrageous behavior of his stuck-up and moralistic Italian wife, the evening could end up costing him millions if not billions of dollars' worth of deals gone down the drain—!

"In retrospect, what Joe Stabat did next was at least from his point of view as logical and inevitable as was his marriage to Luminella di Constantino in the first place when, some thirty or so years before, he had had no choice but to propose marriage when she told him she was pregnant with his child—

"What he did that 'Plantation Dinner Evening'—and I swear I'm not making this up—was grab his wife by the hair, give her a smack across the cheek with the back of his hand, bad cop style, then, while a rare smirk of approval slowly began to appear on the dour-faced countenance of his mother (who if truth be told had all that evening been sitting in her high-backed pope chair with a sour amused smirk on her face but who now could barely contain her joy seeing that her overly sensitive boy, whose potentially glorious military career had been cruelly wasted on a bunch of ungrateful low-life Negro GIs, was now and at long last showing some gumption for a change by giving this snooty highborn Tuscan wife of his just what she deserved and badly needed, a good ass-kicking in front of his powerful business associates—)

"As it turned out, that same night, the night of that overwrought and ill-timed revival of our wartime 'Plantation Dinner,' after all the guests had left and everybody in the mansion except me had gone to bed, Joe Stabat, bleary-eyed and wild-looking, suddenly appeared in the arched doorway of the kitchen where I had been listlessly cleaning up and, just between you and me, getting high on a couple of reefers I'd brought with me from down home—

"He had a bottle and two glasses in his hand which he placed on the huge kitchen table, then ceremoniously pulled out two chairs, helped me into mine, and then pulled his chair around so that we were seated face to face—

"He was bleary-eyed, distraught and there was a zig-zag bloodied bruise on his forehead where he must have fallen on the edge of that high old-fashioned bathtub of his while taking a shower to sober up—

"'You see why I needed you?' he said, 'I made an ass out of myself, didn't I?'

"And when I didn't reply—

"'—but what could I do? She doesn't have any respect for me, she made me look weak and helpless in front of my business partners, what the fuck does she care, they're laughing their asses off at me, all the way from Newark to Las Vegas, I don't know what is with those people, they got it in their veins, for them it's an art form making those they consider beneath them feel like dirt, so what else is new?

"'But goddamit to hell, Tillman, old buddy, if we're dirt, they're shit, 100% merde, what the fuck they care if we working class stiffs have been catching hell since the beginning of time, on the other hand the muthafuckers can't get along without us and that includes you, our colored brothers! Shee-it, man! Who'd till the fucking fields, who'd make the wine, slaughter the fucking pigs while they lounge around sniffing coke or whatever they call that shit they stick up their nose, in the old days it was snuff, right? Right, what I'm getting at, the muthers don't give a shit about us—!'

"Now pay attention! So that you understand what I'm getting at, what you've got to understand is that in all our years together including World War II, I'd never seen Joe Stabat like this, childish, helpless, on the verge of tears but, pardon my language, excruciatingly sincere—so goddamn sincere, to keep from bursting into tears myself, I had to keep my eyes lowered so as to avoid looking at that childish, piggish, whining-ass-face of his, tears pouring down his cheeks, until finally he got down to what was really on his mind, and if you don't believe what I'm willing to swear on a stack of Bibles happened next, I swear, you won't be the first and only one and you damn sure won't be the last—!

"Be that as it may, Joe Stabat offered me another drink even though I was damn sure I wasn't going to finish, come what may—

" 'So what, kismet!' and I don't know what movie he'd gotten this 'kismet' shit from but that's what he said and then went on to say, 'And they can all kiss my ass, for all I care!' (Now he's talking in that fake snarling Jimmy Cagney accent he always goes into when he's trying to create the impression he's delivering a message of gold from the Big Man himself.) 'So I'm an immigrant and you're black and you and me fought a fucking war together which we won, so for Christ Sake, what right do they have to lord it over us, for Christ Sake, she's a fucking emigrant too, but does she give a fuck about America, that's what happens when you marry one of those foreign so-called aristocrats, you always end up cow-towing to them like they got some fucking magic secret hold on us, keep us from revolting or if we do revolt invite us to one of their fancy-dancy high-fashion parties and lay out some coke to buy off our dignity and then expect us to roll over with gratitude and become their fucking slaves—

"'And speaking of slaves, you listen to me, Tillman, you're a good man and you've got dignity, you've got pride and you got class and most important of all you got intelligence and insight enough to understand what I'm about to propose, which is why I called you and asked you to come work for me in the first place, and believe me it wasn't easy finding you—

"'But to stay on message and get back to what I'm really about to propose! Sure slavery was hell, but it was hell only because you had to work in the fucking cotton fields without getting paid for your labor, what I'm about to offer you is something entirely different, you stick with me and I'll make you the fucking richest black man in America, in the fucking world for that matter, you stick with me and I'll make you a fucking king, but only if you sign on as my slave, let me buy you so I own you lock stock and barrel and have the legal papers to prove it—even if the only ones will know you're my legal slave are you and me and my lawyers who, however, will think the whole thing's some cute but sick little joke, and why do I want you to become my legally constituted slave—?

"'Because there's not a fucking person in the world I can trust, especially now that that highborn wife of mine has turned against me, but for you and me and all our World War II buddies, we lived together, fucked together and died together and our blood made every fucking inch of the land we conquered together sacred ground, understand what I'm saying? I want you to be my slave but legally, officially and on the books, and in exchange I'll make you a royal fucking king and the richest black man in America to boot, but it'll all be just between you and me, we'll have this little secret that you belong to me and to me alone, in other words, I know this is a difficult concept to understand, especially now that honest Abe Lincoln officially declared you free, but what I'm talking about is something never been attempted before, something legal and illegal at the same time, our little secret, which is to say you'll still be my slave even though nobody will know that you're legally my slave, nobody but you and me and my lawyers, now does that sound like something you could get your teeth into? Or rather than be the richest black man in America would you prefer to be like all the other nine-to-five working class slobs in this great freak show nation of ours they love to call God's country—

" 'The truth is, Tillman, and I'm going to say it again and I'll repeat it over and over until we both got it tattooed on our brain, there's not a fucking person in this world I can trust, especially now that that highborn wife of mine has turned against me, but you and me and all our World War II buddies who fucked together, suffered together, lived together and died together so that our blood made every fucking square foot of land we liberated sacred ground, which is exactly why I say in World War II, the so-called War of Liberation, we liberated first of all all us working class slobs never been away from home before, and it was as good as it gets, black and white together, shit, every race and color, one for all and all for one, all liberated from our inferiority complexes which made that war as good a war as they make—

"'On the other hand you take someone like the countess, I've given her the best years of my life, worked my ass off to please her and she still blames me because our only child's a fucking dwarf, shit, we never had no dwarfs or retards in my family, my family roots go back thousands of years in Europe so far back nobody in that valley on the Italian side of the Alps knew where the fuck we came from, so fucking far back there weren't even any Christians around breaking everybody's balls, and yet she's always complaining about my 'peasant roots' as if my peasant roots is some kind of a fucking communicable disease—

"'I say shee-it! Fuck them all, who needs them—what I really need, and I've been thinking about this for months, is someone like you, old buddy, somebody who'll always be on my side, someone who'll always be there in my corner when I need you, and not because of your low poor-ass station in life, but because we both have the same need to get back our rightful share; be my slave, Tillman, be my fucking loyal and faithful slave, with papers all legal and official to prove you belong to me and only me and nobody fucking else, whether by common law, commercial law, corporate law, canonical law, any kind of fucking kind of law there is on the books, all you have to do is agree to go along with this one time offer, and I promise I'll make you the richest fucking Negro in America, bar none!'

"By then we'd started on our second bottle of Joe Stabat's premium-label scotch so, as you can well understand, it's hard for me to remember whether I'd actually agreed to go through with his nutty proposal or had just kept my mouth shut and since I didn't say I wouldn't go through with it he assumed I would—

"Anyway, be that as it may, a week or so later, still mellow and high, because after that disastrous so-called 'Plantation Dinner' nobody had come around to tell me exactly what my duties were going to be, or for that matter whether I'd actually been hired or not—

"But then, after nearly a week of sitting around in the kitchen, eating one TV breakfast after the other and washing it down with some of the captain's private stock (to which he graciously gave me the key) all of a sudden and entirely out of the blue I get this call from Joe Stabat to call a taxi 'right now this minute!' and have the driver drive me to a certain address in Rockefeller Plaza he gave me and told me to write down so I'd be sure not to forget, an address on about the one-thousandth floor of one of those Rockefeller Plaza skyscrapers—you know where the skating rink is—and the first thing you know I find myself riding to the top of one of those scary snooty buildings to some posh legal office with a lot of foxy secretaries and carpets so thick it was like I was in Heaven, walking on clouds—

"Finally after a doorman tells me how to get to exactly where I want to get to, I get in another elevator and ride about a hundred floors to the top of the fucking skyscraper itself where this legal office is, and where a teenage girl dressed up like an undertaker's apprentice tells me to wait in a tiny cubbyhole of a room with benches instead of chairs and where I wait and wait and wait until finally Joe Stabat, dressed in a black suit made him look like a preacher appears in the doorway and motions me to follow him down another long hallway to another office looked more like a church than a lawyer's office only there weren't any candles or crucifixes, just stack after stack of old law books, some of them dating all the way back to the days of the Pilgrims (or so at the time my feverish state of mind led me to imagine) and where three very young-looking guys, looked to me like college-boy lawyers were seated around an enormous carved oak table, the highly polished top of which was littered with huge law books, each opened to a page indicated by an ornate red and gold velvet book marker imprinted with the law firm's name, like as if the team of pink-cheeked college-boy lawyers had been up all night studying those ancient law books for an exam—

"'You're very lucky, sir,' one of the bright young pink-cheeked lawyers said, smiling like a fat bishop, 'it was one chance in about six hundred I'd say, but we finally found what we were looking for—'

"By then the mood had begun to change to something very close to academic excitement as one of the bright young men said cheerfully to Joe Stabat as we entered, 'We finally found what we think you're looking for, here it is right here, a legal caveat right here making you the rightful owner, so to speak, of your employee's services and legal identity until such time as he is declared legally dead or retires, whichever comes first, as good a definition of slavery as you're likely to find anywhere and just as legally binding—'

"And weird as it might seem, and I've heard every conceivable argument to the contrary, the simple incontrovertible fact remains that on that morning and in that office high on the top floor of one of those somber skyscrapers in Rockefeller Center, whatever else took place, I legally became Joe Stabat's perfectly legal slave—

"And, in fact, almost as a warning of the kind of nightmarish complexities I would now be exposed to, when we finally reached the Belt Parkway and were moving at a snail's pace toward the exit for Staten Island and finally now were approaching the mansion's ornate gate, we suddenly found the mansion ablaze with every light turned on and the spot lights of at least twelve police cars wildly probing the darkness of the surrounding woods as police dogs yapped in the distance and countless flashlight beams bobbed up and down and crisscrossed and erratically embroidered the deep darkness of the surrounding woods—

" 'She's left, the countess and Little Constantine have left—!'

"It was I who said that, not Joe Stabat, but it could've been either one of us because the same horrible thought had crossed our minds at exactly the same moment—

" 'Something has happened to Luminella!'

"And when Joe Stabat, white as a sheet, repeated his fears (and mine) I knew he was right on target, because ever since her ghastly display of disgust during that misguided replay of our wartime 'Plantation Dinner' Luminella and Little Constantine had remained locked up in her bedroom, refusing even to unlock the door that separated the master bedroom suite from the more modest two-bedroom suite she had claimed for herself and Little Constantine when some twenty years or so ago they moved into Joe Stabat's spooky Prohibition-era mansion buried deep in the Staten Island woods—

" 'I knew it!' Joe Stabat said, shaking his head with pessimistic dismay, 'I knew she was going to do it sooner or later, anything to bring me down, personally and professionally, and—goddamit to hell—this time her timing is going to bury me in a hole I won't be able to dig myself out of even if I live to be a thousand years old!'

"What Joe Stabat was talking about, something so far beyond the boundaries of sanity, was known about by everyone in the mansion but out of necessity was completely ignored since any acknowledgement of the truth would have meant doing something about it and no one had the slightest clue what to do other than pretend it wasn't taking place—

"What had been taking place for months was simply that, every single morning of the week except Sunday when she attended mass at the local Catholic church, Luminella dressed up like a poor emigrant in a long grey dress and a black shawl around her shoulders and, promptly at six o'clock on the dot, she and Little Constantine would get into a taxi pre-hired for the purpose and be driven down to the Staten Island Ferry Terminal where they would join the surging mass of commuters boarding the six-thirty ferry to Manhattan which when it pulled into the dock on the Manhattan side, instead of debarking with the stampeding horde of daily commuters Luminella and Little Constantine would remain aboard, occupying a bench on the top deck set between two lifeboats, and there remain all day with an occasional stroll to the upper deck or to one of the several hot dog stands, pretending to be poor emigrants arriving in New York from Italy for the first time, pretending to speak no English, but speaking Italian—mostly her local Tuscan dialect—to herself and to the dwarf, occasionally engaging someone in a conversation in a kind of ignorant pig-Latin of her own invention, but mostly talking to herself or to Little Constantine and observing the sights, the colorful tourists, an occasional drunk, or a Negro couple, occasionally giving a blind musician a ten dollar bill, or comforting a harassed young mother's crying baby—

"Back and forth, back and forth, all day long Luminella and Little Constantine would ride the ferry without getting off, often engaging out-of-towners in lively conversations in pig-Latin complete with elaborate gestures, roaming the ferry like tourists and admiring the landscape, back and forth, back and forth until almost sunset when promptly at seven-thirty they would join the crowd pushing and shoving ashore and board the taxi they had previously reserved and paid for and return to the mansion exactly an hour and a half before dinner—

"No one challenged her right to do this, and we all understood it had something to do with the vision she had of herself as a homeless, rootless wanderer in the world, a perpetual emigrant, perhaps even a holy beggar—

"We all had opinions as to why she did it but in the end we said nothing to Mr. Stabat nor notified the police—

"But I think it was the chauffeur who finally got around to telling him, and that very night after she and the dwarf went to bed, Joe Stabat called all the help into the kitchen and in the most serious terms instructed us to ignore what she was doing, humor her, so to speak, ask no questions and go along with whatever craziness had affected her mind—

"But now—as a police captain and a detective (hats in hand and sorrowful expressions of Irish mourning and grief engraved on their freshly shaven cheeks) explain the results of their investigation carried out shortly after the 5:30 ferry pulled into its docking space with its man-overboard siren sounding so loud it could be heard from one end of the island to the other—that

Luminella di Constantino and their son Little Constantine have, it is now assumed, committed suicide by jumping overboard at some time between 5:30 p.m. and 3:43, the last time of day a witness remembers seeing them still aboard the ferry—"

"What really happened to her, Joe Stabat's wife, Luminella—?"

"Nobody really knows because no body has ever washed ashore—"

For a long time I sat there stunned and depressed and for a long time I said nothing.

"You know I just lost my wife, Lucia?"

Tillman made no comment but just sat there deep in thought, a faraway look in his eyes—

"That makes two of you—two brothers with dead wives—

"Not that I consider Joe Stabat a brother but he's rich enough to be any fucking thing he wants, which means he could pass if he wanted to—

"Why do you think he's investing all this money in Little Antioch and this cockamamie Gospel Summit—?"

I was staring at Tillman with an expression of total disbelief:

"You mean Joe Stabat is bankrolling this Gospel Summit himself out of his own pocket? Come on, man, what is all this—?"

"Whatever it is it's not a joke, he's dead serious, like everything he does it's another desperate ploy to vindicate himself with his wife's family, finally earn their respect, in fact he's already put in motion a worldwide media strategy that will not only get his name back in the news and make him more bankable than ever—but also—so he hopes and dreams will reconcile him with Luminella's family while impressing her snooty friends. The Gospel Summit, among other things, is going to be like a giant high-powered public relations vindication of Luminella di Constantino's family name—!"

I was shocked and unable to believe what I was hearing—

"Look, man, he has no choice—," Tillman said moving very close and whispering hoarsely into my ear, "—you know it and I know it and now the world's going to know it: Joe Stabat is a madman and a criminal who'll do anything—and I mean anything—to get what he wants, especially if it has to do with his status in life, who he thinks he is and the glory he thinks he deserves! Guys like that who are driven to kingship by the power of their own imagination will go to any length—do anything—to prove that their own high evaluation of themselves is true—

"Shit! Thomas Jefferson was like that! George Washington was like that! All the Rockefellers and Roosevelts were like that! And they all had one thing in common: they surrounded themselves with a few faithful crazy niggers! And you know why? Because crazy niggers have been there, that's why they're crazy! Know all the ins and outs of dealing with the Devil and coming out alive!"

"And Little Antioch? Is Joe Stabat in love with her?"

"You want to know my opinion. Joe Stabat's in love with the idea of making Little Antioch the biggest thing in gospel, the biggest thing in show business, and for that matter the biggest thing in religion—and when she's filled all those slots, become the biggest of the biggest, not only in gospel but in all aspects of the show-business side of religion and to the point she begins sprouting wings—he'll think up something even bigger to satisfy his lust for power and glory—

"I know like you know there were plenty people in the audience of that Bedford-Stuyvesant Church, black people and white people too who were embarrassed seeing this stocky ethnic white man jump up on the gospel concert stage and start yelling at the top of his voice that he'd got religion while at the same time doing that freaky version of the polka he was doing while jerking his arms up and down like it was morning calisthenics time, but who are we to say who can get religion and who can't and why, for Christ's sake, give the man a break, after all, sincere or not Joe Stabat had just lost his wife and son and no doubt like most guys in the same circumstances he was clutching at straws!

"As for what actually happened to his wife I'm absolutely convinced Joe Stabat still believes that one day, some day, his aristocratic and religious wife will come back to him on her knees—

"Indeed, I was shocked by the dire rhetoric Luminella di Constantino's presumed 'disappearance' was beginning to inspire. But on the other hand I wasn't so surprised since from her first appearance at our camp those many years ago to her outburst at dinner the night before, everything she did no matter how innocent seemed to provoke an over-reaction on the part of people intimidated by that air of stern religiosity that was like her trademark—"

"Damn, Tillman, you're making all this sound like—I mean why are you trying to turn Luminella's disappearance into some kind of cosmic historical event? Something for the record books? Shit, wives leave their husbands all the time, and most of them after a quick trip to Disneyland or the Grand Canyon come back and ask to have the locks changed. Aren't you letting yourself be carried away by something that in the end is bound to have a simple explanation?"

"Nothing that woman does is simple, even if she's just another runaway bride, she comes from a family that looks upon itself as being in a special relationship with History, I've heard her say as much, phrases like 'History is made by the bold moves of people who don't give a damn what other people think!' "

"And Joe Stabat? How does Little Antioch fit into all this? Are she and Joe Stabat really thinking of getting married?"

Tillman laughed a private laugh and reared back against the white kid leather of the limo's back seat and folded his long thin hands over the sunken 'skinny man' stomach and closed his eyes—

"Now we're getting to the nitty-gritty, you and me have always been buddies, and our friendship goes back a fairly long time, to when we both were young men who believed in the tooth-fairy, so to speak—

"But now, D., I want you to listen to me carefully because what I have to say I'm only going to say once because you don't get it the first time around means it's non-gettable or you're fucking with me and don't want to get involved—

"But on the other hand, since I have personal experience of how smart you are—for Christ's sake man, you've been a famous writer ever since you started writing probably even before that—but what I'm talking about now is another kind of smartness, life and death smartness, and even though you don't come from a down-home black background like me, you've travelled enough and read enough books to understand that when there's something in the air with a funny smell to it and then everything else starts smelling funny too, make no mistake about it, that means, even if you yourself aren't aware of it, everything else is smelling funny too—!

"Which is why for big-stake gamblers like our man, Joe Stabat, the word 'lose' doesn't even exist in his dictionary because for the likes of Joe Stabat all the excitement, as well as all the money is in the next game, not the game he just lost, fuck the fucking game you just lost, in other words, what're the odds on this hot new game you just been telling me about?

"And as a matter of fact, I'm glad you asked—because now I'm going to tell you! And you can count yourself lucky because you're among the very first to know!

"It's her! Joe Stabat's hot new game is that cute little brown-skinned beauty sitting behind the wheel of this glorified Rolls-Royce pimp-mobile you can't keep your eyes off, who, just for the record, happens to be my great-great-niece and, if certain gossip going around town in Lawton a few months after our outfit went overseas proves credible, she may become your great-great-niece too, something sooner or later you and me, old buddy, are going to have to sit down and come to grips with—

"One thing is sure, she sure has worked her magic on our old commanding officer who, for better or worse, seems determined to make her a world class super-star capable of making black gospel music the hottest new thing in show business, worldwide! And the Gospel Summit is the way he's going to do it!"

"How did they meet?"

"It's not so much how they met as why did it take so long?

Since obviously they were made for each other, a Fate and Destiny brother-sister act bound to happen come hell or high water!

"So how did they meet, Joe Stabat and that charming brown-skinned beauty chauffeuring us to her historic rendezvous with Show Business Glory, well let's see now, how much time do you got?"

5

"Anyway, and to make a long story short, with his highborn Italian wife Luminella and their son Little Constantine either dead, vanished off the face of the earth, or who knows where? Joe Stabat had no choice but to stay out of sight so as to avoid having to discuss the mysterious disappearance of his Italian wife and son with his business cronies and especially the press—

"In fact he began spending less and less time at his office in Rockefeller Plaza and more and more time just sitting around the kitchen with me, shooting the breeze and watching the daytime talk shows on cable TV, while snacking on hot dogs and potato chips, the food the man loves most in the world, especially washed down with expensive scotch—

"It was after about a week or so of goofing off like this that I discovered I was beginning to miss my privacy and was beginning to tire of his whining and implacable gloom, though I was damned always damned careful not to hurt his feelings, and began looking around for an excuse to get him out of the house, and it was around that time I got a phone call from my niece, Little Antioch, actually she was calling from Oklahoma, saying she'd just found out I'd left Lawton for New York and was working as the private cook for some rich man on Staten Island who'd been my commanding officer in Italy during the war, so since we hadn't seen each other since she was a little girl—now that she's a big star why don't we try to get together after the gospel show she's going to be performing in Bedford-Stuyvesant, Brooklyn, which she understands isn't more than half an hour or so from Staten Island, why don't we all get together after the concert and catch up with old times, and when I told her I wasn't sure about my boss but that I'd be there with bells on! a few days later a Fed-Ex envelope arrived special delivery from somewhere in California with two tickets to some event called 'The Gospel Experience,' or something like that, a four-hour concert of gospel music featuring among a long list of other gospel choirs and singers, the night's star performer, 'Little Antioch, the Angel of Salvation—'

"Now remember all this is going on less than a month after Luminella di Constantino and her son, the dwarf, had vanished from the Staten Island ferry (and presumably from the face of the earth) and Joe Stabat was still having one hell of a time getting over his guilt-ridden consternation and grief—

"As for me, you can imagine there was damn little for me to do in the way of cooking or cleaning up the kitchen to take my mind off what happened and, in fact, only once since I had officially become Joe Stabat's slave had Joe Stabat failed to corner me in the kitchen for yet another weepy discussion as to what might have happened to his wife and it was that night or a night like it, that when the conversation inevitably began to drift toward his wife's disappearance and the same desperately packaged homilies and clichés about what a wonderful woman she had been—always now in the past tense—inevitably bringing him to the verge of tears of self-incrimination I suggested out of desperation that he come with me to a concert of gospel music featuring a hot, new, up and coming gospel singer who though her professional name was Little Antioch was a great-niece of mine and (he'd suddenly turned around and was now looking me straight in the eyes with what at the time seemed exaggerated intensity) the daughter of Hopeful, one of Aunt Harriet's 'girls,' who I understand you all had a great time with at that memorable Thanksgiving Dinner at the Tillman Mansion the year I was away at cook's school—

"To make a long story short Joe Stabat almost broke out in tears he was so grateful I had invited him to the gospel concert, which, frankly, started me wondering if I was doing the right thing, especially at a time like this when Joe Stabat was experiencing what certainly must have been the deepest and most emotional void of his life—

"When finally, after inching its way through the largest and most emotionally charged crowd I'd experienced in my life our taxi pulled up in front of the church, a red-brick 19th century structure that occupied almost the entire city block and was crowded and filled beyond imagination with an overflow crowd occupying four city blocks, who would be listening to the gospel concert through loudspeakers mounted on soundtrucks and on the roofs of adjacent buildings, creating a desperate 'end of the world' kind of atmosphere that was selling tickets as fast as they could be printed—

"I still don't know how we got through the milling hordes

blocking the main entrance of the church to go inside the vestibule and then to the front row seats beneath the altar reserved for guest celebrities which, it soon became evident, our gilt-emblazoned invitations signed personally by Little Antioch herself, entitled us to—apparently the burly ushers in whose care Joe Stabat and I had been placed had been hired especially for the occasion and had in their possession some minute electronic device which when turned on emitted a soundless electronic signal which somehow and immediately caused the crowd to hastily move aside to let our party through in such a manner that, while for most of the audience finding a seat could take anywhere from twenty minutes to more than half an hour, Joe Stabat and I (both of us clean-shaved and elegant in dark blue suits Joe Stabat had had made by his personal tailor, two for each of us, one single-breasted and the other double-breasted but with a hint of sheen on the lapel, which suits, I understand, cost seven-thousand dollars each and had been sent to Valentino's in Rome for finishing), as it turns out our seats were right beneath the dais though between our row of super-front row seats there was a kind of red-velvet covered praying zone and a walkway about five yards wide the purpose of which became evident soon after the concert began when streams of people from the audience, carried away by religious fervor and the urge to move rhythmically to the hand-clapping beat of whatever gospel hymn was being sung (as often as not accompanied by some huge but invisible deep-voiced electronic organ and various percussionary devices and live drummers, they too invisible from where we were seated)—all of which contributed to a mood of expectancy that mysterious things and wonders were about to occur—

"And in fact, at a certain climax of hand-clapping and foot-stomping excitement Joe Stabat suddenly jumped to his feet and before I became fully aware of what was happening the next thing I knew there he was up on the red velvet walkway beneath the dais where at the beginning of the concert Little Antioch had made a few remarks welcoming her fans and making special reference to her uncle and his World War II commanding officer, heroes of a war she herself was too young to remember but which we should never forget—and was now prancing around with his arms jerking wildly up and down toward heaven and with tears streaming down his cheeks, dancing wildly in place while shouting 'Glory! Glory! Glory!' loud enough to be heard above the throbbing beat of the gospel chorus and its electronic percussion section, 'I am a sinner, I demand forgiveness, Get Thee Forever Behind me, Satan! Lord, My Lord, I beseech Thee set me free!'

"There was so much Glory and Hallelujah going on I forget the exact sequence in which what happened happened, but what I do remember clear as crystal was suddenly there was an enormous flash of light, like somewhere there had just occurred a short circuit (something entirely possible because of the incredible tangle of electrical cables attached to organs, lights, amplifiers, etc.—it was almost impossible to cross the jumbled stage without tripping on some electrical connection), so after the great explosion of light, the next thing I knew there was Joe Stabat like lifted up onto the stage and by the time I'd jumped to my feet to figure out what in the hell was going on (because all this was happening like in a matter of a few seconds) he, Joe Stabat, was stretched out unconscious on the red velvet walkway and Little Antioch who had been in the final glory ending to the song she had been singing, 'Lord, Lordy Lord, I Need an Explanation' from her latest hit album of the same name, was kneeling down beside him, tears streaming down her cheeks, shouting at the top of her voice, 'God has worked His first miracle tonight on this pilgrim and henceforth this white man shall be blessed and all glory to His name!'

"That night when all three of us got back to Joe Stabat's mansion in the Staten Island woods the lights were all ablaze but there wasn't a soul on hand to greet us, everybody, which meant Mrs. Meany had left and Joe Stabat, Little Antioch and I had the whole mansion to ourselves—

"Now I know, D., you're just like me and you got it all figured out just like I thought I had it all figured out—but just like I was wrong, you're dead wrong too—

"No hanky-panky between Little Antioch and Joe Stabat took place and the reason I know no hanky-panky took place is because of something happened to her about six or seven months before the concert in Bed-Stuy—

"What happened was that at the time, this is just before she started becoming a big time gospel star, Gospel Lights of Nashville, Tennessee, who was managing her and getting her ready to become the biggest star in gospel, they noticed that when she finished whatever song she was singing with a high-A note the audience could notice her bottom teeth were crooked and badly needed fixing and they went to a dentist called Benny Lincoln to do the job and he botched it so badly he lost control of the drill which unfortunately pierced her vocal chords and put her in a special research hospital for the next six months during which time she became very religious and promised the Lord if she got her teeth back and her voice back she would remain chaste as a nun and never have sex with a man, period.

"In fact it was while she was in a hospital in Denver, Colorado, recovering from the accident and had time to read all kinds of books in the hospital library that she got the idea for a World Gospel Summit that could be held on the sacred grounds where the Emperor Constantine had experienced the 'Vision of the Cross' which as you well know was how Christianity began—

"So the reason, apart from my niece's saintly nature, the reason I know there wasn't no hanky-panky and hasn't been none since—none whatsoever—is that they spent practically all that night in the kitchen planning how they could make the Gospel Summit happen—which right then and there Joe Stabat promised to organize and help finance in memory of his missing wife and their dwarf son, Little Constantine, and the only one who went to bed that night in Joe Stabat's mansion was me and when I woke up about seven-thirty the next morning, the big kitchen table was covered with sheets of paper on which were written long lists of gospel choirs from all over the world which Little Antioch knew about from the concerts she had been giving since she started singing gospel at the age of twelve—"

"And you think Joe Stabat is sincere? He really got religion?" I was asking as abruptly Tillman stopped talking and instead began to stare out the window obviously deep in thought.

"I think he's convinced himself he's sincere which for Joe Stabat is the same as actually being sincere—

"On the other hand it's not all that difficult to understand how someone like my niece has become not only as chaste as a nun but in the same breath finds herself violently attracted to a blundering bully like our former commanding officer, Joe Stabat—

"As for Joe Stabat himself, on one level Little Antioch is this powerful moneymaking star who—and no one can explain why—has placed her trust in him the way little girls trust their fathers which is an entirely new experience for him, almost as if for the very first time in his life he feels connected to a woman in a kind of chaste father-daughter relationship, something he was never able to experience with Luminella who as a countess was above him in class, caste and character and who, therefore, and from his point of view could only be viewed as an enemy to subdue—

"Then there's this business of his climbing up on the stage and acting the fool like he'd just gotten religion, and as far as I'm concerned the man deserves some slack, because as they say God moves in mysterious ways!

"Because for once, I think he was sincere and that he was in some kind of a religious trance when he did it, and that includes all the weird dancing and acrobatics!

"Whatever the explanation Joe Stabat at that gospel concert in Bedford-Stuyvesant was having some kind of medieval religious experience, some unaccustomed, for him, holy-roller episode even if he did make a fool of himself, hopping around like that, and yelling at the top of his voice that he'd got religion!

"In fact that night after the concert when the three of us got back to the mansion, after Joe Stabat promised Little Antioch's manager we would put her on a plane the following afternoon in time for her next concert which, if I remember correctly, was in Pittsburgh before the whole gospel troupe would meet in Detroit for a Baptist revival to be televised nationally on cable TV—

"In the meantime, Joe Stabat was bubbling over with energy and was going around saying to anyone who would listen that gospel was what the world had been waiting for and needed and was capable of changing the course of history and, of course, the Gospel Summit was meant to do exactly that!

"The truth was Joe Stabat was inspired as if something or somebody was putting words into his mouth and by then he had convinced himself that an international Gospel Summit to be held on the sacred ground where Constantine I had had his 'Vision of the Cross' could actually change the world!

"And it was then Joe Stabat began raving about a Gospel Summit to anyone who was willing to listen that would be held in Italy, maybe even on the site where Constantine I had experienced his 'Vision of the Cross,' and that night in his mansion after his gospel experience at the Bedford-Stuyvesant church he wouldn't let us go to bed but kept us up all night discussing a wild plan that had just popped into his head and insisted we stay up with him and discuss the plan with him, a World Gospel Summit, gospel choirs from all over the world meeting somewhere in Italy near Constantine's Holy Site (at first he said it like that 'the Gospel Summit would take place somewhere in the world') but then he stopped, his eyes started popping and he said like as if he had just had the biggest revelation of his life, that if the Gospel Summit was to happen anywhere why not have it happen at the very site where Constantine had had his 'Vision of the Cross,' but at the time I hadn't the slightest idea what they were talking about, but Joe Stabat, bless his heart, knew who the Emperor Constantine was, his wife must have told him, and I suddenly remembered the dwarf, his son, was named Little Constantine, so by then all the pieces were starting to fall together—

"When we got back to Joe Stabat's mansion in Staten Island he was still raving and after Little Antioch went to bed in what had been Luminella's bedroom but was now—so Joe Stabat said—until further notice the guest bedroom, he and I sat down in the kitchen until almost three o'clock in the morning while he raved on and on about what almost hysterically he kept describing as the most important cultural event of the century—

"Anyway and to make a long story short the next morning when I got up Joe Stabat had already left for his office and Little Antioch was still fast asleep and snoring in Luminella's bedroom when around ten o'clock in the morning I get this hysterical phone call from Joe Stabat telling me that Little Antioch and I should immediately drop whatever we're doing and call a cab immediately and get our asses to his office in Rockefeller Plaza because 'everything was arranged—'

"What it was that had been arranged was, number one, a fabulous contract that annulled all Little Antioch's previous contracts with Gospel Lights of Nashville, Tennessee, and placed her under the exclusive management of Joe Stabat.com—

"Don't ask me how he did it but he did do it, and when the two of us—Little Antioch and I—later the next morning finally got to Joe Stabat's office, the very same office, filled with smart-ass young lawyers I already told you about when I 'officially' became Joe Stabat's slave, right then and there and with all the necessary contracts ready to be signed, the World Gospel Summit, featuring gospel choirs from all over the world performing nonstop for forty-eight hours at the very site where the Emperor

Constantine had had his 'Vision of the Cross' became not only a reality but as the ensuing publicity began to proclaim relentlessly on every major television network and in every major language in the world, was destined to become 'the most publicized event in the history of the world, surpassed only by the as yet unproclaimed Second Coming of Christ—' "

When I heard that, I looked at Tillman with outraged eyes.

"Do you expect me to believe some outrageous bullshit like that?"

"Of course I don't expect you to believe it, to tell you the truth, I didn't believe it either—"

"Then why are you fucking with me like this?"

"Because you have no choice but to come with us and see what happens!"

"What do you mean I have no choice?"

"Exactly what I said—having come this far, for you there's no turning back—"

Frantically I grabbed hold of the door latch but found it locked—

"Don't waste your time, whether you want to or not you have no choice but to come with us, because, frankly, there is no force in Heaven or Hell that can save you from what now has become foreordained—!"

"But Tillman, you're Tillman, how can you expect me to believe some crazy bullshit like this?"

"Believe what? That what I say is true? I just told you it's true, you have no choice but to believe me and if you still choose not to believe me then you have no choice but to accept the consequences—"

“Consequences? What consequences?”

“Consequences, you’re a college boy, you know what consequences are! Consequences that by now should be self-evident!”

In the meantime Joe Stabat had turned around and was looking at us with suspicious but mirthful eyes—

“What’ve you and Tillman been yapping about all this time back there! It’s about time you two realize this is a team effort and that we’re all in this together!”

“You’re a great man, and we trust you!” Little Antioch said, giving Joe Stabat an affectionate kiss on the cheek, “At least I do, I can’t speak for those two so-called veterans back there who from the way they talk you’d think they won the war singlehanded!”

“No one said we WON the war what it was we were observing was that all three of us were in the war at the same time and in the same place and therefore we have every right to call each other ‘old buddy!’

“And what I was about to point out—,” Joe Stabat growled, “this Gospel Summit we’re about to set in motion could turn out to be a bigger deal than World War I, World II, and World War III all together—”

“Maybe so, I’m not disputing the value of hyperbole as a motivating factor,” I said, my voice breaking squeakily, “—but will somebody please tell me what the plan is, what it is we’re supposed to be doing when we get to where we’re going?”

In response Joe Stabat slammed the partition shut and hunkered down in his seat so that all we could see of him was the fringe of gray hair on his wrinkled pate—

“You should be careful making the man angry like that,” Tillman said, his voice dripping with hurt and genuine concern,

"Joe Stabat may be an asshole but the man's been through hell since his wife disappeared and you and me and Little Antioch should be pooling our resources to help him through what obviously is the biggest crisis of his life—!"

"His crisis? What about my crisis? You guys just show up out of nowhere and expect me not to complain when I tell you I haven't the slightest idea what this is all about or where we're going and what we're going to do when we get there!

"All I'm asking—," I said by way of conclusion, "—is a simple explanation!

And when I said that Little Antioch let out a shriek—

"That's it—!" she yelled, "That's the title of the song—"

"Title of what song?" I yelled growing angrier and more frustrated by the minute.

"'Lord, Lordy Lord, I Need an Explanation!'"

And so saying she pulled over to the side of the road and parked in the lane set aside for emergencies and suddenly in that thrilling throaty contralto of hers she began to sing what was destined to become her signature spiritual, the spiritual that has since thrilled audiences all over the world but which we were hearing for the very first time: "Lord, Lordy Lord, I Need an Explanation!"

Lord, Lordy Lord
I need an explanation
The Sadness of the World
Has trodden me down
All this grief, all this Sorrow
Little Children Without Joy

If this is how it is and how it has to be
Lord, Lordy Lord
I need You to explain!
If you know his Name
This Savior Without Fame
Come Sweet Lord and Tell Me
So I Can Tell the World!

PART III

1

Both here in Rome and back home in New York those bankers and their banks who throughout his years as a Wall Street insider Joe Stabat had always been able to count on to finance his frequently ingenious but always controversial investment "strategies," "whims," and "no problem, sure things," suddenly and without any explanation nor even so much as an ingeniously crafted "letter of regret" had become uncharacteristically skittish and evasive and now were taking their time making good on their promises of even those minimal start-up funds (usually referred to as "chickenfeed") to help get off the ground this latest and most ingenious but also, and in the opinion of certain ultra-conservative Roman bankers, the most risky and suspect project Joe Stabat Inc. had ever proposed, the so-called "Gospel Summit"—

Which was why at three a.m. this morning (and in spite of his basic rule: "Never, Repeat, Never Beg") Joe Stabat actually phoned his brother-in-law, Riccardo, who was in Buenos Aires on some tainted but no doubt lucrative business venture, to ask "in the name of family solidarity" his help in a matter of serious concern to both of them, only to be told in no uncertain terms that given Luminella's still unsolved disappearance and Joe Stabat's "blatant and unforgivable dalliance with that sexy Negro gospel singer friend of yours" there was nothing he nor anyone else in their circle could or was likely to do for him even though a powerful mob figure and stock broker they both knew had told him in strict confidence that "there were still plenty hard-nosed music industry wise guys out there on both sides of the Atlantic" who still considered Joe Stabat the "best in the money-making business" and this latest brainstorm of his, one of the most timely, innovative and surefire moneymaking projects to come down the pike since Woodstock!

The project everybody in Rome was talking about, the "Talk of the Town" so to speak, was of course Joe Stabat's "Gospel Summit" now widely advertised as a "three-day festival of Black American and International Gospel Music to be sung by a great variety of Gospel Choral Ensembles from all over the world," and scheduled to take place in two weeks' time but at a site yet to be announced by the competent authorities within the Italian government apparatus, even though at least twenty-eight gospel choirs or choral groups had already confirmed their participation and time of arrival.

Which is why, after having been holed up here in Rome for the better part of three weeks, most of the time right here in the Hotel d'Inghilterra Bar, like everybody else connected to the Gospel Summit waiting in vain for the still lacking but now desperately needed start-up funds to be released as promised by the competent government agencies I had become painfully aware that a mood not quite yet of desperation but certainly of rapidly approaching despondency was beginning to settle over the entire enterprise like a pall, so that this very morning when a prominent Rome newspaper columnist pointed out in today's daily column what by now was becoming painfully obvious to all, that "if the so-called Gospel Summit is really for real, is indeed the popular expression of a by now accepted popular art form, how come the responsible government agency still hasn't assigned the event a site?" those of us closest to the Gospel Summit Project became darkly convinced that what we were beginning to witness at this point was nothing less than the handwriting on the wall—

In fact just this morning the site originally assigned the "late Gospel Summit Project" (as it was now derisively being described by both government agencies and the press), a vast park-like meadow six kilometers northwest of the spot historians say Constantine I experienced his "Dream-Vision of the Cross" had unceremoniously been taken off the bargaining table by the finicky but ultra-powerful and authoritative Belle Arte Commission because suddenly it had been discovered (again just that morning) that that particularly lovely and grassy patch of meadowland several kilometers north of the Milvio Bridge had already been set aside as the hallowed site for a monument to the military dead of the Iraq War.

Which led most of us close to the project to the conclusion that just days before the Gospel Summit was scheduled to begin advanced planning for the event suddenly and ignominiously was about to come to a final halt—

True enough there were still those few pious smiles of encouragement and the occasional comradely slap on the back, usually accompanied by a whispered and conspiratorial "corraggio!" from various minor and therefore still friendly Gospel Summit enthusiasts among certain junior government officials and foreign journalists still streaming in and out of Joe Stabat's sumptuous "foreign press headquarters" with its continuous 24-hour-a-day buffet table and open bar and where the main news this morning was an article that had appeared in today's edition of the right-wing tabloid *SCANDALA*, in which Joe Stabat, "the colorful and mercurial one-man army behind the well-meaning but perhaps misguided Gospel Summit has just been identified by sources close to the intelligence community as that same 'Captain Joe Stabat' who both British and American Intelligence Services had identified as the infamous former World War II black marketeer and trafficker in illegally dug-up art objects from the Etruscan tombs with secret ties to the wartime Fascist Underground," which acidulously defamatory article ended with the provocative crowd-pleasing rhetorical challenge: "What does it say about the tenor of the times when one of Christianity's most cherished founding myths is being so blatantly vilified by an American war criminal in the name of vulgar and crowd-pleasing American show business sleight of hand—?"

It was during these darkest of hours (during one of which I had sneaked off alone to the American Express Office in Piazza di Spagna to protest an unfounded charge on my American Express Card account) that unexpectedly I ran into Joe Stabat, Tillman and Little Antioch having a late lunch at the fashionable insider's restaurant in the heart of Old Rome, Otello's, on Via della Croce, which apparently had been recommended to them by the venerable journalist and literary critic, Paolo Moroso, the very same Paolo Moroso who in that day's column in *La Repubblica* had claimed (in his own words) to have become "morbidly fascinated by the poisonous medieval intrigue swirling around this so-called Gospel Summit like so much chaff from a hateful prayer wheel" which "atmosphere of poisonous medieval intrigue" apparently hadn't discouraged him from seeking out even more "lurid dark secrets" about the Gospel Summit's travails for a final two-part series of articles, the first of which was scheduled to appear that weekend in *La Repubblica*'s Sunday edition; and for which—judging from the uninhibited and wine-stimulated conversation around our table (at which he, Joe Stabat, Little Antioch, Tillman and now I were impatiently awaiting the arrival of our first course)—he was now eagerly looking forward to gathering even more "lurid and colorful" insights and, indeed, this very moment, as I came rushing in the crowded restaurant and now and at the very moment I was being seated was asking his fellow guests at the table the apparently innocent question, "—exactly how did it come about that an idea so exquisitely non-Catholic for a Catholic city par-excellence like Rome was chosen for your Gospel Summit Project, did the idea come about in the first place, from a dream perhaps?"

In retrospect and thinking back to that day and especially to that specifically loaded question in particular, it now seems all the more striking that at the exact moment a plate of steaming creamy, bacon-flecked and peppercorn-littered plate of "spaghetti alla carbonara" was being placed before each of us seated around that conspicuously visible "private party" table in front of a covered-over fireplace, the famed restaurant's "place of honor" usually reserved for movie starlets on the make, publicity-seeking celebrities and public figures, and on a day that the mood and mindset of even the most hardcore Gospel Summit enthusiast had sunk to its lowest ebb, yet another journalist—this one, however, a colorful and internationally known British print and television journalist who actually in private is a red-bearded Scot who naively has forbidden me to mention his name which is Brent Scowler usually identified on his frequent appearances on Italian TV as the "Dean of the Rome Foreign Press Corps" and who apparently had been following the ups and downs of the star-crossed Gospel Summit in both his daily column and weekly TV appearances, suddenly in this moment comes rushing over to our table holding up over his head a tiny high-powered AM/FM radio which suddenly now he plops down in the center of the tablecloth next to a fiasco of Chianti wine, just in time for us to hear with our own ears a special BBC news bulletin (and don't forget this is the night before a final decision on the part of several crucial Italian government agencies was to be made as to whether or not the government would be issuing certain crucial permits which in turn would determine whether or not the Gospel Summit would take place as planned) which special BBC news bulletin now began to report (somewhat blandly and entirely without emphasis), that a certain private "entity" (later and in the same broadcast identified as "The Lord Demby Evangelical Choral Society, founded in London in the Year 1806, by Negro slaves newly arrived from

Long Island where they had fought bravely alongside the British Army against the American Rebels in the American Revolutionary War, and who at the time of their arrival in London at a time of dire economic depression had been considered unemployed refugees and a burden to the depressed economy but who now [at the time of the writing of this novel] having been sent to Sierra Leone as colonists and become enriched by mining gold and raking up diamonds, were devout members of a rich and powerful evangelical congregation in the hinterland of that tiny but proud African nation where the founders of the above mentioned choral society had now settled and apparently [and now quite obviously] prospered), has just confirmed that, in a special convocation of its Board of Missionaries, the sum of 'six bags of gem grade diamonds' each bag worth the sum of at least three million and a half U.S. dollars for a total dollar value of the gift amounting to approximately twenty-one million dollars, depending on the previous day's market quotations, is immediately being dispatched by Federal Express overnight mail to the competent Gospel Summit authorities at its Rome, Italy, headquarters in the Hotel d'Inghilterra for the precise purpose of having erected above the soon to be sanctified site of the Gospel Summit a huge Gospel Summit Cross to be judiciously studded with these troubled diamonds from the battlefields of tribal animosity and corporate greed to now do the Good Work of Our Lord!"

Moments later, hardly before we could catch our breath and realize our fantastic good fortune, the same BBC broadcast went on to announce what for Joe Stabat, Little Antioch, Tillman and me was perhaps the most invigorating good news of all, that following one of the most raucously contentious sessions of parliament in recent memory, the Italian government through its International Public Events Office had just voted unanimous approval of a unique "Memorandum of Collaboration between the Italian government and the Central Planning Committee of the American Gospel Singer Little Antioch's much-anticipated Gospel Summit," which memorandum provides for the "immediate issuance of all relevant permits" and a "memorandum of understanding" between all interested parties that the Gospel Summit Events shall now take place as scheduled at the site of the former "Italo Balbo Military Airport, now abandoned and out of use but capable of rapid adaptation as the site of the American Negro gospel singer, Little Antioch's so-called Gospel Summit which rehabilitation and restoration, to begin immediately, shall include the priority construction of a circular outdoor theatre with seating for at least 2500 persons around the still-existing and structurally sound control tower atop of which shall be erected an iron and steel architectural trellis as structural support for a revolving Gospel Summit Cross of monumental size and construction to be embedded with a portion of the diamonds donated by the Lord Demby Choral Society of Sierra Leone and that on the grounds outside the former control tower and in addition to the dressing rooms and other amenities appropriate for an international-class outdoor theatre there shall be constructed inside the tower, and technical provisions made for a battery of the most powerful search lights available to light up the Gospel Summit Cross at night that it may be visible as far away as Anzio to the south and Viareggio to the north, in this way reminding one and all of the universal relativity, even in the jaded popular music world of today's youth, of the divine inspiration of the Roman Emperor Constantine's 'Vision of the Cross' and, finally, that provision be made immediately to insure the safety and security of the site, the visiting artists and the vast audience expected to attend what promises to be a unique and world-class three-day musical event that can only do honor to the Italian nation and its hallowed tradition of religious, racial and artistic tolerance and understanding—

"It is further stipulated, that to insure the safety and comfort of the thousands of music lovers expected to attend the Gospel Summit arrangements be made to seat them comfortably and tranquilly on the surrounding hillside and in a special fenced-in area that guarantees as much comfort and safety as can be arranged in the short time at our disposal, including ample sanitary facilities, emergency food supplies and water outlets for personal hygiene for all those Third World dissidents and nay-sayers who in recent days have been crowding the streets of Rome and its airports and central train station of the city and in endless processions and marches and noisy motorcades apparently arriving from all over Europe and the Middle East shouting, 'Prester John is coming back, coming back, coming back, Prester John is coming back, coming back!' creating in this inconsiderate manner an atmosphere of public tension and anxiety as much by the paranoiac violence of their chanting as by the overwhelming numbers of their unannounced, inconsiderate and undocumented presences, which comfortable seating and toilet facilities shall be made available to the above-mentioned nay-sayers and dissidents in such a manner that they too, the dissidents, may watch from a distance and hear over a powerful sound system the same concerts as those with tickets, and in such a manner (given the massive security force circumstances dictate that shall be on duty) the Gospel Summit concerts may at last proceed without risk of misguided and noisy protests on the part of outside hooligans and naysayers, avoiding in this manner the risk of misguided attempts to interrupt the proceedings—"

All's well that ends well, but if the truth be known our jubilation was perforce tempered by the knowledge that our tiny grassroots initiative had now not only been taken completely and unceremoniously out of our hands but suddenly overnight had become transformed into a megalomaniacal world-class super-event over which we had lost all control—

But it was of course Joe Stabat who, having characteristically remained stubbornly fixated on the gift of conflict diamonds, was now, therefore, the first to regain some small measure of control over his own behavior especially as regards what he would do next—

Which, to everyone at the table's astonishment, was to push his chair back, rise unsteadily to his feet, and, with tears streaming down his cheeks, fall down heavily on his knees in front of Tillman and begin to pray:

"Forgive me, dear Tillman, for I know not what I did, forgive me, my dear Army buddy and friend, for having made you my slave, and yet, may God and everyone present be my witness, once again Thee and Thy People have seen fit to save my worthless butt!"

Infuriated and embarrassed that Joe Stabat would choose a poignant moment like this to reveal what was certainly the most shameful and horrid dark secret between them, Tillman suddenly and wildly delivered one of those now old-fashioned but highly effective roundhouse punches to the side of Joe Stabat's head, which sent him flying off his seat (to say the least) in a sprawling and entirely indecorous manner!

"It's not my people saving your ass, you conceited, overbearing and overgrown piece of shit—!" Tillman shrieked, ready if necessary to top off his long-overdue vendetta with a vicious kick for good measure in his master's butt—,"What's saving your worthless ass are those fucking conflict diamonds, which I hope to God you have sense enough to deposit in some reputable bank vault before, fucked up drunk as you've been getting these last few days, you'll probably end up vomiting down the toilet by mistake!"

Now I'd be the first to admit this is heavy stuff even for an ancient and some say (I don't agree) cynical city like Rome, and to this day I haven't the slightest idea how the local press corps got wind of these dramatic goings-on in that tiny but fashionable Roman restaurant nor how seemingly everybody in the world heard about what was going on seemingly almost before it happened—

Be that as it may, suddenly now here comes Tillman who moments before had been retreating sulkingly to a corner out of sight and out of mind, but who now, and all of a sudden and at the exact moment Little Antioch finished her emotional prayer, springs sprightly to his feet and proceeds to seize Little Antioch by the hand and start leading her (all the while peremptorily waving everybody else in the restaurant to their feet) in what for want of a more accurate description was becoming a kind of joyful "Strutting Parade" around the room, me, Little Antioch, Joe Stabat, the BBC reporter, Otello's wife and daughter in the lead, and now suddenly here comes Otello's ancient cook along with the Moroccan busboy, round and round and back and forth until in that memorable moment when Little Antioch stopped in her tracks and scrambled atop a table hastily pushed into the very center of the incredibly crowded room, waited Marion Anderson fashion, eyes closed and hands quiet and dignified at her sides, and then, suddenly and with both her hands raised entreatingly as an almost terrifying silence suddenly fell, and with tears of some enigmatic joy streaming down her cheeks, began to sing that most mysterious and enimatic gospel song in recent gospel song history, "Lord, Lordy Lord, I Need an Explanation—"

2

Later that same night in yet another BBC special broadcast, one in which a scholarly voice attempted to place the extravagant gift of three bags of gem-quality diamonds in a deeper and more rational historical context, the mysterious donor (or donors) of the three bags of gem-quality diamonds was identified as "His Excellency, Sir James Steven Demby, Director-General of the Falcon Mining Trust and Hereditary Patron of the Famed 'Lord Demby Evangelical Gospel Choir,' organized in London in the Year 1806 by former African slaves who having fought bravely with the British Armies in the American Revolutionary War and who had subsequently been brought to London from Long Island, New York, aboard the warships of the defeated but still proud British General Sir William Howe and who, as a reward for their loyal and valiant service alongside the defeated British Expeditionary Force, had been 'repatriated' as privileged colonists to the tiny British colony of Sierra Leone on the West Coast of Africa where an unusually large number of the original colonists had prospered, especially in both the mining and marketing of gold and diamonds, and thus—having heard of this 'holy and inspired "Gospel Summit" initiative of their American brothers and sisters in slavery'—had been proud and eager to announce the Society's joyous participation in that God-inspired Gospel Summit to be held in Rome at or near the site of Constantine I's 'Vision of the Cross,' which unprecedented gift of diamonds and public affirmation of faith has now, and in the words of a front page editorial in that morning's edition of *La Repubblica,* 'Once and for all and effectively removed from the arena of public debate that exquisitely philological question of government financing for popular events of an inspirational or religious nature—' "

3

And now just four days before the Gospel Summit is scheduled to begin and at exactly 4:45 in the morning, someone is knocking at the door to my "mini-suite" in this new and just-completed luxury resort hotel an easy walking distance from the grassy banks of the Tiber which here extend the entire length of this abandoned military airport site where already at least five separate construction crews are hard at work rushing to complete the transformation of what just a few weeks ago was for all practical purposes a squalid public dump into an outdoor theatre capable of seating the four thousand or more gospel music fans expected to attend this by now historical and highly publicized musical event, and the airport's still valid but long-unused control tower into an ingenious revolving stage capable of being moved upwards or downwards by the simple pressing of a button on a control panel and which by means of electronic sensors scattered throughout the site can automatically detect the audience's emotional index which index, translated into an electronic signal, can automatically adjust the psychedelic lighting effects to conform immediately to the audience's collective emotional mood—

In fact, rock concert devotees will have by now recognized, in such gorgeous attention to artistic and psychological detail, the handiwork of the much sought after sound and light technician, M'bela Levine, whose father, a legendary and industry-savvy sound technician and innovator in his own right, had been one of the early prime movers and technical advisors to that wild and wooly band of rock music enthusiasts and music industry insiders who somehow and against all odds ended up producing the history-making, trend-setting and politics-conditioning Woodstock Festival, which (now it can be told) is why, late the day before yesterday and without telling a soul what he was up to, Joe Stabat flew to London to sign a contract with the recording genius' son and thus insure for the two of them (providing M'bela Levine could be persuaded to come aboard on Joe Stabat's terms) not only the best deal possible for the worldwide marketing of the Gospel Summit Album, but (as a secret clause would guarantee) the lion's share of the profits—

But getting back to this mysterious knock at my door (it was of course Little Antioch, smartly dressed in spite of the pre-dawn hour in a light blue, nautically inspired and high-fashion linen jacket, white silk blouse open to her navel and blinding white linen slacks which flatter her long legs and tiny feet, daintily covered by a pair of obviously handmade sandals of the finest leather thongs woven at the forefoot into an intricate Coptic design, meant, she is quick to explain, to foster a "quiet meditative mood of grounded peace" which Coptic design, however, is having the exact opposite effect on me, awakening in my loins a disturbing tug of early morning lust which under the circumstances has emboldened me to throw my arms around her and cop a kiss, which aborted kiss, however, and I must say at the speed of light, she counters with some exotic jiu-jitsu move after which I suddenly find myself face down on the floor, not quite dead but with tears in my eyes and grinning like the fool I now know myself to be—

"Where did you learn to do that?"

"I'm sorry, but you forget I come from Oklahoma where as you well know sexual matters between men and women can get pretty mixed up, which is why no doubt my grandmother gave me this to give to you in case I ever ran into you; actually what she said on her death bed was, 'Go find him and tell him and give him this!' What I'm about to give you is a deathbed command—"

And so saying she handed me one of those dingy brown oversized bank envelopes tied with a black string and with the name Lawton First National Bank printed on the side which she primly put aside until she had pulled me to my feet at which time she picked up the brown bank envelope from the table where she had laid it and which she then ceremoniously pressed it into my hand—

"What's this?" I asked, gingerly turning the battered old bank envelope over in my hand and noting with alarm the words "Cpl First Class" clumsily printed in front of my name, a sure sign that ghosts from the distant past were not only about to catch up with me but violently change my life—

"Well I've done my part!" she said, obviously enjoying my by now all too visible discomfort.

And when I still didn't move she took me gently by the hand

and said, "I have no idea what's inside, all I know is my grandmother gave this scruffy old bank envelope to me on her death bed and told me, '*Go find him, and tell him, and give him this—*' "

And when I still hadn't moved—

"Now don't be silly, it's not like it's a 'death warrant,' come inside and have a seat on the sofa, take a deep breath and open it, in the meantime I'm going into the bedroom to get into something more comfortable than this ridiculous admiral's uniform—"

The moment the bedroom door closed behind her I untied the faded black ribbon that held the scruffy old bank envelope together and gently dumped the contents on the glass top of the coffee table in front of me—

Inside were five pebbles each of which had been wrapped in tissue paper so old the tiny squares of parchment-like paper had almost become transparent—

And each small pebble was a different shade of turquoise blue or violet—

Along with the mysterious pebbles there was a small old-fashioned Kodak snapshot of what looked like a tiny newborn baby—

And there was a note written in careful old-fashioned perfectly legible handwriting, though what the handwriting said sent a cold shiver of fear down my spine—

"Guard these pebbles with your life because for more years than I care to count or think about they have passed through many hands and now come down to you through the ages to explain who you are, where you come from and why you were chosen to become the father of this blessed child!

"Always remember, you don't belong to yourself no more, you belong to The Tribe, which still walks and breathes, and wants you back because of my dreams and what has since come to pass that you and nobody else but you are the elder and therefore the Chief!!!"

* * *

(King Comus pulled his heavy Colt service revolver out of its holster and shot the skinny trembling horse straight between the eyes and then watched expressionless as his once proud stallion shivered all over and became a frail jittery sack of bones and desperately tried to right itself but instead stumbled on three legs and gave one last open-mouthed grunt and collapsed and with King Comus looking on with tears overflowing in his eyes what was left of his horse slid slowly down the muddy bank into the frothy and stubbornly foaming flood waters of the Raglan River gone wild and in less time than it would have taken him to utter a respectful "Rest in peace, Old Friend" the dead horse sank out of sight and suddenly King Comus felt more frightened and alone than he had ever felt in his life—

And though his mind was in no condition to remember or even recall how many days and how many nights it had been since the flimsy jerry-built bridge his mounted reconnaissance patrol with King Comus himself bringing up the rear had been trying gingerly to cross when instead the raging flood waters suddenly tore it apart into grotesque jagged hunks in such a way that he himself was saved but there was nothing he could do to save his men, leaving him all alone in the universe to face this very worst of human terrors, this brand new terror of being totally alone with his loss without anyone to talk to or share his grief, for his men and his horse for too long had been the only friends he had had in the world and all he was left with now was the haunted look of lost sanity in his eyes which even that he could not see—

But now as he continued to stand there gazing as if hypnotized at the place where his horse had finally sunk out of sight, suddenly he felt a presence behind him and waited just an instant before making a wild and sudden grab for his revolver and had even spun around ready to shoot when—

"Put your gun back in its holster," the old Indian said, raising his hand with the palm facing King Comus as a sign his intentions were not hostile but of peace—

In reply, instinctively, as if remembering something in a dream, King Comus spoke a phrase he had learned when he lived with the Cherokee tribe that had plucked him out of the Mississippi so many years ago it was like it had happened in someone else's life—

The old Indian spoke in tribal-accented English—

"I know who you are," the old Indian said, "—and if I told you my name you would know who I am too and why I am here—did you drop these?"

The old Indian was holding a tiny leather bag with something in it that rattled—

"You must have dropped these because they were there on the ground at your feet—"

King Comus took the tiny leather bag out of the old Indian's hand, took a peek, and promptly hid the bag behind his back—

"You're a shaman!" King Comus said, almost accusingly, "—These are divining stones, where did you get these?"

"Then my dreams told me the truth, they do belong to you!"

"Where did you get them?" King Comus asked almost angrily.

"They are yours, they were given to you the day your son was born—"

"I did not deserve a son, I had no power and therefore I wasn't a good father to him and thus failed to protect him when he needed it most—!" King Comus said, hoping against hope the old Indian would go away and let him alone.

"They belong to you and nobody else on the face of this earth, they are the source of your immense power—"

"It is easy for you to say such things because you are a shaman and you want to work your magic on me because I am weak and lonely and have nowhere to go in the whole wide world—"

And when the old Indian did not reply but allowed the hint of a smile to play briefly on his lips, King Comus repeated what he had said just a few moments before though with the slightest change in the arrangement of his words—

"You are a shaman and you have come to me out of nowhere like this because I am dead and have nowhere to go—"

"I am here to give you what is yours by right, I consider it a great fortune and an honor to have finally found you, so have no fear, I have not come to harm you but to restore to you what is yours by right—"

When he said that the old Indian smiled a broader more relaxed smile and rubbed the palms of his hands together in the ancient manner of a Cherokee chief as a sign that he was pleased to have finally acted in accordance with the will of his Cherokee forefathers—

"You are not dead, but neither you nor I are meant to understand how the mission I am about to give you will be accomplished, nor even exactly what the mission is—"

It is not true that King Comus had forgotten all about his son—

Sometimes, more often than he cared to remember he would dream long complicated dreams about his life with the general's widow, especially here in the wilderness and in the darkness of some cold and lonely night, perhaps while on patrol, he would squinch his eyes tight and dream of the stern and starched comfort of the general's mansion and the kind, lavender-scented hospitality the general's widow so generously gave him with no questions asked, and he would dream too of that day she so unexpectedly agreed to allow him to live there in that mansion as husband and wife, sometimes he dreamed of the baron but that was a dream of slavery not at all like his most favorite dream of all, the dream he seldom had but always enjoyed when it would come, the dream of the day he had gone to the convent to fetch his son and bring him home to the widow's mansion, but the most painful dream of all, a nightmare he feared because when he dreamed it he would shiver and his body would become stiff and rigid and he would try to cry but no tears would come to his eyes so horrid was this dream, the dream of how cruelly the Cherokee women chased him away when his wife died from the winter pox and the women of the tribe laughed behind his back and finally told him what they had already decided among themselves, that there would be no more food to feed his son and the two of them, father and son, since they were not truly born into the tribe they would have to go away and seek their fortune elsewhere and only the widow took them in—

A mystery then and a mystery now, for if the shaman could indeed hear and understand even the most secret thoughts of who it was he was talking to and now seemed to know more about this skinny black cavalryman's life than even the skinny black cavalryman himself knew, knew or could remember, why now had he King Comus been so willing to give up and sink into the wild flood waters and become forever forgotten and silent?

It was then the shaman looked deeply into King Comus' eyes and addressed him in an entirely different tone of voice, a tone of formality and ancient ceremonies—

"I have come to bring you good tidings, not to remind you of the injustice done you in the past—!"

And so saying the shaman took King Comus by the hand and led him to a quiet spot on what before the flood must have been the top of a wooded hill and where now they settled down side by side, beneath a gnarled and ancient apple tree whose branches were so laden with large red, yellow and green apples that it was as if they had suddenly stumbled on the Garden of Eden—

And in fact that is exactly what King Comus said:

"Then it is true, I am dead and you are dead and this is the Garden of Eden!"

The shaman laughed heartily, but when he finished laughing he said very solemnly and in a deeper voice than he had been speaking in up to now—

"No, my son, you are not dead, not because it would be impossible for you to be dead, but because it is not yet your time to be dead but a time for you to be both alive and dead at the same

time, a privilege bestowed only rarely and only when according to the gods the world has gone out of kilter—"

"—so listen to me carefully because I am allowed to ask you only once, if you were indeed dead which, I assure you, you are not, where would you like to go, to the Past, to the Future, or perhaps somewhere now that is in the Present—"

When the shaman said that and even though the shaman had claimed otherwise King Comus knew without any further doubt left in his mind that he was definitely dead, and that since he was definitely dead—and even if it turned out he was only dreaming—he might as well go along with the shaman's stupid game and have himself a little fun!

"Well, sir—," King Comus said in what he thought was a respectful tone of voice but which in reality was a tone of barroom mockery, the tone he sometimes used when talking to a rookie officer who hadn't yet learned what was what in the Army and what was the best way to go about getting it, "—if you put it like that I think that since there's not a soul I give a damn about here in this godforsaken Indian Territory, if I had my druthers I think I'd like to go somewhere where there ain't no slavery no more, somewhere in the Future, see how my loved ones and my kinfolk are doing, now that everybody's free—"

The shaman seemed pleased by King Comus' reply and smiled a wise and peaceful smile—

"Nobody told you everybody's free, but godspeed to you anyway, my son, and in the name of a just God who sometimes makes mistakes but at least two times out of three gets it right, your wish is hereby granted!"

5

From the night of the Gospel Summit's premiere, those journalists (radio, TV and print but predominately print) attempting to describe both the mood of the huge audiences Joe Stabat's three-day and three-night concert series of gospel music universally advertised as "The Gospel Summit" often resorted to language usually reserved for learned academic theses about aberrant crowd behavior in the late Middle Ages, the music correspondent for *Il Giorno*, for example, describing the "strange atmosphere of expectancy that hung over the event like a fog over a marsh," while the music critic of *L'Osservatore Romano* described the mood of the audiences as being "—at once raucous and mystical, a sense of holiness unprecedented in our time," both critics referring of course to both the event itself and the incredible size of the first night audience, which five hours before the first concert was to begin had already filled to overflowing the outdoor theatre's 4500 authorized seating capacity by perhaps a third and, by the time the first concert was to begin, had already spilled out to blanket the banks of the Tiber River and the surrounding hillside towns with a respectful but wildly enthusiastic overflow crowd almost double that occupying the ticketed seats of the outdoor theatre in the valley below—

But only *Il Tempo* in its following morning commentary mentioned what was now the talk of Rome, and indeed all of Italy, a mysterious night sky display of "dancing triangles of light" which first appeared in the sky over the concert site immediately after sunset the first night of the concert and which some astronomers, interviewed on the late night news and on BBC TV broadcasts were tentatively attributing to certain "unexplained and perhaps even inexplicable phenomenon creating electrical charges connected to the erratic movements of unknown objects in the subionosphere though as yet there has been no available theory to explain why the above-mentioned unknown objects have consistently seemed to maintain an observable triangular shape—"

"What I think it is—," Tillman was saying, "—is God thinking in 'threes' again, you know what I mean? Father, Son and the Holy Ghost! That's why you see them only over the concert, to remind all those crazy people out there what gospel music is all about and what it's not about! You know what I'm sayin'? A lotta people out there think rock music and gospel music is one and the same thing!"

"You may be right—," Little Antioch said (but you could tell her mind was elsewhere by the frown on her forehead and the nervous way she was playing with the sugar spoon), "What really worries me about it is—"

Joe Stabat interrupted what she had been about to say and

in fact he was so pleased by the way things were now going he'd ordered the only thing not even mentioned on the hotel menu: pancakes and syrup, for which he'd given a twenty-dollar tip to the waiter to persuade the chief cook who had worked at the Sheraton in New York to make special for him, and which he now stopped pouring syrup on long enough to observe:

"Take my word for it, it's some kinda new optical weapon, you know, uses atomic energy to blow away the enemy after first locating them, naturally with the help of the microwave oven from the kitchen of some navy submarine on maneuvers out there somewhere off the shore of Sardinia—"

At which point Joe Stabat laughed and laughed and laughed, like he was working off his pent-up nervousness, like he was never going to stop laughing, and more than at his stupid idiot joke, he was laughing out of control like that out of a deep-felt sense of relief that finally at long last he was going to get out of the financial grave he had dug for himself by embarking on a financial venture as doomed to failure as this his new girl-friend's cockamamie 'Gospel Summit'!

"You wait and see—," Tillman said, picking his rear gold tooth with a toothpick he'd just discovered in a tiny ceramic container in the middle of the breakfast-cluttered table, "When God speaks with authority he speaks with authority, God doesn't speak in no silly-ass jokes! Ain't that right, schoolboy, you a college professor and got all the answers, what's your opinion? Are those dancing triangle lights real, or are they some kind of optical illusion?"

I had no intention of falling into a cunning trap like that but at the same time I knew I had to say something, no matter how pompous or silly or risk further humiliation; and what I finally ended up saying was something I'd once read in a book but which nevertheless was as close to the truth as I was likely ever to get:

"All I know—and for that matter all anybody really knows—is that when the world's in trouble—really in trouble, everybody starts looking up at the sky!"

Little Antioch who was sitting next to me at the breakfast table let her hand fall softly on my knee as if to tell me that whatever we were talking about she was with me and to tell you the truth that secret gesture of hers suddenly and inexplicably almost made me cry—

But by this time the mood at this final Gospel Summit concert was suddenly beginning to change and entire sections of the audience that for this final concert had been blanketing the landscape as far as the eye could see and in any direction, suddenly now began to demand by shouts, stamping feet, and by the loudest mass chanting I have ever heard in my life, "Prester John is coming back, Prester John is coming back!" over and over again and progressively louder and louder and so out of control the police came running—

In short the huge crowd attending that famous final concert began demanding—clamorously, especially that part of the crowd made up mostly of out of town brown and black youth and young ladies gathered as far as the eye could see on the surrounding hills overlooking the site of the concert—that their idol Little Antioch sing yet another, the fourth demand encore of the evening of "Lord, Lordy Lord, I Need an Explanation!" even though it had been secretly decided by the security details present that for purposes of public safety the most exhilarating open-air concert ever held in modern times must be brought to a close and the area cleared—which official announcement over the commandeered microphone had just provoked a loud and prolonged sigh of sorrow such as I have never heard before, and in that haunting interlude of silence that followed, moments before Little Antioch began to sing her final encore of "Lord, Lordy Lord, I Need an Explanation!" and as a terrifying hush fell over the audience of which now there were more people standing than it was possible by any standard to seat, as one and all began quietly to join in singing and in a quiet sea-surge of sound the enigmatic words of the century's most mysterious and controversial gospel song—

Lord, Lordy Lord, I need an explanation
The sadness of the world has trodden me into the ground
The grief, the sorrow
The children without joy
If this is how it is,
And this is how it must be
Lord, Lordy Lord, I Need an Explanation!
But if you know his name
This savior without fame
Come Sweet Lord and tell me
And I will tell the World—

It was in that precise moment—and believe me, there have been as many claims and descriptions as there were people in the audience, with the predictable result that there is on record no single authoritative account; but almost as many accounts and versions of accounts as there were people present that night, what I most vividly remember of that mysterious event and think I saw with my own eyes is, to the best of my recollection, the following:

True, what happened happened while Little Antioch was singing the final chorus of her signature gospel song, "Lord, Lordy Lord, I Need an Explanation!"

And as during all previous performances the so-called dancing triangles had again appeared inexplicably in the sky, but this time with a difference—

This time while Little Antioch was singing, the dancing triangles suddenly began to spin wildly and seemingly out of control until for the briefest moment of what we presume to know about Time, while continuing to spin out of control the triangles of light seemed to be forming some kind of five-pointed star—

("Lil David, play on your harp, play on your harp,
Lil David play on your harp, Hallelujah—")

—which however almost immediately and inexplicably began to shrink into what can only be described as an astonishingly glimmering and pulsating pinpoint of light which in turn and in the blink of an eye became a soundless explosion of light lasting only a few seconds until perhaps in a minute or so gradually began to shrink, became very small and increasingly tiny until it was just a pinpoint of light in the sky, something like a falling star, but somehow a star falling in a purposeful direction, and this falling pinpoint of light continued for about five or ten minutes longer, until suddenly and directly over our heads there was yet another terrifying explosion of light, this one engulfing apparently the entire sky as far as the eye could see, after which we heard a kind of BOOM sound, but this time there was no after-BOOM sound as obviously there should have been since the disturbance we all saw must have been seen and heard over half of Italy but instead all became silent, there was no sound at all, only a strange sucking sound like a distant whistle blowing during which again (this much I am absolutely sure of) I heard the old woman's voice singing inside my head the old Negro spiritual "Lil David play on your harp, play on your harp, play on your harp, Lil David play on your harp, hallelujah" and then all of a sudden he was here, King Comus was here, in a tattered 19th-century horse cavalry trooper's uniform, and all became deadly silent, a silence so cosmic and terrifying it was as if all the universe had come to a halt, as though suddenly all the life had been sucked out of the universe—

And it was then as with bated breath we continued to watch the pathetic figure of the man dressed as I said in the tattered uniform of a 19th-century horse cavalryman, standing on the stage very close to Little Antioch, and in the same moment that he arrived, a great yell rose from the back seats of the audience a huge inchoate roaring avalanche of a rolling sound like "Ohhhhhhhh—" which spooky outcry lasted for almost five minutes until suddenly, thunderously (seemingly shaking asunder the entire planet) the inchoate explosion of sound began to reverberate and gradually become a unified outcry of joy, "He is here, he is here, he is here with us—," and then they came running, pushing and shoving from far back in the audience like an hysterical invasion of pilgrims upon the promised arrival of the one they had been secretly expecting to arrive, the long hoped for redeemer of their ancient dreams, suddenly there he was, after all these endless years here he was here among them, and they came running, pushing and shoving their way through the terrified paying audience who had no escape so vast was the thunderous rush toward the stage of the growing horde of hundreds now perhaps thousands appearing out of nowhere many from the distant hills that overlooked the abandoned military airport, all shouting and chanting, "He is here, he is here, Prester John is here, our prayers have been answered, Prester John has come—," and as all those who had been sitting in the front rows began to stand up and become aware of the thundering herd of pilgrims stampeding wildly through their silent dumbfounded midst the rapidly panicking crowd now about to be crushed under the incredible din of yelling, screaming and futile invocations of help, the incredible spectacle in moments becoming more than is humanly possible to endure, more than is humanly possible even to dream about, at once a nightmare and a holy dream—on the stage and while the object of all this fear and wonder (of course not Prester John but King Comus himself, come to see his kinfolk, how they came out with the passing of time and with all the tribulation they have been through; King Comus in flesh and blood and yet so ethereal he appeared as in some vaporous dream and in some unnatural state of being, but have no doubt about it, it was indeed King Comus, King Comus in flesh and blood, a quiet smile on his face as he gazed into Little Antioch's eyes, causing her to faint and fall unconscious at his feet, which now frightened King Comus himself who, ghost or apparition that he was, quickly bent over to lift her up, uttering all the murmuring words of comfort and good tidings he still remembered until suddenly Little Antioch fell in a faint once more and became very limp—

It was then quite unexpectedly a chanter seized the microphone out of Little Antioch's hand and now was thrusting it almost ferociously into King Comus' face, "How long we have awaited your coming and now that you are here you will not speak! How can that be? Speak to us O Esteemed and precious King Prester John, now that you are here and we know you are not an imposter because you have fallen out of the sky as was promised those many centuries ago, Speak to us O John the Conqueror, speak to us and tell us at long last what it is we must do!"

It was then (and there are as many other versions as to the actual sequence of events as there were people present) but in a sudden move that caught every body crowding around King Comus by surprise, another hand grabbed hold of the microphone and began pressing it even more insistently against King Comus' lips almost threateningly as if to force him to speak the words they had so long dreamed he would speak, but so threateningly and with such a violent swing of the hand that almost certainly King Comus must have thought he was being attacked by a dagger or by a sword and to protect himself, good soldier that he was, he held up his arm to guard his face just as a frantic bunch of chanters surrounding him suddenly stooped down as if to seize hold of King Comus' legs but instead lifted him high over their heads and began to spin him around dizzily until finally like a drooping puppet he began to lose his balance and in that moment uttered the only words anyone remembered hearing him say, "For the grace of God, put me down, where are my kinfolks, why don't they come to rescue me? Can't you see I am dead, you only think I am alive! Where are my kinfolks? Tell them I am here before it is too late, tell them to hurry and get here before I run out of time, I tell you I am dead and not alive, where are my kinfolks? Tell them before it is too late. I have finally come, tell them that I'm finally here, that King Comus is not even my real name which I can't even remember what it used to be, King Comus was the name my master gave me, my real name is—"

Those were King Comus' last words and the only one to hear them was Little Antioch who immediately began to weep and at the same time had somehow and in all that incredible chaos managed to fight her way through the angry crowd of chanters surrounding King Comus and was about to throw her arms around him and place a kiss on the top of his head, but by then it was already too late, already too late because at the very moment of her kiss King Comus had begun to disintegrate, and in a matter of a few seconds there was nothing left of him but a tiny pile of dust—

* * *

(Luminella di Constantino, Joe Stabat's long missing Italian wife was well acquainted with the legend of King Comus since Tillman, those first months after he had been hired by Joe Stabat as his right hand man and cook, had spent long hours initiating her into the lore of his family's founder just as he had done with his Army friends and with me, and indeed with anyone willing to listen; so it is not surprising that we now find Joe Stabat's thoroughly Catholic wife, Little Constantine in her arms, both of them slowly making their way down the grass-covered paving stones of what had once been the only road out of Lawton but which now was indeed on U.S. Army property not far from the old artillery range and not many miles away from the site of a large brand new and extremely avant-garde building, the newly built and somewhat controversial site (especially since the graduating class from an exclusive female college had written and signed a well-documented protest against locating the new convent and orphanage so near what had once been an artillery firing range)—

But what Luminella and Little Constantine, her son, are doing there now is following the path of a story about King Comus and his son, how when their wagon had overturned in a ravine the boy had lost the penknife and a saint's card the Ursuline Sisters had given him as a farewell gift when King Comus had come to fetch him and take him to his new home in the widow's mansion she had just inherited from the general, both which Joe Stabat's strong-willed wife has now gone deep into the thicket of the ravine to look for, for it is the penknife and the saint's card of Saint Ursula that she hopes to present to the Ursuline Sisters as a gift and token of her serious intent to finally bring order to her life.

And when, after an hour of searching in the thick damp underbrush she does indeed find what she is looking for she goes straight to the heavy oak front door of the convent and hands the dark-skinned nun who has opened the door for her both the waterlogged but incredibly still recognizable saint's card depicting the Madonna of Guadalupe and the penknife heavily crusted with rust to the plump and jolly nun who has just recently become the convent's Mother Superior, and who now says to Luminella and also to Little Constantine, "I had no doubt you would find what you found and without too much difficulty, I knew because I can see you are of good sturdy stock like us and just as stubborn, therefore, welcome to our order, stay as long as you wish, for however long you stay it is our devout wish that your stay here be fruitful and bring both peace and solace to your heart, all glory be to God, all glory be to our Lord, may the Lord bless you and keep you—"

The End, Sag Harbor, N.Y., May 29. 07.

A Note on the Text

William Demby declared his novel *King Comus* finished at the time he signed off on the final page of the manuscript, printed here in its entirety, with: "The End, Sag Harbor, N.Y., May 29. 07." Extant drafts of the novel are archived in the David M. Rubenstein Rare Book and Manuscript Library at Duke University.

It bears mentioning that, from the novel's earliest pages, Demby attunes readers to his storytelling method, in which the novel's characters are woven into affiliative relations with one another by circumstance and across the expanse of time:

> But forgive me for I am rambling and the truth is I don't know quite how to proceed, for I am an ant traveling over one of those enormous Tapestries of Time, and I shall make mistakes of fact and observation, and may not see in time what was there to see before attempting to climb up yet another mountain of colored thread—so first things first, and so as to doubly reassure ourselves that what follows is the workings of Our Lord and not

> the workings of the Demon it may be wise for us, at least for the time being, to abandon certain vain and useless literary conventions as to the nature or not of narrative realism (which in any case in light of newly discovered laws of physics make such guarantees at best illusory and academically vain).

Readers may wish to wait until finishing the novel before reading further in these notes, as they contain key plot points.

Since this is a posthumous publication, the author could not be consulted, as is typically the case, regarding any editing decisions. A great number of silent copy edits were made to address spelling errors and inconsistencies of punctuation and typography. Where variations occurred, the author's predominant usage prevailed. Demby signaled chapter breaks in his manuscript, partially numbering them himself. The numbering of chapters has been regularized throughout. The author also separated the novel into three sections, though Part III is substantially shorter than Parts I and II.

Keeping Demby's narrative advice regarding realism in mind, there are, nevertheless, some idiosyncrasies or inconsistencies in the text related to plot details and characterization that readers may wish to consider. Such details were not "corrected"; rather, the following notes serve to call them to the reader's attention.

One such inconsistency refers to King Comus' age. In the novel's opening, King Comus is said to have been born in a New Orleans slave market in "1817 c." A few pages later, however, another character, King Comus' soon-to-be enslaver, "Baron von Gugelstein," arrives in New Orleans in the fall of 1815, some months after the historic Congress of Vienna. The baron heads immediately to the slave market, where he purchases a young, unnamed woman and her eleven-year-old son, Cato, whom he renames Comus. Here, in other words, King Comus is said to be eleven years old in 1815, not born circa 1817. Later in the narrative, King Comus' age is referenced again: he is described as a young man "still in his twenties" in the 1840s. This detail supports his being born in the fall of 1815; nevertheless, both dates were left as the author indicated them in the text.

Questions surrounding familial relations and kinship also surface in the novel. For instance, in Joe Stabat's introductory speech to the GIs in Italy, he alludes to his dead mother, but his mother later appears as a menacing figure, a "black-clad tower of wrath," living in his Staten Island mansion. In another instance, the key character Little Antioch is ultimately revealed to be Hopeful and D.'s daughter, conceived on Thanksgiving just before D. deploys to the war. Such a revelation means that Little Antioch is in her fifties at the time of the Gospel Summit in Rome in the 1990s. Little Antioch's lineage in King Comus' family, however, remains ambiguous. Little Antioch's mother, Hopeful, is described as one of Tillman's Aunt Harriet's "girls," and it is suggested that she, like the other young women living in the mansion in Oklahoma, is not a blood relation. Harriet takes care to introduce herself to D. as "Miss," stating that she never married; a few pages later, however, she refers to her "husband." Aunt Harriet's nephew, Tillman, calls Little Antioch his niece, his great-niece, and his great-great-niece in the novel, but is himself said to be the last of King Comus' line. Such details generate compelling questions related to affiliative and biological kinship; this dynamic recurs when D. is named chief of

King Comus' tribe upon receiving Little Antioch's gift of King Comus' divining stones near the end of the novel.

Another notable discrepancy in the novel relates to acts of naming. Tillman explains to D. that Little Antioch has a hit gospel song "Lord, Lordy Lord, I Need an Explanation!" that she performs at a concert that Tillman and Joe Stabat attend in Bedford-Stuyvesant prior to coming to Italy for the Gospel Summit. On the first page of the novel D. informs readers that this song was written by "a black teenage gospel singer from a Bedford-Stuyvesant housing project in Brooklyn, New York, known to her millions of fans around the world as 'Little Antioch.'" Given Little Antioch's age at the time of the Gospel Summit, this would mean that she wrote the song decades beforehand. Later in the novel, however, D. expresses his need for "a simple explanation," in reference to the plans for the Gospel Summit in Rome, and Little Antioch responds with elation, declaring that she will use D.'s words in her title, "Lord, Lordy Lord, I Need an Explanation!" as though naming what would become a chart-topping success for the first time.

Given the novel's ambitious engagement with multiple temporalities, embracing these alternative plotlines and simultaneities, even contradictions, enriches the text's experimentalism. Fittingly, on the subject of chronology, Tillman tells D., "I'm not going to get into the exact dates everything happened because I've never been sure of the exact dates myself." This insight affords another model for reading this posthumous novel, which relies on oral storytelling for much of its delivery, in a mode that welcomes embellishment, flexibility and panache. In keeping with *King Comus'* interest in the fungibility of temporality and memory, both subjective and historical, the aforementioned details remain dynamic and refuse standardization. These variations alternately compete with and complement each other, eliciting an active reader to draw her or his own correlations in order to carry the tale forward.

—Melanie Masterton

ALSO BY

WILLIAM DEMBY

THE CATACOMBS

In this masterpiece of metafiction set in the Rome of the tumultuous 1960s, Black American expatriate Bill Demby narrates his attempts to write a novel about his friend Doris, a Black American actress working as one of Elizabeth Taylor's handmaidens in the film *Cleopatra*. Utterly dependent upon Doris for the development of his novel, Demby is both a participant in and observer of her life as she begins an affair with an Italian count. Demby's growing emotional and artistic involvement in the affair of his character-friend leads him on an existential quest for the meaning of truth and fiction, both lived and created, in a world torn by the social upheaval of the time period.

Fiction

LOVE STORY BLACK

In the midst of the turbulent 1970s, Edwards, a freelance writer and Black Studies professor at a small college in New York City, is assigned a story for *New Black Woman* magazine: a profile of Mona Pariss, an aging former singer whose popularity once rivaled Josephine Baker's. With his creditors at the door, Professor Edwards beats a path to the crumbling Harlem apartment house where Mona, once the toast of Europe for her singing, now lives in squalid obscurity. As his interviews progress, Edwards is gradually drawn into Mona's strange world. At the same time, he finds himself entering into an affair with Hortense, a beautiful young assistant at *New Black Woman*. From revolutionary downtown poetry readings to a hospital bed on the Continent and back, becoming entangled in the lives of both women might turn Edwards's bourgeois life upside down for good.

Fiction

BEETLECREEK

After years of seclusion in the Black quarter of Beetlecreek, West Virginia, in the precarious 1930s, a retired carnival worker named Bill Trapp strikes up a chance friendship with Johnny Johnson, a Pittsburgh teenager transplanted into his uncle's home. Bill is white. Johnny is Black. Both are searching for acceptance, something that will give meaning to their lives. While Bill tries to court favor in the community, Johnny joins a local gang; meanwhile, their new friendship kindles hope that there is something for each of them beyond the bounds of Beetlecreek. But as the church society's Fall Festival approaches, the battle between the repressive small town and the aspirations of its trapped inhabitants comes to a nail-biting head. First published in 1950, *Beetlecreek* stands as a moving condemnation of provincialism and fundamentalism, and a classic of Black American literature. Both a critique of racial hypocrisy and a new direction for the African American novel, it occupies fresh territory that is neither the gritty realism of Richard Wright nor the ironic modernism of Ralph Ellison.

Fiction

VINTAGE BOOKS
Available wherever books are sold.
vintagebooks.com